A Small Fire Burned on Windy Hill

A Small Fire Burned on Windy Hill

Marlow Peerse Weaver

NPI

Northwest Publishing, Inc.
Salt Lake City, Utah

A Small Fire Burned on Windy Hill

All rights reserved.
Copyright © 1995 Northwest Publishing, Inc.

Reproduction in any manner, in whole or in part,
in English or in other languages, or otherwise
without written permission of the publisher is prohibited.

This is a work of fiction.
All characters and events portrayed in this book are fictional,
and any resemblance to real people or incidents is purely coincidental.

For information address: Northwest Publishing, Inc.
6906 South 300 West, Salt Lake City, Utah 84047
JC 5.24.95 / JP

PRINTING HISTORY
First Printing 1995

ISBN: 1-56901-882-0

NPI books are published by Northwest Publishing, Incorporated,
6906 South 300 West, Salt Lake City, Utah 84047.
The name "NPI" and the "NPI" logo are trademarks belonging to
Northwest Publishing, Incorporated.

PRINTED IN THE UNITED STATES OF AMERICA.
10 9 8 7 6 5 4 3 2 1

Dedicated to
Laura's unconditional belief,
Anna's spiritual questioning,
and God's gracious tolerance.

Preface

    Who of us hasn't, quietly within us or out loud, cried out, as Christ did, "Father, why have You forsaken me?" Who of us hasn't strived to perceive paternal expectations only to be met with silence? Who of us hasn't begged for enlightenment, begged to understand what offers us entry into eternity?
    It is said a Messiah shall come to us at the end of time. What layers of cynicism, the innumerable times we've been forsaken, would blind us to this event if it were imminent? How would such a Messiah reveal itself to us? From above us, within us, among us? Would such a Messiah also harbor the lingering doubts that torment us, that tormented Christ?

Another question of a child in search of guidance, in search of enlightenment. What is an "X"? A cross sagging and falling on its side? A void, an emptiness where something of significance should stand, as in "Xmas" or "X generation"? Does "X" mark an old, musty map the place where something bountiful would fill us, the treasure we cannot find? Is "X" the silence we encounter when we ask of those preceding us where the journey, the quest will end?

I wanted to disclaim *Windy Hill* being in any way a religious book, but then I read Merriam-Webster's definition of that word, "relating to any acknowledged ultimate reality." I will graciously concede to writing about the quest to find that "ultimate reality." If reading this book in any way brings energy into that process, I will be gratified as a humble "weaver of words."

I thank Vienna, West Virginia; Houston, Texas; Raleigh, North Carolina; the contemplative dreariness of northern Germany; a small fire in South Kensington; and countless airport waiting areas for inspirational moments that led to this book.

1

"Hi, Mom. Freddie. Sorry it's so late. Hope I didn't wake you up."

"No. What's wrong, baby?"

"If only I knew. Chris flew out of town this morning. A big meeting. This evening, I went to the airport to pick him up…"

"You, Freddie?"

"Yes, as much as I hate airports. It was Chris's biggest contract ever, probably the big slammer for his career, and I wanted to surprise him, and go somewhere and celebrate it with him. But, that's it. He didn't show."

"That is a surprise. I thought you two have your lives

programmed like clockwork. I'm sure…"

"Whatever happened, Mom, I'm pissed. I've got voice mail, fax machines, both at work and at home. Chris knows to use them."

Freddie's mother paused. "It's none of my business, I know, baby, but do you two have any kind of problem?"

"A problem? We? Unequivocally, no! Hey, look, I'm sorry I called so late. I'm sure you think I'm blowing the whole thing out of proportion."

"No, no, Freddie, it's okay. I guess I'd be worried, too."

"You're just saying that. Forget I called. I'll just sleep on it and let it clear itself up in the morning."

"But you will tell me if there's a problem, won't you, Freddie?"

"If you mean trash—no, Mom. My private life's off limits. To everyone."

Far outside the urban sprawl of the city of Pontifica, nestled in a relatively isolated area of rolling hills and forest, was a large, expansive estate, the centerpiece a huge, bunkerlike building, its facades covered with gray and red slate slabs.

There, within its confines, two men sat in a large, understated but expensively furnished den, a setting hinting of self-confident power, the kind that requires no additional outward embellishment to assert itself. The older of the two men was Koan Angstrom, the other, Paul Wahrmacher, Koan's assistant and his sole intimate confidant.

"Paul, are the preparations nearing completion?"

"Yes, sir. We're ready to proceed." Paul hesitated, battling with himself. His role wasn't to question Koan's judgment, at best to offer additional information that might lead to alternative conclusions, yet this rare time he felt compelled to challenge the path they were taking. "Sir, I still have my reservations."

"Not concerning my intentions?"

"Certainly not that, sir. It's the procedures. I've taken great pains to assess their feasibility, and the uncertainties continue to remain unacceptably high. Perhaps it would be judicious to allow ourselves more time?"

Koan slapped his thick, meaty hand against the leather armrest of his chair. "Damn this passivity! I've listened to too many ticks of the clock in this otherwise silent room." Koan expanded his full chest outward, then slumped back into his chair, his steely eyes narrowing. "I'm supposed to possess such great powers, yet, what has it brought me? Nothing but this damned wealth. For what is it good? To build monuments to me? Only children need affirmation for their self-esteem. But this standing aside, damn it, I sometimes feel like God in heaven, sitting here peacefully, above it all, listening to angels playing their harps, while a cacophony rages in the background, the dischordant noises of mankind in the process of destroying itself? I can hide my being from the world, but my soul nags, prods, torments me to be involved."

Paul let Koan's words quiet before responding. "I understand that, sir, and do not wish to even suggest we change course. I'd simply much prefer we find alternatives with far less incertitude. I'm speaking only of the vehicle, not the destination."

"I know that, Paul, but even I am capable of impatience. I'm terribly weary. Especially of this image, this mythical figure I've become, the one created by journalists and would-be biographers. Reduced to an illusion, that's what I am, an old, reclusive man spouting abstract wisdoms. It's been a testing exercise in will and fortitude to await until we had everything assembled. And now we're there."

"Fine, sir. We'll leave things as planned."

Sighing deeply, Koan folded his hands together at his waist. A thick cloud of tentativeness continued to hang in the room, but Koan chose to ignore it. And Paul knew he'd pushed his role as far as allowed.

In the same large estate, in another wing, the body of a

young man, nearly motionless, lay on a bed. His eyes scanned a high, ornate white ceiling, then traveled down a bare wall to a brightly lit window. Birds sang, and off in the distance a dog barked. These were registered, but using the senses required great effort. Relenting to a feeling of intoxication, the young man's mind drifted once again back into semi-conscious wanderings.

The house. I see it. The chimney. Smoke. Mom and Dad are there. But it's so far away. I'm cold, my legs so heavy.

My God, Dad's gonna be pissed. I'm late. I know those words, "Why didn't you use that compass, boy, the one I gave you for Christmas? A man can get lost out there, or even killed. Perish. You possess so little faith, Son, only in yourself, and that's not enough..."

Fighting to remain conscious, the young man, Chris Folkstone, massaged his eyes, then twisted his body and fell off the bed. The brightness of a window had drawn his attention to it, and now he lay on the floor, oblivious to whether or not he felt pain. He tried to crawl toward the window, but when he put weight on his arms, they collapsed. Soon exhaustion and sleep overcame him.

The previous afternoon, a precipitous event had befallen Chris. An hour earlier, he had tied the ribbons on a contract that was sure to springboard his career. Nothing beckoned stronger than to get to the airport and fly home, then celebrate his great achievement with his wife, Freddie. He, however, never made it to the airport.

The fateful incident had played itself out in the parking lot of a large shopping mall. Minutes earlier in a trendy, upscale gift shop, Chris had bought an unusual wine dispenser for his wife. As he walked across the asphalt parking lot between rows of parked cars, his mind was preoccupied with how Freddie was going to react to his greatest yet professional coup, as well as the gift he was bringing her.

Freddie wasn't a homemaker, mother of Chris's children, none of the traditional roles. She embodied instead what

Chris most dearly sought, recognition. To impress her, accomplishments had to be superlatives. Chris knew the contract he'd been working toward was in that league, and he was anticipating Freddie's admiration. While searching for an appropriate present in the gift shop, Chris hadn't been able to repress an urge to make a statement. Freddie didn't desire presents as an act of love, rather she valued what was socially utilitarian; something that set them apart from the crowd and put the two of them one step ahead. The wine dispenser Chris bought provided him with a subtle extra, a little jab at what he considered a facade of rigid morality held up by Freddie.

Chris hadn't had any choices concerning religious indoctrination. In his birthplace, Shepherdstown, church was the hub of social interaction. In contrast, Freddie couldn't even name one book from the Bible. Her moral values were fluid and mostly situational, based more than anything on immediate utilitarian considerations. Chris's feelings about this were highly ambiguous, a blend of admiration and resentment. But what could light his fuse were the occasional charades Freddie played out, especially her extreme prudishness. Chris's present begged for a small confrontation. The wine dispenser was a convincing copy of an object from the Italian Renaissance, a satyr figure, half-man, half-goat, with a lustful smile on its face. As the sales woman had demonstrated, one inserted a wine bottle in an inverted position inside the figure. Dispensing the wine was accomplished by pushing downward an erect but not too graphic penis in the front. While Chris envisioned it as a wonderful attention-getter for the frequent cocktail parties they held at their house, he could also imagine Freddie tossing it with great indignity into the trash.

Such thoughts were whirling through Chris's mind as he walked across the mall parking lot to his rental car. His attention hadn't registered a white van traveling down the row of parked cars he was crossing. The screeching of tires snapped him to attention as the van's front bumper nearly slammed into his shins. Chris let out a profanity, more out of fright than anger, but before he was able to gather his senses, men jumped out of the van and grabbed him. Seconds later he found himself on the floor of the van, a strongly scented cloth pressed over his face, then moments later he was unconscious.

Lying in the strange room, Chris still hadn't recalled this event. Cobwebs filled his head, and the grogginess he experienced was overpowering. In fact, the present moment was absent from his thoughts, which focused more on fragmentary episodes from his childhood.

Cub Scouts. The Pack? Dad said, "Chris, a pack's a lesson for life."

A pack? Like lions or wolves? I liked the solitary fox. But Dad was a wolf, and proud to be a member of the pack. Yeah, he'd also pack me by the scruff of my neck and try to shake sense into me. No use, though. His wolf pup was a little fox.

That's when Dad really died, not later. It was when he found out he'd sired a fox.

He fell silent long before his heartbeat did. He no longer howled around me, or at the moon. I preferred the golden sun. Or was it the night?

Bread was dead, too. He'd say, "Chris, life's the bread. Our soul. While partaking of it, we break it and share of it with others."

"No, Dad, bread's to buy things. Before others do. It was your pack, not mine."

This last shred of thought completed, Chris once again passed out.

2

Chris Folkstone was again awake and becoming more coherent. The stubble on his face clashed with his usual suave appearance, that polished look of a mid-thirties senior associate with Warwick & Albright, an international management consulting firm. To assure his career was firmly established, Chris had sacrificed much.

Among other things, he had put off marriage until after thirty, as had his wife, Freddie, a rising account executive in media advertising. Chris and Freddie hadn't sought each other out. In fact, if they'd met, there may've been little attraction. Mutual acquaintances, seeing in them a nice, pleasing fit, had maneuvered them together, declaring their marriage to be predestined. Indeed, as man and wife, Chris and Freddie created a slick partnership, fashioning an apart image, one that expressed itself in everything from their striking, self-designed house to their exclusive choice of friends. Lying there on the bed in the strange room, his head still heavy and aching, Chris concentrated hard, recalling when he'd last seen Freddie. It had been early morning on what Chris assumed was the previous day. Though still rather groggy, he tried to play the scene through in detail in his mind.

"It's 6 A.M." This announcement, in a synthesized voice, came from the digital clock perched on the microwave in Chris and Freddie Folkstone's kitchen. Chris sat in the breakfast nook, a folded newspaper under his nose. He lifted his personalized, custom-made stone mug to his lips, looking into it before taking a sip.

"Manic Mouse, this tea's dreadful!" Chris's half-pained expression was one of unrelinquished adolescence. "I just wasn't created for herbal teas. Some morning, I'm going to gag on this stuff, cinnamon-scented vomit and all." Chris ignored Freddie's frown, rolling his eyes up toward the ceiling. "Ah, for those days of yore, when a couple cigarettes and a strong coffee flicked the invisible switch. Wake up time for the bowels! And these fiber substitutes, Freddie, frankly, they're yuck!"

Freddie glared at Chris. "Dear old Hickory Harry, such crude outbursts are uncouth, and entirely detrimental to your image." Freddie shook her head from side to side, then planted her hand firmly on her flat, boyish hip. "New subject. What about vacation?"

"Vacation?" There was irritation in Chris's tone.

"Yes, vacation. Any thoughts about where?"

"The *in* place, or my preference?"

"The inniest place, dear."

"To impress our friends?"

"Yes, Mr. Trendsetter?"

Chris shrugged his shoulders. "Well, I guess I'm not the

authority. Besides, Manic Mouse, I've got a ton-plus-one things to do."

Freddie lifted her short, tight body to make herself look bigger. "Who's the consultant here?" Chris only shrugged again. "Okay, okay. I already carry the weight of the world on my tiny shoulders. But don't forget, if we don't book early, we're stuck spending Thanksgiving with my parents. Need I say more?"

Chris twisted his face into a dumbish, smart-assed look. "Got it. Nothing wrecks an image faster than vulgar displays of family ties, right, Mouse?"

"I believe that was a quote from me." Freddie glanced at the clock. "Chris, your taxi!" Chris was flying to a meeting with a major client and needed to be at the airport in about an hour. Freddie paused to sort her thoughts. "Chris, would you do me a big favor and pick up a gadget?"

"A gadget? You mean something no one needs, but can't live without? An ingenious wonder that saves minutes, but takes hours to figure out?"

"I hear old Hickory Harry coming through."

"Yes, Manic Mouse, ole Hickory Harry, tough as nails and clever as hell!" Chris raised his balled hand to his mouth like he was blowing a horn. "Tatatta ta ta ta! Time to go and get with the flow." Chris wiped his mouth and disappeared into the bathroom.

After ten minutes had passed, Freddie shouted, "My God, hurry, Chris! I'll die if we don't have time for a kiss. It's chilling, but I think I'm getting used to them."

Chris finally emerged from the bathroom, brushing stray hairs from his suit, too engrossed in his preparations to hear Freddie's teasing. "Do I look perfect?"

Freddie leaned against the wall, inspecting Chris. "Do we kiss today like Bogie and Ingrid? After all, you're flying."

"It was Ingrid who was flying. Bogie just stood there and smoked."

"While they were kissing?"

Chris lowered his bold chin, inserting his little finger into the corner of his mouth. "Bogie could hang his fag in the corner of his mouth, like this, yeah, even while they were kissing. Wanna give it a try?"

"No, thanks. A peck and squeeze will do. Burning passion's not my thing."

Chris went to get his things. Minutes later his taxi arrived. At the door, Chris struck a Rudolf Valentino pose, throwing his arms out to Freddie. "Just once, my dear, just once, let's make some old-passioned love!"

The honking of a taxi in the driveway interrupted Freddie's stilted laugh. "Chris, don't forget that gadget. We need something for the big cocktail gig this weekend. If you want to stay in the game, you have to score points, and new toys impress. How about a fig peeler?" Freddie giggled.

"Think that'll get our sex life going?"

Freddie's face twisted. "That was a low blow. Oh, forget it. No, don't forget it—the gadget, that is."

Chris saluted Freddie as he walked out the door. "Gotcha, chief. I'm outta here. See ya tonight."

Lying in the white, sterile room, Chris's thoughts drifted back to his immediate reality. *Damn, if there's anything Freddie hates, it's waiting. Someone must've notified her. Maybe she's here? Sure. This must be a hospital. She's probably outside raising hell to see me. Freddie, the control freak, won't let anyone tell her no. She'll be in here in a flash.*

God, this numbness in my head is unreal. This heaviness. I feel like a dinosaur.

This is too much effort, being alive.

Then, silently and effectively, the drugs took over again and Chris sank into darkness.

Koan Angstrom and Paul Wahrmacher conversed for hours, nearly every day, but much of it wasn't real conversation. Mostly Paul listened, and it often sounded as if Koan were speaking into an empty space.

"Paul, contrivance is unavoidable. Unfortunately, it's what's understood."

"Contrivance, sir?"

Koan Angstrom's hand slipped down from where it was smoothing his white hair away from his ear to the joint of his square jaw. "Yes, Paul. Except for the occasional instinctual twitch, the human species has hardly the faintest recollection of its natural niche within existence? In grandiose fashion, it uses the term civilization, a synthetic term created by those who would wish to elevate mankind above nature, its genesis womb, the providing ancestor from which it arose. And in trying to rise above creation itself, Man, unwittingly, is gradually sinking into a mire of its own self-destruction."

Koan Angstrom wasn't lecturing Paul, nor even trying to make a point of any urgency. His words were wrapped in a tone of sadness, like that of a father reflecting on a son who had fallen far short of his expectations.

"To listen to gifted people talk, humankind is standing on the threshold of mastering the universe. But that's like a fetus seeking to declare it omnipotence over its mother's womb." Koan's head sank to where his chin was nearly touching his broad chest. "The blindness of self-focus. Not only is the context being lost, but also being removed, destroyed. How long still? Seconds, perhaps, generously, minutes in celestial time? Our dear human species becomes suspended more and more on a solitary thread, a fragile, artificial thread. It may take only an insignificant natural event, then, snap, what is called social order, even the species itself, is gone, no longer existent. A minor role, a brief appearance in a much larger, eternal play, one that grinds forward without all those rules conceived by one, single species, an incidental corpse dragged behind the curtains and quickly forgotten."

Paul Wahrmacher nodded in silent agreement. His acceptance of what Koan said wasn't out of blind duty to a master, rather internalized faith. Paul's faith was based on never having experienced Koan Angstrom err in his observations.

"But why babble on endlessly? It's just words. I value your companionship, Paul. You are the consummate listener. But what I say is not something the common man wishes to hear." Koan paused, massaging his now uplifted chin. "Common man? When did I last read or hear that term? It implied so wonderfully that common denominator that bonds together all things. Holda.

"Paul, if one looks back on the passage of time, what is it that has shaken mankind back to some vestige of sobriety? Not bigger-than-life leaders. They have only led down paths of destruction. No, it's been one of its own kind. Its mirror image. A humble servant from among them. De couer, Paul. That's been your point, remarks I have not taken as dissent. To work it must be contrived."

"I don't believe I've said contrived, sir?"

"No, you prefer the phrase 'create a vehicle,' however, that is indisputably contrivance."

"I guess I must agree."

Koan Angstrom, who seemed entirely incognizant of his own appearance, was a solidly built man of average height. His white hair and a certain crustiness belied his age, but there were no signs of deterioration or loss of vigor. And beyond his outward image, his resolute spirit was truly ageless. Paul often thought of Koan as someone who could live on forever. The masses perceived Koan Angstrom, and his conglomerate, Angstrom Unlimited, in one, singular dimension: immense wealth. No one and nothing controlled more financial resources, although it was impossible to determine the exact numbers. His wealth, however, was merely a coincidental facet of Koan Angstrom's life. To those who tried to delve deeper into his identity and comprehend him, he was reclusive, mystical; complex beyond understanding. Amid often nonsensical speculation, one rumor was persistent, that he cursed his financial worth as a damnable by-product of his life, an accurate and definitive facet of the man. Koan spent much time envisioning how he could dispose of his wealth in some humble and meaningful way, however the sheer magnitude of such an endeavor frustrated him. Humble contradicted the dimensions of his power.

"Paul, what does time mean to our world? You've seen as often as I have that term, 'living legend.' How can I be immortalized while still alive?" A soft, sarcastic laugh eased out of Koan. "Is that not a desperate attempt to obliterate what is incomprehensible? As if the world fears an old man could spring some new surprises. Better to freeze him in an inanimate image."

While Koan Angstrom obsessively resisted attempts to immortalize his person, there were repeated attempts to do so, oftentimes triggering ridicule from him, or an act of humiliation. There was, for example, the government of the city, where his conglomerate's headquarters were located. To assure that Angstrom Industries and its enormous taxes would remain in their municipality, the city fathers made Koan an unusual offer. They asked him to rename the city, assuring him that any name he chose who be acceptable.

Upon hearing of this offer, Koan Angstrom had broken into uncontrolled laughter. Later, however, he suggested the name Pontifica. When Paul passed this onto the city council, there was bafflement, but a short time later, the name change was announced, and the official ceremonies were scheduled so that they synchronized with the construction of the new Angstrom Industries headquarters building.

The council had envisioned a dazzling structure that would become a landmark showpiece of the city skyline. To their dismay, the finished building turned out to be an amorphous, dull-black granite blob, cutely dubbed in the press as "the slag heap."

Most perceived this episode as an evasive and potent put down, exemplifying Koan's cynical and often devious defiance of worldly definitions.

While Koan Angstrom remained an enigma to the general public, it was imaginable that Paul Wahrmacher, his constant companion, possessed the insight to define him. Paul, however, never tried. Either he respected Koan Angstrom too greatly or was uncertain who the man really was. The only reference Paul ever made to his superior's identity was to cite a singular incident. That was Koan's response to a magazine article, from which he read a quote several times out loud to Paul. "Koan Angstrom is undoubtedly a man immersed in the perpetual pursuit of spiritual truths." That terse portrayal appeared to have gratified Koan.

Paul Wahrmacher carried many titles, but these were simply business formalities. He was president or chairman of dozens of companies within the Angstrom Industries conglomerate. But titles were not what defined him to others. Paul was variously described as polished, sleek, immaculately groomed, yet unobtrusive and never self-promoting, heartless in execution, always the epitome of efficiency. His bold forehead and slicked-back, dark hair gave him the appearance of one who moved deftly through obstacles. His eyes, nearly colorless, were as boringly intense as a narrowly focused laser beam, able to disrobe anyone confronting him of their every pretense. And if these characteristics weren't intimidating enough, there was that which was ever presently implied, that Paul Wahrmacher had Koan Angstrom's unconditional trust.

As in so many consummately functioning partnerships, Koan and Paul were wholly different beings yet faultlessly matched in complementing each other. Koan's intuition was his soul, godlike in its accuracy, with an uncanny ability to anticipate events. It was if he had access to the most intimate essence of existence itself. In contrast, Paul's mind was coldly analytical, skillful at structuring and carrying out intricate plans with incredible effectiveness. At the most basic level, Koan sketched outlines on a canvas and Paul filled in the forms and colors.

"Paul, it's a burden to be the object of so much speculation. Do I even need an identity? I would be most at ease perceived as a spirit, a boundless existence that permeates everything yet escapes tacit descriptions. Yes, that would give me peace."

While Koan and Paul functioned in tandem, a seamless mesh of two beings, there were times when Paul was left grasping for comprehension. He understood and mastered the concrete world, the rules that governed social interaction, negotiation, one upmanship. But when Koan wandered off into a spiritual realm, Paul fathomed him, at best, incompletely. Koan was careful never to deride Paul for his focused obsessions with tangible accomplishments. And he never lost a glimmer of hope that Paul might someday enter with him into a mystical state of cognition. That hope was dear to Koan Angstrom, for he felt himself in that province absolutely alone.

"Yes, Paul, a spirit could commune with souls, speak through their hearts. That would be the perfect existence. Holda. But look what mankind does, this compulsion it has. Even God must be something concrete, an image, a statue, a golden calf, an old man with white hair like mine." Koan allowed himself an amused smile. "Paul, I know you're not a religious man, but how do you know God?"

It was one of those moments in their conversations where Paul felt ill at ease, incompetent to be a worthy partner. "I guess it's as often said, God is revealed through the Bible, the prophets. Distilled out of that is an image of God, a mosaic of interpretations, if you like. But I confess, I haven't been one to read the Bible."

"Just as well, Paul. Why would God demand that, when one who is illiterate or deaf and blind can feel His spirit too? Why would a true God feel compelled to speak through mortal agents, prophets, or messiahs."

"I understand, sir."

"But you don't recognize the flaw?"

"No, sir. I'm confused. I find your argument very convincing, that God need be no more than a spirit mortal beings can perceive."

"The point, Paul, is our contrivance?"

"Oh, I see. You mean the creation of what you termed a mortal agent to interpret was seems too esoteric or spiritual. Yes, there's ambiguity in that."

"A very strong paradox."

"Yes, a paradox. Something you thrive on."

"Yes, Paul. It's not only in my name, but in my very nature. Paradoxes help unravel knots of misunderstanding."

Many an astute journalist in researching Koan Angstrom was frustrated to find his past was unusually murky. Though numerous theories had been concocted, no one ever established where he came from, or who his parents were. Paul guessed Koan to be around seventy, but there was nothing to affirm that. Koan had a few times joked that he had come to life as an adult, having no use for the trial-and-error searching of youth. Koan never reminisced about his past, and on those rarest of occasions when he took stock of his life, he didn't cite concrete worldly events, rather moments he called "elucidations," experiences that provided a clearer comprehension of life and existence. These he felt were the only real milestones in the passage of time, or a person's life.

"Paul, for the sake of discussion, what happens if I should die?" Paul professed he'd never considered the possibility, but Paul's evasiveness didn't satisfy Koan. "The possibility presents interesting questions, doesn't it? For example, what does mankind consider enduring? Would there be a temptation to place me together with a Carnegie, Mellon, or Rockefeller? That romantic myth of a robber baron turned Robin Hood? Such nonsense." Koan twisted his neck, as if it was stiffening, and let his eyes close. "A flawed equation, that power comes with an anguished conscience seeking redemption? But that's precisely how it would be presented, if I were to channel my wealth back into the potentials of mankind. The bitter old man so fearing to relinquish his wealth to his adversaries, presenting it instead to charity. That's contrivance of the worse kind. That charity, human potential, fear and altruism could share the same arena—precisely that stands between us and moving forward."

"I understand the dilemma, sir."

"Paul, I've shunned the public simply out of pure cynicism for the images that would be created."

"Something I fully respect, sir."

"Yes, you have, Paul. But that does give rise to chilling thoughts."

"How's that, sir?"

"What happens when there's no one left to unconditionally respect, to hold in high esteem and emulate? I can imagine life descending to a level of basic survival, the end of order as we know it. Perhaps better so. Man might then slip back into a humble but viable niche within Nature. From the perspective of the All, the human species is no more than an experiment, an attempt to see if worldly perception and comprehension of what lies beyond mortal existence can coexist with the raw instincts to survive? A species created out of grace, or a diabolical gesture?"

Paul felt prompted for a response, one for which he had no conviction. "Certainly, that sounds like a monumental test, or perhaps a curse?"

"I'd prefer not to believe it was a failed experiment." Koan slapped down loudly on the armrest. "Paul, the world should spend less energy trying to speculate who I am."

"I agree, sir. Elucidation is in what you stand for."

Koan smiled. "Very good, Paul. You are indeed a rare man, one who never allows himself the luxury of sentimentalities. I can imagine you won't want a tombstone to remind the world that you once were. Paul, point blank from your perspective, do you ever look at what we are about to do as nothing more than an experiment?"

Paul felt himself abruptly and unexpectedly pushed up against a granite wall. "Experiment? How do you mean that, sir?"

"Do you sense that I too may be caught up in an illusion, one that may be doomed to failure?"

"Sir, I've always said, with the highest of respect, that it isn't among my gifts to grasp everything you master and truly understand. And that offers me no substance with which I could form an opinion. My role is to facilitate, not question you."

Compassion arose in Koan and he conveyed it with a smile, before lifting himself from his chair. "It's time. I'm ready. As soon as the doctors give the go ahead, let's get on with it. Life and time don't come with reverse gears." At the door, Koan turned around. "Is our guest well?"

"Physically, yes, sir. And I have confidence in the measures to deal with the anticipated rebellion and resistance. The medical staff expects to run through their testing right on plan."

"That's in your hands, Paul. I wish there were some way to assure he maintains high spirits. Without having met face to face, I already feel a kinship with him."

3

For the first time Chris felt reasonably alert. During his semi-consciousness, he was certain he'd seen the blurred image of doctors, which buoyed his suspicions he was in a hospital. On the other hand, he didn't feel ill, nor did he detect any injuries from an accident. When he finally tried to rise from the bed, he was relieved to find he could walk.

The sole window in the room promised to provide some orientation, but the view offered few answers to Chris's questions. Near and far were nothing but well-landscaped gardens, rolling fields, and forests. From the distance to the ground below, he guessed he was on a second or third floor. Only a few times did he catch a glimpse of a person, and missing was the hustle and bustle one would expect outside a hospital.

Next Chris studied the room, but this too offered him little insight. Despite the high, ornate ceiling, the furnishings were more Spartan than the cheapest motel. The only piece of furniture, a chest of drawers, contained underwear, socks, sweat suits, and towels, but nothing like writing paper, information sheets, or pamphlets, which might hint at where he was. Chris casually gripped the knob on the only door, startled that it was locked. Confused, he laid back down on the bed, trying to reconstruct what had brought him there.

Let's see, I was at Transworld. Yeah, I really pulled that one off! The capital coup! A multi-million dollar contract! Watch out, bonus time's coming! I was off for home and the big celebration. Freddie the super striver was going to get a big, juicy bite of humble pie.

Hey, yes, that was it! Freddie! I'd forgotten the gadget I promised her. I stopped at the big mall on the way to the airport, and...wham, now I've got it!

I was going to my car, and that van almost ran over me. Men grabbed...no, that can't be?! I've been kidnapped!

No, why? Ransom? Absurd. Shit, we're in debt up to our ears. Come on, who'd want me? Yeah, like it was the Mafia, or the CIA. That's bullshit.

I do remember that, the van, the men. That must've gone fast. No fluke. But why me? And where am I?

No, no. I've got it. There was an accident or something. That was an ambulance. And this is a hospital. But why is the door locked?

Cool now, real cool, Chris. We're going to talk to someone. As quickly as possible. And with Freddie, and the office. We'll get this straightened out. Stay cool, diplomatic, real cool. As old Hickory Harry would say when things get hairy, "We need a fright blight, anxiety sobriety, ice in our veins."

Koan ran his thick fingers back through his silver gray

hair. He'd been going through an organizer of papers prepared for him by Paul. This was a daily morning routine, time set aside to expedite ongoing business matters. Completing the last required signature, Koan slapped the organizer shut, impatient to get onto other issues.

"Paul, I find it extremely difficult to refrain from talking to our young man."

"I understand, sir."

Koan clenched his hands together, tilting his head backward, closing his steely-gray eyes. "I wonder if he has any sense of his destiny? There was a time when young people perceived a thread of life, a continuity of time, real purpose. Not that I've ever viewed nostalgia with any admiration. Sense of tradition is perhaps a more acceptable term. Contrast that with that almost gleefully used expression, instant gratification. What is an instant? Not an explosion, nor creation, not even death. All involve factors and forces coming together, often painfully slow, to enable a leap to a different threshold. Certainly mankind didn't evolve in an instant. Is the very essence of living not a grappling with choices with far-reaching consequences?"

"Sir, as I know you, I agree."

"Then you must understand, Paul, why I want to know this young man?"

"I do understand, sir, however, our selection was made from a different perspective. We searched for someone in the mainstream of contemporary culture, an every man, if you will. Our man profiles as extremely self-centered, strongly inclined toward material pursuit, peer recognition, embellishment of his personal status. There's little pointing to any spiritual or intellectual development, though there are hints that such a basis may have been in place during his youth. We decided he should be someone most people can identify with. It's significant that he fits very well to the target audience of most advertising, which allowed us to conclude, that, at least in image, he would be a generally accepted stereotype.

Finally, it was essential, from the medical standpoint, that we establish perfect health and genetic strength."

Koan sighed deeply. "At least he valued his health. Of course, you're right, Paul. What could we hope to gain, if he were in my image? I admit it was easier to deal with this as an abstraction. Confronted with this person, it uncovers a disdain in me I'm not particularly proud of, one that has kept me apart from the world. In reading the description of the young man, I couldn't suppress the thought, how he and I could be merged into one? Maybe it's that question that fuels this burning urge to talk with him, like I'm hoping to discover some faint core of idealism within him, an ember that will ignite into a fire?"

"Sir, I don't wish to deter you from conversing with him. My comments were merely to guard against expectations. Perhaps when he's reached the compliant stage?"

"Fine. Tell me your opinion, Paul, is he a man among the people? What I mean is, are there substantial bonds between him and those around him?"

Paul hesitated, this time not to find the right phrasing. "Sir, I'm at a loss for an answer. He and his wife appeared to be nearly obsessed with knowing great numbers of people. Connecting, as they call it. They directed considerable time and effort into that."

"So, they sought out friends? That's hardly a negative attribute."

"If one takes a very broad definition of the term friendship, yes, however, in monitoring the response to his abduction, hardly anyone has rallied to his aid, or to the side of his wife. Surprisingly, no one, not even his firm, has prompted the authorities to expand their investigations."

Koan pawed with a hand over his face as if weary. "I hear that with concern, Paul." Koan's head sank, then raised again. "Perhaps he's as typical a person as we can find. Sadly. You're right, Paul. He will not be the same person. And wherein lies our oneness? Not in our bodies or minds, no, in our souls."

Chris was confident he'd be able to talk his way out of his situation. However, the opportunity didn't present itself. The only time the door was unlocked was to let two robotlike men enter to bring him meals and fresh laundry. They totally ignored his questions, acting as if he weren't there. Finally, someone else came in, three physicians, accompanied by the same two men. Chris unloaded his questions in complete expectation of answers, but to his amazement they also disregarded him.

Everyone there seemed to be stoics. The physicians went about doing tests, making notes, everything in near silence. Chris raised his tone a notch or two, but all that got was threatening looks from the two bodyguard-like characters, who approached him as if they were going to hold him down.

As days slipped by, Chris went without conducting anything worthy of the term conversation, despite his frequent medical visitors, or those who brought him meals and fresh laundry, and the silence made him increasingly disoriented. He tried joking with himself, creating his own dialogues, but even that took on an edge of fear.

"Chris, we want your body for science."

"Why me? I'm so perfect. There are plenty of ugly specimens lying around in the streets. If fact, taking them would beautify our city."

"We agree, Chris, but our purpose is to clone you. And your wife. You see, we're trying to create a world of perfect people."

"Pretty clever. Okay, but only on one condition. No herbal teas or fiber substitutes. And if detesting such things is an imperfection, hah, I don't qualify."

"Well, what about your wife?"

"Look, if you promise not to tell her I told you, the little lady has a thousand flaws, but not ones she'd ever admit to."

As such self-amusement became increasingly boring,

Chris spent more and more time lying on the bed trying to sleep. Sleep, however, didn't offer a comforting escape from his anxieties. Over the years, Chris had come to dream less and less. Now he was dreaming constantly, and most of the dreams related back to his childhood.

A dream that surfaced several times involved a hermit in a forest. There had been, in fact, such an old man, back in the small, remote town of Chris's youth, Shepherdstown. As kids they were warned to run, if they ever met the old hermit in the woods. Supposedly he was crazy, wandering about aimlessly like a wild animal.

Chris's dreams also included a person who was inseparable from any recollections of his childhood years. Moss was more than a buddy. He was a confidant, co-conspirator; his secret sharer in most everything he did. Their regular wanderings, disclosed to no one else, not even their families, took them far back into the forest, where they often met the old hermit, the one everyone in Shepherdstown seemed to fear.

The first time they ran into the old, scraggly man, he scared the wits out of them. His wild mane of whitish-gray hair matched his long beard, and he wore nothing more than stitched-together feed sacks, resembling an aged bale of cotton with arms and legs. Curiosity quickly overcame their fear, and Chris and Moss tried to get the old hermit to talk to them. To their surprise and amazement, his speech was clear and articulate, and an aura of gentleness and profound understanding surrounded him that contrasted wholly with his appearance.

This, their friendship with the old hermit, became one of Moss and Chris's many shared secrets. They loved to chew the fat with him, as seemingly aimless discussions were called in Shepherdstown. A mystical kind of wisdom that came through in his words fascinated them. Staring up at the white ceiling, Chris smiled, recalling that they had asked the old hermit what crazy people were, not saying to him that people in Shepherdstown categorized him as such.

It was great how he'd grab that long beard and look off somewhere far away, as if there was something out there sending him thoughts. He believed the minds of crazy people drifted away from them, like animals that weren't properly fenced in, sometimes returning, but usually not. We asked him where those minds went, and he said they probably got into other people's heads, made them a little different, maybe wiser, or more gifted. He even thought one of those minds had drifted into his head, giving him understanding he'd never had before. And then he said we might all be crazy, if we wanted to call it that, because he thought our minds, and our spirits, just floated about, and we could never know who was with us or where we were at any time. That made Moss and me feel so spooky, but there was something in it. We knew that. Seems funny now.

That was an incredible guy, that old hermit. Those people in Shepherdstown couldn't handle him. So? What's new? They couldn't handle me either. But it didn't mean I was crazy.

Oh, that too. He loved to talk about the trees. He loved them as if he were one of them. He'd say a tree doesn't know it's a tree. He said a tree was really the leaves it discarded and gave the forest floor to build new soil, or the branches and holes it provided to build nests. He often said that about the trees, and anything living, for that matter, that they were simply there for things around them, that everything in nature lived because it provided for everything else. And every once in awhile he'd blurt out that word, holda. Holda? Moss and I never found that word in a dictionary or encyclopedia. And he never explained it to us.

I sometimes wanted so badly to protest when he said that, that a tree isn't a tree. Only one time I did. He simply smiled, not in a condescending way, asking me why a tree would even be there if it weren't there to do all those things for everything around it. That sounded too much like something my dad would say. What I wanted to say was that I was Chris

Folkstone, that I could stand on my own, lead my life any way I wished, without regard for anything around me. Funny, I couldn't say that to the hermit, though I did, many times, to my father.

"How's our young man doing, Paul?"

Paul leafed through a file of papers, his eyes rapidly evaluating key notations. "Here in the medical team's report, everything looks fine, sir. Not one negative test result."

"Isn't he at least raising hell?"

"Of course. Let's see. That is surprising. There are five compliance phases here, and he's already rated a three."

"Paul, I detest that term, compliance, but I'm sure the team has a reason for using it. Cooperation would better please me."

"I can change that. Here's a note that might provide some insight. 'Rootedness seems weak. Possible loner mentality. Self-identity dependent on environment. Likely to encounter sharp defiance, but resistance to molding should be low.'"

"Paul, correct me, if you wish, but I don't perceive in that description any sign of character strength, or integrity. Weak rootedness? That equates, in my mind, with a lack of community bonds. Have we erred?"

"Sir, the team has assured us many times that none of his present traits will carry over after the procedure."

Koan's face mirrored an inner anguish. "Why, Paul, do I have this burning desire to converse with him? You needn't answer that. I must follow my instincts."

"Sir, if you allow me, I rather doubt he would comprehend you."

"You may be right, Paul, but I feel I must do it."

The physicians continued to test Chris with seeming obsession. Their attitude was as impersonal as a medical student's relationship to his cadaver. More than once, Chris jumped on a flash of compassion, like when one of them excused himself for his clumsy insertion of a needle into Chris's elbow vein. No conversations ensued. Chris even caught himself admiring the physicians for their self-discipline and the purposefulness of their professional procedurism.

Numerous times Chris simply lost it, delivering tirades and chains of profanities. On one such occasion, Chris's ego was getting a thorough bruising. He was strapped down and his head being shaved.

"You bastards! Do you know how long it took to nurse that hairdo? If I ever get your asses, I'm going to kick them from here to there and back again! And lawsuits? You're going to have enough of them to keep an army of attorneys busy."

Chris's outbursts and exaggerated machismo couldn't veil his increasing sense of isolation. Despite wild outbursts, even an hour of fist pounding against the door, Chris's will eroded.

The same evening his hair was removed, Chris had a strange dream. In it, he was disembarking from an airplane and walking up the gate ramp to the waiting area. It was the day on which he had landed the big new account for his firm. He could see Freddie waiting at the head of the gate, her arms opened wide to greet him, a magnum of Don Perignon on a chair next to her, the cork already popped and two champagne glasses filled. Then, as Chris was but a few steps from Freddie's embrace, men grabbed him by his arms, yanking him away. Chris cried out, 'Freddie, stop them, get help!' but Freddie's face broke out in a big grin, then laughter escaped her. Chris screamed at her to stop laughing and get someone to free him from the men, but Freddie only laughed louder, shouting sharply at Chris, 'Do you think I'm going to let you get one up on me, put me in your shadow, humiliate me? Not on your life, Chris. Take him!'

When Chris shook himself out of this dream, his first urge was to cry, but he fought it back, even though he was in total solitude. He found it hard to go back to sleep, disturbed that his mind could put Freddie in such a role.

A couple days later, Chris finally got a break from the monotony. A TV set and a video camera were rolled in, then the face of an old man appeared on the monitor. He was sitting in front of a big fireplace looking stern yet contented. On the old man's face was a strained smile.

"Hello, Chris. I want to welcome you as my guest. My name is Koan. I hope things have been comfortable for you."

Except for a crisp hello, Chris didn't reply. Too many thoughts were going through his head.

The man's face took on a concerned look. "Chris, I know you have lots of questions, but you have no reason to feel anxious. Everything's fine. You've cooperated surprisingly well." Again the face on the TV monitor smiled. "Chris, you're an exceptionally healthy young man. We assumed that, but had to make sure. I'm very pleased."

Chris couldn't hold back any longer. "Can you hear me?"

"Yes, I can."

"I have no idea why I'm here, or where I am. For starters, I would like to…"

"Chris! I will answer the questions I feel are important." The old man had a feisty look, stern, his voice slightly raspy, yet bold, determined, and confident. His commanding presence triggered an involuntary sense of respect in Chris, compelling him to hold back his questions. "Chris, because you're in such perfect health, you'll be taking part in something of immense value to mankind. You should feel very proud to be offered this opportunity. No, proud is inappropriate. This is an honor. Imagine the billions of human beings out there dashing about in the pursuit of empty activities, and you, yes, you, were plucked out of that mass to help save them, give them purpose. I could imagine it might make you feel very humble."

Chris listened like someone waiting for the punch line of a long joke, however, the old man continued without addressing Chris's questions. Chris's emotions were in conflict.

While his primal concern was his well-being, he sensed he was in something way over his head, and the rather grand style and tone of the old man was catching his imagination. When Chris finally pleaded again for explanations, he sounded muddled and unconvincing.

"Chris, why be preoccupied with such things in the face of such a great moment? Questions are superfluous when inevitability grasps us and elevates our potentialities to a higher level. You should summon your vitality and center on what will be. Again, Chris, I wish to apologize for the unpleasantness you've had to endure. I urge you to keep up the good spirits. The journey's worth it. Trust me."

Chris wanted to say something, but what he'd heard churned too powerfully through his mind.

Maybe there's going to be a big payout for this? This guy's big time. Maybe I just need to sit tight? There might be a good explanation for all the secretiveness and crap I'm going through. He said there's a big reward. Who am I to say I couldn't use one? Besides, making a big fuss isn't cool. I'd like to show this guy, Koan, yes, Koan, I'd like to show him I have a little savvy myself.

As the days of confinement became weeks, Chris's thoughts began to haunt him. He tried focusing on concrete things; his job, plans he and Freddie had made, friends and their competitive games to keep one step ahead of each other. These were, however, only brief reprieves from more basic deliberations, ones he didn't dwell on often; his childhood, his identity, his very existence.

Dad said men don't make a big fuss. He'd be disappointed if I were scared. He never complained, not even when he was dying. I wanted to hear that it hurt him, that there was something I could do to help. Pain was an abstraction for him. I never understood that.

Chris's father had died only a couple years earlier. He'd suffered a massive stroke and been hospitalized for the first time in his life. They had brought him to Pontifica so he could get the best possible treatment. That also allowed Chris to spend long evenings, sometimes all-night vigils, at his father's bedside. The only sound in that darkened room had been the beep of the heart monitor, and his father's heavy breathing. His father never regained consciousness, and even before he died, Chris sensed the loss, the escaping chance to put things right.

Chris hadn't told anyone he'd cried, but one person knew. She was a nurse and had entered the hospital room so softly Chris hadn't noticed. Without a word exchanged, that nurse, named Hope, offered Chris comfort.

After his father's death, Chris sought out Hope, and what he found was more than comfort for his loss. No one else in his contrived world allowed him to question himself, and Hope provided injections of sobriety to which he gradually became addicted.

Chris's thoughts went back to his last visit with Hope.

Chris's face betrayed in tight lines a genuine agony. "I wish I had the balls to change things." Chris stopped himself, falling back into dark silence.

Slivers of light knifed through the narrow opening between the drawn curtains, cutting across the modest living room, illuminating the face of the woman sitting cross-legged on the floor. Hope had that plain, ageless look established in a girl's teens and carried over into adulthood. Full figured, she gave an impression of nurturing tenderness. Her cuteness was that of the waitress you found at hamburger and coffee dives. While the face was nondescript, the yellow-brown eyes, even without makeup, could penetrate with intensity, mellowed by an edge of compassion.

"Chris, bitching's just misspent energy. And brooding only intensifies it."

Chris continued to stare at the ceiling. His attire was in marked contrast to Hope's. Her faded jeans and cotton blouse defined her as a someone whose priority was the price tag, not the label inside. In contrast, Chris's suit was designer styled, the uniform of the young, upwardly mobile businessman.

Chris looked around at Hope's small, cramped living room, the furnishings inexpensive and mostly passed on. "Why don't you find a better place?"

"Simple. I can't afford it."

When Chris suggested she find a better job, Hope barked back, "You know, there's some theory that I can't be happy just as I am. Well, that theory sucks."

Hope took a hasty swig of beer, her voice taking on an intentionally whining tone. "'Hope, why can't you find something more befitting to an image we'd all feel comfortable with?' Really, Chris, look at your happy little world. Before you lecture me about choices, what about yours?"

Chris climbed up from his prone position, lighting one of Hope's cigarettes and blowing a billow of smoke into the sunlight illuminating her. "So, you're the expert on choices. Tell me about them. What magical formulas do you apply?"

Hope's face twisted, her pale lips moving as if limbering themselves for a fight. "Formulas? Business school formulas? Plug in numbers and out comes the truth? Hah." Hope took a drag on her cigarette, the smoke surging through her nostrils like a comic strip bull, an utter contrast to the plain, sweet innocence of her face. "I've heard your macho stories, Chris, how you manipulate people, rip them off, sitting there smiling like you're proud of it." Hope pointed to her chest. "This is where the real choices come from."

Chris's smart smile left his face, and Hope asked if he was pissed.

"No, I understand. Leave my shit outside." Chris's head sank. "My world doesn't interest you, does it?"

"No, it doesn't, Chris. I find that world as plastic as all those self-identifying cards you carry. It reminds me of my brother. He had a little railroad set, with plastic buildings, and tiny plastic people. He lived in that world, creating things that took him far away. But it was dead world. Nothing ever moved or made a sound. The expressions on people's faces never changed. But it numbed him to the painful realities he couldn't face, the realities of the real world." Hope's eyes were damp, her throat tightened. "He put a graveyard in that railroad set. A family graveyard. And, one day, he chose death to leaving that world."

Chris got up and walked out, leaving Hope to anticipate the exit Chris so often made when she got too close. Instead she heard the toilet flush at the other end of the apartment, and a short while later sobbing. Hope arose and found Chris in her bedroom, sprawled face down on the bed. She snuggled up next to him and stroked his dark, well-styled hair, but Chris pressed his face into the bedspread like he wanted to hide, halfheartedly pushing Hope away.

"Hope, why do I come here? It's always the same crap."

"Take it easy, Chris." Hope laid her head next to his and embraced him.

They laid there in the half-darkness until the sunlight behind the drawn curtains began to fade. Finally, Chris rolled over onto his side.

"Hope, somewhere back as a kid, I believed I'd contribute something to the world." Chris went silent again, his eyes staring off into nowhere, wrestling with the chasm between his inner feelings and his external self. It was as different as the Rolex he wore, and the simple Timex strapped around Hope's wrist. "Hope, there are realities we can't change. Professions force us into attitudes. It narrows our choices. There're things you do to succeed."

"Chris, nothing compels us to give up our most basic choices," Hope playfully squeezed the tip of Chris's nose. "And I don't think you'll have to become a nurse to discover that." Hope moved closer and whispered into Chris's ear, "Dear buddy, you have your world out there waiting for you, not to mention a wife."

"Sometimes I wish…"

"Shhh. You're married. That's a reality."

Chris gave Hope a warm kiss. "Sometimes I wonder why you put up with this."

"Because I care about you." Hope gave Chris a passionate kiss. "Get your ass moving. And call me the next time you want to share the bed. At least I can phrase it that way, can't I?"

Chris was already up, standing in front of the mirror, making sure his clothes and hair were in order. "What's that, Hope?"

"I said, that's what I can tell myself. That…oh, nothing."

Chris kissed Hope on her pale forehead. "Thanks from the heart."

Chris shook himself, conscious again of his confinement, and the gathering dusk.

I can't cry. If Hope were here, maybe I could. But not alone. Tears beg for compassion.

Hope liked to joke about that, about the popularity of effeminate rock singers singing about hurting, how that let males emote vicariously, while assuring females that somewhere down deep in men there was a well-hidden ability to scream and sob. She understood those inner realms.

Hope must wonder why I haven't called. I always have, like clockwork. As if I feel more obligated to her than Freddie. If this were the hospital where Hope works, she'd walk in, put her arms around me, and I could let it all come rolling out. I wish.

God knows I need that. I need Hope.

4

The police had located Chris's rental car in a shopping center parking lot, but, after that, no further clues or leads materialized. It was as if he'd ceased to exist.

Calling it an investigative formality, the police twice interrogated Freddie, the first time to establish a personal background on Chris, the second interrogation concentrating on possible motives. The questions asked pushed Freddie past her limits, implying things she found utterly absurd.

"Was he disturbed about anything. Things, for example, that woke him up in the night? Were there any indications that he might have desperate concerns, like credit problems, or gambling debts? Did he sometimes seem distant, sensitive about discussing certain topics, have irrational outbursts? What about mood swings, depression? Did he ever get abusive? Was there another relationship, another woman he might've been seeing? Or a man?"

Again and again Freddie answered, "No." She found the questions insulting and once lost it, calling her interrogators amateur psychologists, suggesting a more systematic and focused investigation would've already located Chris.

Months later, after losing faith in the police, or the private investigator she and her father had hired, Freddie began her own search for clues and explanations. One of Freddie's extreme character traits was persistence, and her grilling of almost anyone who knew Chris began getting on a lot of nerves, especially those she interviewed numerous times. No one knew anything that even hinted at what may have happened to Chris. But then Freddie sensed a lead, a flimsy one, an inconsistency in someone's behavior.

It was Everett, one of Chris's assistants. Hired out of college, Everett had been assigned to Chris as an understudy. During Freddie's talks with people in Chris's firm, she had noticed a conspicuous hesitancy in Everett. Going on little more than intuition, Freddie invited Everett to dinner.

Everett was almost too sweet-looking to be called masculine, having the milk-fed, fresh look of a church choir boy. Sitting with him at the upscale restaurant *Chez Leon*, Freddie viewed Everett more as someone who could be her kid brother rather than her peer.

"Freddie, I can imagine it's awfully tough to deal with, I mean Chris, uh, his... his...I mean, that must be hard, uh...it is for me, uh, to understand it."

Outwardly, Everett looked so perfect, like all the other clones in Chris's firm, but when he opened his mouth, it fanned an ember of cynicism in Freddie. After the exchange of pleasantries, Freddie dug into what Everett might know.

"Everett, I'm sure you guys all have your places you go; watering holes, hang outs, places to unwind."

"Yeah, sometimes that's salvation itself."

"And acquaintances you see occasionally. People you know, just so."

Everett's negative response came too quickly.

"Look, Everett. Chris and I didn't always bother each other with casual acquaintances, but now such things could have meaning. I'm looking for clues, even little ones. You understand that, don't you?"

Everett was rescued by the appetizers being served. He dipped into his onion soup like he'd been starving for days. The interruption peeved Freddie, who glared at the waiter with a look that said, 'I'm paying for this, so I'll run the show, thank you.' Freddie continued her questioning, and Everett seemed to loosen up some.

"Okay. Let me think. Chris often went with us to The Rat Race. Know the place?" Everett named other places that were familiar to Freddie, but then hesitated. "Actually…no. Chris didn't really go there often."

Freddie leaned forward, as if she was going to reach out and shake Everett. He raised a hand like a policeman stopping traffic. "Really, I shouldn't be telling you this. Chris'd be totally pissed at me for shooting off my mouth."

"Chris's ass is in enough trouble."

"Okay. Good. It had something to do with bridges. Let's see…there was a song or something. Oh yeah. Burning Bridges. That's it. No idea where the place is, but that's where he went. I'm sure now. It was called Burning Bridges."

Freddie held the telephone receiver tensely with both hands, listening to the crackling ring at the other end of the line.

"Hi, Jack at da Bridges! Hooz dare?"

Freddie's breath caught in her throat. "Hello. I'm trying to locate someone."

The man on the phone yelled out to someone. "Ids some dame! Howda hell should ah know?" Freddie almost hung up.

"Wads dat ya said, lady?"

"I said I'm trying to locate someone. Someone who's been there."

"Al giva holler. Whad's da name?"

Freddie went rigid and hung up.

An hour passed before Freddie approached the phone again, sucking in air before dialing. The voice from earlier sent a rush of dread through her body.

"Whad's wrong, honey, drop yer coins?"

The sleazy cackle gave Freddie goose bumps. She straightened her torso, mustering up a determined composure. "Look, I'm trying to locate someone who occasionally frequented your bar. I'm trying to ascertain whether anyone there remembers him."

"Ya wanna asser what? Hey, dis lady's haifalutin'!" Another terrible cackle rolled through the phone.

The man's tone angered Freddie. "This is serious! Okay?"

The man finally agreed to ask if anyone knew Chris. For what seemed an eternity, Freddie heard only a muffled collection of garbled talk and laughter. Suddenly, the voice returned. "Lady, we may be in bisnuss, if id's da character ah think id is. Hardta ferget one like dat. Only saw 'em once. Mr. Moneybags! Lucky no one hit 'im up. Ya know whad ah mean? Much too classy fer deez parts."

"Has anyone seem him lately?"

"Jus' god through tellin' ya, ah only seen 'im once. Ya deaf or sumptin'? Ya sound like someone's wife."

"I'm not his wife!" Freddie's body trembled. "Look, is there anyone who can tell me more about him?"

"Led's see. Yeah. Ah think he used to talk to Fatha Nick."

"Is he there?"

"Fatha Nick only shows up when he wantsa. Ah'd had his ass outta here a long time ago, but he getsum talkin' their shit and drinkin'. When he's here. Give me yer nummer, and ah'll tell 'im ya called."

Freddie gave a false number and hung up.

Freddie would never have ventured into such surroundings intentionally. Several times, her low slung sports car scraped bottom on the pot-holed, litter-strewn streets. She found the Burning Bridges bar, which was one of only a few buildings still standing on a dark street. Freddie circled the block several times, but each time she slowed down to stop, fear overcame her. Finally, her foot hit the gas pedal, and her car sped off for home, accompanied by a sense of relief and safety.

Freddie phoned the Burning Bridges bar at intervals, usually getting the same person. Then one day, a man who said he was Father Nick was on the phone.

"Chris? Hmm…let me think. Chris, ya say?" There was a pause that Freddie wanted to help along. "You sound like a classy lady. Yeah. That coulda been the one. A kinda hotshot sorta guy? Yeah, I know 'im."

"Do you know where he might be?"

"Ah'm sorry, ma'am, could ya say dat louder?!" The background noise was overbearing. The man sounded like he knew something, but he insisted Freddie would have to come talk to him personally. Freddie kept on talking, even though it had clicked on the other end of the line. Realizing, finally, the call had ended, she dropped the receiver, her head sinking forward onto the desk.

Freddie had been rummaging through a chest of drawers with Chris's things in it and found a stash of scribbled papers. She sank down to the floor to read them.

Is the past ever past? Is the future but a continuum of what has come before? Are we but responsible for the here and now, or also obligated to that before us, and that which will come?

Freddie threw the paper down and grabbed another.

Was it Pavlov who discovered the dogs in us? Why then, I ask myself, do we go to church? Does the church fill our bellies, tickle the pleasure centers of our minds? Or even

promise to do so?
Move aside, you houses of worship. Make room for those almighty offerers who paint us those wonderfully gaudy images of satisfaction, gratification and pleasure.
Let them pass before us their collection plates. Plastic cards will do. Their icons offer us more variety, not merely a sad figure hanging on a butchered tree. We want the new, the ever changing. Where do we spend more time? In those sacred, stained-glass mausoleums, or before our flickering wonder boxes?
Yes, it was I, Pavlov who found the dog's button, and Madison Avenue discovered ours.

Freddie let her head sink back, her eyes shut, wondering if Chris had written as a diversion to amuse himself, dismissing as playful sarcasm the implied hostilities toward her profession. She picked up another sheet of paper.

Oh, Moses. Why did you spend so much time on the mountain? For ten lousy commandments? In just one night on Windy Hill, Moss and I came up with more. No wonder no one wanted to read yours. You took too long, Moses. People want instant gratification.

Freddie was agitated enough to need a couple tranquilizers from her stash of prescription drugs. Chris's preoccupation with religious themes was grotesquely out of character, territory she and he had never discussed. The name Moss, which came up numerous times, was foreign to her. Her voyeurism into Chris's secret life, while also repulsing her, spurred her curiosity to know more. And the only door ajar was the Burning Bridges bar.

Freddie stood in front of the cracked, peeling facade. Above her, a buzzing neon sign flickered inconsistently, lighting up the first four letters, "BURN." The building next door had done just that and was nothing more than a scorched skeleton.

In an attempt to look less conspicuous, Freddie wore old

jeans and a turtleneck sweater. Just down the street, a tattered man stared at her sports car with its personalized "FREDDIE" plates. She felt an urge to go over and cover it up.

From the other side of the dented metal door, Freddie heard a yelling voice, accompanied by a menacing, high-pitched laugh. She gingerly touched the dirty doorknob, pulling the door open. Immediately, air heavy with the repulsive smells engulfed her, making her cough.

Freddie looked around the dusky, smoke-filled room. At a larger table, a group of shaggy-headed men muttered and laughed in muted tones. Suddenly, one of them spotted her. "Hey, look! Id's the Virgin Mary!" The man crossed himself, while the other men gaped at Freddie as if she were a vision. Freddie froze to the spot.

"Ma'am, is dat you!?" The voice sounded familiar, yet Freddie couldn't move. Worse yet, she felt she was going to pee.

"Ma'am, ma'am!"

Freddie turned her head toward the voice, her face the picture of terror. A large, rotund man stood behind the bar at the end of the room, his round face, jolly in any other setting, framed by curly, unkempt hair.

"Ma'am, come over here!"

To murmurs and a few hoots, Freddie stumbled on an unevenness in the linoleum, falling up against a table that screeched loudly against the floor.

"She's hadda few."

"Cute bitch."

The voice from the bar broke in again. "Don't mind 'em, ma'am!"

Freddie reached a rusted chrome barstool with a torn and heavily taped plastic seat. It looked wretched but stable. She recognized the bartender's voice as that of Father Nick. He shoved a chipped glass across the bar. Freddie grasped the glass, her hand shaking as she lifted it to her mouth. The cheap whiskey made her cough.

"Take it easy, ma'am. Yer safe here."

Freddie straightened up, focusing as intensely as she could on the reasons she was there. "You're Nick?"

"Better known as Father Nick." The huge man in front of her made a proud pose. "Ya found me. But ah still don't know who you are."

"It doesn't matter."

"Chris's wife?"

Freddie flinched. "I'm not his wife!" Realizing her hefty response might be drawing the focus onto her identity and not the reasons she had come there, Freddie recomposed herself. "I've been asked to help locate Chris. A friend of his family. He disappeared without a trace, and the police investigation hasn't been that thorough. I'm checking out some loose ends."

Nick confirmed that Chris had been there quite a few times. "Had more money in his pocket dan mosta deez bastards will see in der lives. Guarantee ya dat."

A large cockroach rambled over the bar. Father Nick's hamlike hand smashed down and crushed it with a crackling sound. "He was ma bread, 'til he stopped comin'."

"When was that?"

"Months ago. Haven' seen 'im since."

A dirty hand slipped around Freddie's shoulder. "How's about a drink, baby?"

Freddie screamed.

"John! Get da hell away from da lady or ah'll kill ya! Ya bastard! Do ya hear me?! Git!" The hand disappeared, accompanied by cursing and muttering. "Don't worry 'bout dem, ma'am. Day all got shit in der pants. Jus' loud and smelly."

Freddie shuddered, but set forth her questions. "Why did Chris come here?"

"Why does anyone go anywhere? When ah first saw 'im, ah thought he was a pimp, or one of doze collecting guys. Until he opened his mouth. Only fine people talk dat way."

Freddie took another sip of her drink. It burned her throat, but helped her speak. "Did you talk much with Chris?"

"Oh, yeah. Ah'm a fine list'ner, and he hadda whole lot on his mind." Freddie prodded Father Nick to go into some of the subjects they'd discussed. Nick's eyes focused on Freddie's. "Fer example, his job. He didn't like dat one bit. He called id a buncha crap, a buncha assholes. Yeah, dat's whad he called 'im." Nick laughed loudly, his rotund body shaking. "Assholes! He had fire inniz eyes when he said dat. 'Assholes!'"

"Are you sure he meant his job?"

"Ah'm just tellin' ya whad ah heard, ma'am. He called 'em assholes. Id really tickled me how he'd say dat. 'Assholes!'"

"What else? Did Chris talk about anything else besides his job?"

Nick wiggled a fat finger in his ear, then coughed deeply without covering his mouth. "Damn place. Id'll be my death." Nick rubbed his bulbous chin slowly and deliberately. "Der wuz one thing, sumptin' worse dan his work."

"And that was?"

Nick leaned forward, closer than Freddie wished him to be. His breath smelled rancid. "There was some bitch."

"I beg your pardon?"

"Some bitch." Nick picked up a dirty towel and rubbed his hands in it. "She was a real pain in da ass to 'im."

"And who was this person? This woman, I assume?"

"Aw, ya know, ah didn't believe dat name. Not at first. Guess wealthy people use names like dat. He always said sumptin' like...led's see, ah've nearly forgotten it now. Id'll come." Father Nick turned away as if looking at Freddie disoriented him.

"Yeah, Manic Mouse! Dat's id! Manic Mouse. Kinda weird, dontcha think?"

"I think you're making that up."

Freddie's accusation caught Father Nick by surprise.

"No, ma'am. Dat's da truth." Nick chuckled, leaning forward with both elbows on the bar. "Sure sounds like sumptin' you'd make up, doesn't id. Can't imagine how anyone getsa name like Manic Mouse. 'Cept some of doze goofy rock stars. Thought he was puttin' me on."

Freddie fought back anger. "And what did Chris say about this woman?"

Nick leaned discretely closer. "Ya see, he had some beef with dis gal, da Manic Mouse one. Ice cold when id come to sex. 'Scuse me if ah'm gettin' too sensitive or sumptin'." Again, Nick couldn't hold back a rolling laugh. "She musta been half-crazy. He'd show me how she made all kinda lists, right here on da bar, scribblin' things all over da place. He said she even made notes to know when ta shit. 'Scuse me, but ain't that funny?"

Freddie's face reddened. There was too much truth in what she was hearing. It had embarrassed and disgusted her that her husband could have even frequented such a place, and confided in a loser, which was her judgment of Nick. But to hear that Chris had ridiculed her, that was too much. Freddie fought a growing nausea, forcing herself to ask with all the self-discipline she could muster whether Chris talked about other people. Father Nick was hazy about details, but all of a sudden he banged his fist against his round head.

"Ah nearly forgot dat. Yeah, dat was about da only time he wasn't all mad and angry. Her name? Led's see. Ah used to be sharper. Hold on." Nick clawed his head like a big bear, his forehead deeply wrinkled. "Got it! Cathy. No. Sumptin' real close to dat. Led's see." Freddie sat baffled, waiting, until Nick suddenly shouted, "Hope! Damn id! Dat's id! Hope."

"Hope what?"

"Not hope what? Dat was the damned name."

Freddie drew a blank.

Father Nick slapped at a roach with the towel, knocking it off the bar. "She's a nurse. He carried on an awful lot 'bout dat, dat she's a nurse. Helpin' people and all dat. 'She did it right.' Dat's what he'd say. He thought a lot a' dat lady."

Freddie didn't know any Hope, nor any nurses. "Was she a friend, acquaintance, or what?"

"Naw, not by da way he talked about her. She was more than a friend. He said she wouldn't fit in with his crowd, the asshole ones." Father Nick chuckled again. "Said she was dignified in a different way. Not like dem. He called id blood and guts. Ah'd say she was his girlfriend."

Freddie searched hurriedly in her purse for a twenty-dollar bill, put it on the bar, and briskly made her way out to her car. Sobbing briefly, she turned the ignition, accelerating away with a screech of the tires. It occurred to her that she hadn't asked directly about Chris's disappearance, or his possible whereabouts. It angered her, but she knew she wouldn't return.

Whether or not she'd ever find Chris had lost some of its significance. Chris had obviously betrayed her. It wasn't that he'd had an affair with another woman; Freddie felt she might be capable of forgiving him for that. What singed her ego too intensely was his denigration of her self-discipline and control. Freddie castigated herself over and over again for putting herself through such a humiliation, swearing her next challenge was to erase Chris completely from her mind. At home she showered nearly an hour, as if the visit to the Burning Bridge bar had left stains on her.

5

From his confinement, which in a macabre way he was coming to accept, Chris stared out the window. The fields and distant forest reminded him of Shepherdstown and the countryside around it, the setting of his boyhood he recalled with fondness. Chris reminisced how friends had ribbed him about his enthusiasm for writing. In their view, writing was something girls or sissies did. The only person he got encouragement from was an old-maid high school teacher, Miss Scribner, who died his senior year.

Chris cursed. There was nothing in the room to write on, and he felt an intense desire to do so. Finally, he began composing in his head, repeating the words again and again until he had each composition down pat.

"The rustling of leaves so often evoked a certain joy. Memories of the rich hues of autumn, smoldering smokiness in the air, dew heavy Friday evening football games. Those were yesterdays. Now my feet shuffle with tentativeness, tossing from my toes the browning carcasses of a tree's summer glory. Silence falls under my steps, which cease before a gray, pitted stone; a monument, not to my life, but to its ending."

Chris's creeping despondency, which he was having difficulty countering, was broken by several visits from an unusually impressive person. He had introduced himself as Paul. Chris felt intimidated by the man's polished presence, unable to summon the boldness necessary to present his many questions with any compelling edge. Paul's composure and command were far beyond the carefully rehearsed veneer Chris encountered daily in his now past business world.

It comforted Chris some when Paul expressed compassion for his plight. Paul, however, didn't dwell long on such emotions, rather, he spoke repeatedly of a great challenge Chris was going to face.

"Chris, this is the breed of challenge that most of us only fantasize about, the kind that fills us with exhilaration in our dreams. Mediocrity is something we can resign ourselves to, but never in our hearts really accept. We all long for something more heroic. More than anything else, Chris, this is what I would like you to understand. You are being offered that rare chance."

Half in jest, Chris said, "You know, Paul, they sent us to all kinds of motivational seminars, but none of those clowns came on like you do."

Paul glided smoothly past this attempt at flattery, making Chris deflatingly aware that his old rules of making it with others were totally out of place. Paul wasn't needy of any pats on the back or "attaboys."

"I understand your questions, Chris, but fate walks away

from those who confront it with suspicion. The hero who thrust himself onto a grenade, saving his buddy's life, he grasped destiny, if only in a split second. We all ask ourselves, if such a moment came our way, would we be able or willing to rise above ourselves? Ponder that, and not details and specifics, all of which will seem petty to you later. Grasp this moment to focus on possibilities that transcend who you are."

Chris ached to learn what the specifics were going to be, but he felt he would be insulting Paul if he pressed him with further questions. This reaction within him angered him somewhat, but he had reached a point where he was more inclined to let someone lead him out rather than to try to bust out on his own will.

"Chris, Mr. Angstrom has made a choice, a monumental choice, that you should join him. That will first reveal itself to you when you get there, but it's a noble choice. Free yourself as much as possible of your past, and prepare yourself for a new beginning of your life."

The uplifting shots of adrenaline Paul's visits provided couldn't abate the anxiety Chris was experiencing. And thoughts were all Chris had. In fact, verbal dialogue began to seem trite to Chris. He began to view much of his past intercourse with people as insignificant and empty. But his thoughts were also driving him to the brink of sanity, and they wound themselves into ever-tighter spirals.

Charlie, at the office, talked about staging his own wake. He wanted to lie in an open casket so he could hear what people were saying about him. He had said that was the only time anyone says anything near the truth about us.

What would they say at my wake? Would Freddie shoot from the hip, or just be Miss Nimblefoot, the grand mistress at side-stepping straight talk, except when there's an advantage to be gained from it? I can hear her talking about her good dude, happy-go-lucky Hickory Harry. Thanks, but I don't need to die for that great insight.

Chris took socks, balled them up, laid on the bed tossing them at an open drawer, doing an accompanying basketball play-by-play. A half-hour later, this became old.

That heroic stuff Paul talked about sounds great, but it's got to be cornballs. I mean, what happened to John in the contracts department? Blew the horn on a client who was overcharging government contracts. Fine and good, someone was breaking laws, but what did he have from being a hero? A moment of glory, and now his career's down the tubes. Well, at least he's not competing with me for the next promotion. Shit, what promotion? Will I even see my old job again? Doesn't sound like it.

Chris tried again and again to go back to composing little things in his mind, but it wasn't working. He had just his thoughts, crowded with anxieties.

It's just as well Freddie hasn't tried to find me. Ice cold, I have to say it. I detest the bitch. Why any diplomacy now? I've been nothing but a fucking cheerleader, a pump for her unquenchable ego, an extra mirror to embellish her image of herself. If I don't get out of here, she'll need a replacement for me. She doesn't function well without someone telling her how great she's doing. Even when it's a pile of lies.

But who the hell am I to crucify her? Good ole Hickory Harry, Freddie's appendage. Man, that Transworld contract was my one chance to prove myself and get the big-time recognition from her I wanted, and, wham, it got snatched away from me. Like she was behind it.

Finding no rope to pull him out of the quicksand of self-pity, Chris rolled over and tried to bury his head under the pillow.

Is there someone waiting behind that black curtain in front of me, ready to ask, when I pass through, 'Hello, Chris, tell me what difference has it made? Tell me about the significance of your life.' God, no, please, I'm not ready to die. And if I must, don't let there be anyone on the other side to greet me. Especially not Dad. I beg you, please, let it be a black void, absolute solitude, with nothing to compare what was with what could have been.

Although his emotions drove him to consider the possibility, Chris was too attached to his living self to seriously entertain suicide. His self-pity didn't equate to self-destruction.

They're saying this is a noble cause. When it's done, will they tell everyone? Can't there be one last cheer or applause? Oh, God, please, don't let me die a selfish bastard. I don't want to spend eternity listening to the echoes of Dad's voice.

The noises were just loud enough to draw Chris from a very deep sleep. His eyes opened. It was dark and he surmised that the sounds had been dreamt, but then someone cleared their throat deeply. They were in the room, in the dark there with him.

"Who is it?"

"I'm sorry I've awakened you."

The voice was familiar, even though Chris had only heard it once. "Is that you, Mr. Angstrom?"

"Yes. What better time than in the deepest hours of the night to talk about that which moves our souls. Do you mind?"

A shudder went through Chris. It wasn't the undercooling of the night. Chris recognized the fear that made him shiver. It was the close proximity of a man of Koan Angstrom's power and prominence, highlighted by the darkness surrounding them.

"What do you want to discuss with me?"

"Us. The larger dimensions of what we are. That which remains of us when we feel our identity has vanished. Holda. Our oneness with others. Holda."

That statement hit an eerie chord within Chris, a recollection back to his college years, to a specific person, a student named Dale who had uttered a sentence very close to the one Chris had just heard. Dale had been an oddball of sorts, shunning the traditional trappings of college life such as fraternities, weekend partying, and other activities Chris had held so dear. No, Dale had not been a nerd. In fact, he was an accomplished mountain climber, regularly repelling down the sides of the dormitory to keep himself in shape. He was a theology student, but without intentions of entering into the service of the church. Dale impressed upon Chris that he pursued the comprehension of higher truths, and this elicited in Chris conscious efforts to avoid Dale, or be seen in his company. Similarly, though, as Koan Angstrom had done, Dale slipped into Chris's room, usually later at night, when Chris couldn't escape conversing with him.

What Chris specifically recalled was a late-night discussion with Dale that had lasted several hours. At some point, Chris began to feel lightheaded. It was as if his words no longer were tied to deliberate thoughts but arose from some part of him over which he had no control. He and Dale had several times remarked with utter calm and peace that they felt like they were sailing through the universe, back to the very dawn of existence itself. That's when Dale said their physical identities had completely vanished and they had become one with all that ever was and ever would be.

"Chris, can you imagine yourself shedding those things that describe you to others, where you live, your profession, yes, your name? Can you imagine that state of being, devoid of all that, and being anew, fresh from scratch?"

"No, sir, I can't."

"What about death? Surely, you do not believe we take all those trappings with us?"

"Of course not."

"Good. Let's say you were resurrected, after your death, however, as you agree, your identity had ceased when you died. Can you imagine that and how you would feel?"

"Dead and resurrected? I guess I'd be a ghost."

"Describe a ghost to me."

"Invisible? I don't know. I guess I'd still have to have an

identity?"

"Yes, perhaps. But not that which, as you say, would be visible to others. You would have no physical dimensions. That's a good word, you would be limitless."

"In what way?" To his surprise, Chris was enjoying the discussion, which reminded him of ones he'd had during his boyhood with Moss, very occasionally and briefly with his father, and another strange partaker in his life, the old hermit in the forest.

"Limitless applies to little or nothing in the concrete world, that which we mistakenly believe to be the only life we have. We're incapable of imagining the concept of being limitless, because we've become dependent on such things as mathematics and physics to tell us our world has bounds. And we are always limited by our personal identities, real or contrived. But a ghost or a spirit, what might place any constraints on such a state? Taking that a bit further, where would one spirit end and the other begin? Are there any compelling arguments that there would be individual spirits, as opposed to just one great unity?"

Again, a shudder shook Chris as the words of the old hermit came to him, "We are for just moments individual drops of rain falling from the heavens to merge again in puddles, streams and rivers as one."

"I suppose you're right, sir. Why should there be lots of ghosts, except maybe to talk to each other."

"About what? Our professional pursuits, our newest acquisitions? Certainly not to talk about the weather, which would become fully irrelevant. Politics? There would no longer be boundaries to separate us, no territories to be occupied, no wants to right where individuals are in conflict. You see, Chris, what would there be to talk about?"

"Maybe about all the crap we did wrong while we were alive?" Chris chuckled, hoping it would lighten up the conversation.

"Good point, Chris. But perhaps we would have resolved

that by merging into a spiritual oneness. After all, is it not our persistence in finding ways to keep ourselves separate from one another as mortal beings that leads to most of what we regret at the ends of our lives?"

Koan Angstrom's point stabbed at Chris's heart, where his alienation from his father hit him. "I suppose you're right, sir."

"It's of little importance to me that I be right, Chris. What interests me is what you believe?"

"Well, I think I believe that, what we've been talking about. In fact, I've had a lot of time to ponder what comes after death. I'd like to believe that's the way it'll be."

"And what about during our mortal lives? Do you not believe a limitless dimension is possible, that it's futile to seek a oneness?"

The urge pushed Chris toward agreement, simply to please Mr. Angstrom, but he also feared his insincerity might be detected. "Mr. Angstrom, can I ask you a question?" Chris got a yes. "You've been extremely successful, and it seems reasonable to wonder how you could have accomplished that without asserting who you are, how unique you are in your abilities and understanding of business and finances?"

Apprehension gripped Chris that he had spoken too freely, but a gentle roll of laughter allowed him to relax.

"Chris, what you know of me is not from me. Any identity I have is the vivid imagination of others. You know more of me from this conversation than from all you may have read or heard. You could be me, and I you, at least a dimension of you, a personal dimension you haven't trusted with too much freedom. Yes, I have a name, a creation to satisfy the cyclical mechanics of the physical world, but it is just one of endless names that could be attached to me. Have you ever known anyone who had no name?"

"Yes, there was an old hermit we talked to in the forest, when I was boy."

"Interesting. Did it matter to you that he had no name?"

"No, actually it didn't."

"Then we have arrived at an understanding that makes us one."

The faint, warm glow inside him seemed terribly inappropriate to Chris, given with whom he was talking.

"So, Chris, I have kept you awake long enough. I'm very contented in leaving you, knowing there is less than we may have thought separating us. Have a good night's sleep."

Days later, Chris was taken to a room and strapped to a table. As the doctors moved about him, he lost it, exploding into a tantrum of abusive language.

"You lousy sons of bitches! You think I'm some stupid asshole, who doesn't care what the hell's going on around here. Well, goddamn you, it's my fucking body you're messing with. And it's my fucking freedom you've taken away. I'll get your asses! You wait! I'll have you arrogant bastards sued, defrocked!"

Chris was restrained and injected with a sedative.

Later, Chris drifted back into semi-consciousness. The scent of disinfectant hung in the air. Lying on a table with bright lights over him, he saw, only a few feet away, a form on another table.

"Hello, Chris, we meet again." It was Koan Angstrom. Chris tried to reply.

"Take it easy, Chris. I'm calm, and you should be, as well."

Chris felt worse than drunk, trying with all his power and energy to speak. "I wena nu was happeenin'...waas...ken ah go now?"

"Everything's just fine, Chris. You may find comfort, if you just listen. Listening's a great virtue, but so rare these days."

Chris's pleading couldn't stir the countenance of supreme satisfaction shrouding the man next to him. "Chris, this is part of the great inevitability. People live in illusions.

They believe they control their destinies. A selfish belief. Most of their lives are simple ties, events that sweep them along. Rarely does a moment of choice confront us, and when it does, most ignore it, pursuing instead their petty obsessions. You stand before a choice, one of the greatest a man could receive. Choose to go into it with grace, Chris, and gratitude that you've been so honored. Holda."

Chris's strength was ebbing. A veil of peace settled over him. His body became light, light enough to be swept up by a wind and carried through the air, over puffy clouds into a realm of beauty and calm.

6

It was a world of faint, pale green, in which nothing changed, a monotonous roaring lightly encroached upon by faint beeps. Thoughts didn't exist, merely occasional fragments, random pieces of remembrance.

Turtle shell. Wet. Stone. Stanley. High. Gone. Colored glass. Snow. Sun. Albright. Hand. Warm. Hope. Windy Hill. Fire.

What seemed a state of eternal bliss was shaken, gently by voices, murmurs rather than recognizable words, like the chanting of Buddhist monks. Still, there were no coherent thoughts.

Angels. Heaven? Dad? Death. Me? Freddie?

The feeling of floating around weightlessly in some huge, hollow dome seemed a passing, post mortem state, stations en route to an afterlife or post-life existence.

Chris felt no emotions, no anxiety or apprehension, no fear, joy, or happiness, only a desolate, empty numbness. Also a sense of relief, an unprecedented state of peace.

"Sir, you're coming along real well. Keep your spirits up. We're making progress."

Weeks had passed and the team of physicians was detecting strengthening life signs in Chris, who was now registering what the voices around him were saying.

Ironically, his revitalization was being fueled by anger and disappointment. The embrace of death had been too inviting, too comforting in its finality. A profanity leaped to his lips, one meant for whoever was talking to him, but he couldn't coordinate his mouth and tongue to speak it.

"Heilgott, pray to whomever you believe in. With gratitude. I now believe he's going to pull through. I feel it."

The room was dark, except for a green-shaded bookkeeper's lamp on Dr. Heilgott's desk. He had been the lead physician in an experiment gone grotesquely awry. He sat there, his hollow, bloodshot eyes staring blankly at Paul, as if all human emotion had left him.

"Paul, I can give no assurances that what we're perceiving is a recovery. The brain waves aren't matching the pre-procedure patterns. But then, what we were measuring weren't normal signals. To use a non-professional expression, there's something eerie about Mr. Angstrom, an electromagnetic dimension we can't explain. But we've talked about that already, and that isn't your concern. If you're asking me if he's recovering, yes, everything points to that. I'm optimistic."

At Koan Angstrom's unwavering demands, an interdisciplinary team had attempted a procedure no one, to their knowledge, had ever undertaken. Koan called it "instilling his soul into the young man." The consensus among the assembled experts had been that the soul resided in the brain, that an extraction of the soul was possible, utilizing a super computer. However, on the question of whether one soul could be "overlayed" onto that of another, the verdict was split. A layman in the technology involved, Paul had had his own grave doubts.

The first crisis occurred after they had downloaded the electromagnetic contents of Chris's and Koan's brains. Hours into the "soul merging" procedure, which was processing within the computer, Chris's vital signs began to wane. In response, the physicians focused themselves completely on reviving Chris, but their efforts were in vain. The next morning, Chris had to be declared dead.

In essence, this tragic turn of events canceled the very purpose of the elaborate proceedings. All that remained was to revive Koan Angstrom out of his induced comatose state. The medical team's greatest apprehension was how they were going to explain their failure to Koan.

That's when the second crisis occurred. Bringing Koan Angstrom back to consciousness failed. Frantic hours were spent brainstorming what to do next, but it produced discord and profound disagreement. Dr. Heilgott, as the group's leader, even cracked a few times under the intense pressure, requiring Paul to step in and coerce him back to sobriety.

"Heilgott, I should have listened to my gut instincts. I had little faith in the technical feasibility. Thank God he's still alive."

Dr. Heilgott wagged a finger limply toward Paul. "Our only doubts were whether we had created the correct matrices in the brain simulator. Locationally, we…"

"That's your realm, Heilgott. I've never professed to understand it. I'll be very relieved when we're back to square one, and remain there."

"If there was a point of origin?" Dr. Heilgott said this with the blank look of a corpse, sending a shiver through Paul.

"Heilgott, if he recovers, I'll take back everything I've accused you of, but I suggest, until then, that you pray."

"You think I haven't? Reloading the contents of his brain back from the computer, no, I didn't know if that would work. Some of my colleagues distanced themselves from it. And I've prayed. At least he seems to be coming out of the coma."

"How much longer will that take?"

"Until he regains full consciousness? Your guess is as good as mine."

"Then continue to pray."

Chris finally recognized a voice. It was the man named Paul, who was encouraging him to be courageous. Thinking was still arduous, his brain a heavy, often painful blackness. Recollections of the past came much easier than focusing on the present.

Dad said we kids lacked discipline. Discipline? I lifted my arms, moved my fingers, felt every muscle contract and relax, asking myself, "Is this what Dad meant by discipline?"

Dad said, "Boot camp, that'd straighten ya out. An ole drill instructor like I had. That'd do it." I went to the army recruiters, over at Christchurch, telling Dad that evening I was gonna sign up. He exploded, but never told me why. Just that one sentence. "Son, going to war wasn't meant to prove anything."

"All the things I wanted to be. A doctor, because old Dr. Lutz was the most respected man in town. A landscaper, because I knew the fields and woods better than my home. But then, the time came when I didn't care. I just wanted to get out of there. And college, thank God, was the escape.

Grades came easy enough. And frat life was fun. Bullshitting. Like my job. Do shit for some shit organization for the shit it gives you, and all the shit you can buy. That was the shit for me. I got lots of good job offers.

But I lost something? It was like that compass Dad gave

me that one Christmas.

I lost a sense of direction. The church spire in Shepherdstown. You could see it from everywhere. Just seeing the church spire, from the distance, you knew where home was, where the doctor's office was, the school. You could tell people, 'It's just a few streets over from the church, over there, the tall steeple.'

That compass wouldn't work in our subdivision, the one we live in now. There's only that water tower, out in a field, but it doesn't tell you where anything is. It's like the streets. In Shepherdstown, Oak Street was draped by big oaks, Park Lane ran by the park. Now our home's on Highland Lane, but there're no hills, or any heather on Heather Crest, the cul de sac behind us. Back in Shepherdstown, things made a lot more sense. And you didn't get lost so easy.

Why is this guy Paul trying to tell me what courage is? I had courage, courage to leave the world of a father I couldn't understand, courage to enter a world that didn't make sense, not like that of the woods, fields, and animals. I had the courage to cast off that identity and assume one that worked. Hell, I became someone I wasn't, like Hope used to say, but that's courage. What more does this Paul expect of me? I dared to forget everything familiar back in Shepherdstown and walk into an unknown and chaotic world. And I was ready to die. That's courage.

Nearly two more weeks passed. Though his sight was still blurred, Chris believed he recognized doctors, and, for the first time, he saw Paul, or at least the discernible outlines of his face.

"Sir, the therapist said you were able to whisper a few words. Keep working on that, like your life depends on it."

"Freddie." Chris's whisper was barely audible. "Freddie. Where? Where?"

Paul's forehead wrinkled in response to a name he'd never heard Koan mention, dismissing it as an act of delirium.

"Everything's just fine, sir. Continue to focus on speaking. I'm convinced it will help with the recovery. You're doing well. Very well."

The increasing clarity of his thoughts, along with the emergence of rudimentary speech, buoyed Chris's spirits, but one day his delicately woven threads of hope were ripped apart. Paul, who spent hours with him, mostly in silence or mindless cheerleading, sounded increasingly agitated by Chris's utterances. Paul leaned very close to Chris, his lips nearly touching Chris's ear, asking slowly and deliberately, "Who are you?"

Finding the question odd, Chris said his name. Paul asked again, twice more, each time hearing "Chris" being whispered. Suddenly, Paul yelled out, "Oh, my God! No, this can't be true! No, it can't be!" Paul stormed out of the room, leaving Chris in a swirl of confusion.

7

One day, as Chris's eyes began focusing more sharply, he was suddenly overcome by a feeling of dread. His hands and arms had changed drastically. They were thick and meaty, appearing aged and covered with a coarse, whitish hair.

Paul continued to visit Chris regularly, but his mood had swung from passionate encouragement to obligatory compassion. Chris, highly attuned to such nuances, concluded there was something wrong about himself, that that was the cause for Paul's shift of attitude. And the alterations in his body he recognized more and more were, he decided, an symptom of what was wrong with him.

"Paul, what has happened to me? Am I sick?"

"No, Chris." Paul sounded sad. "Chris, it's no use to leave you wondering and guessing. You will require time to comprehend everything, but you have left an existence behind you, become a different person. I realize this may alarm you, but there's much to be optimistic about. Believe me, it is so."

In small chewable portions, Paul gradually explained to Chris that his body was now that of Koan Angstrom. When Chris asked why, or how it was possible, Paul's total command and control sometimes wavered. Glossing over technical or medical clarifications, Paul instead concentrated on defining who Koan Angstrom had been.

Chris listened, often with intense fascination, but wondered why he needed to know so much about the man.

"Chris, I'm certain you had aspirations that went unfulfilled because the means and position failed you. Sometimes fate takes twists that suddenly thrust us into a situation where our dreams can come true. That is, if we have the patience and perseverance to deal with our new givens."

Paul's strategy, one he found no viable alternative to, was to drop hints of a new life with greater potentials than before. He knew it was also a gamble, and it failed. When it finally dawned on Chris that Paul wanted him to adopt the role of Koan Angstrom, he was stunned. Instead of seeing that as a thread of hope, Chris focused on his irrevocable loss of his own identity. His physical condition went through setbacks, paralleled by erratic swings of emotion, ranging from cynical laughter to bitter anger, with longer periods of moroseness and depression.

Ironically, Paul finally came face-to-face with his own loss, which he had buried under the urgency of his crisis management. An awareness crept over him that he had to get acquainted with the person in the body in front of him, take him on as a partner, regardless of how difficult this acceptance seemed. Otherwise he was alone, a state he was unable to cope with.

"Chris, I hope you have come to know me, for we will be

spending more and more time together. And I also hope there is trust. No, I understand that might be difficult. You may see me as the cause for your condition. Chris, you must believe me. There were no intentions to change your identity. With God as my witness, you should have been, now, the very person you were before. This outcome is as, how do I say it, tragic, yes, as tragic to me as it is for you."

"But what's happened to me?"

Paul, who hardly exhibited his emotions outwardly, couldn't disguise a look of pain. "I have a fear of telling you."

"Why?"

Paul paused and closed his eyes. "If I were you, it would weigh as heavily on me as anything possibly could. But I don't dare deceive you, as hard as it is to tell you more."

An eerie chill passed through Chris's body. He only knew Paul as an immaculately polished person and knew whatever was tearing him up must be earth shattering. Chris fenced with an urge to beg Paul not to continue, aware he didn't know how close his own sanity was to falling over an abyss.

"Chris, I'm at a total loss for a nicely packaged way to say it. Your body died. It's been disposed of. Cremated."

Chris's eyes fell shut, he wanted to scream, but instead a soft moan eased across his lips, and he nearly slipped into unconsciousness. He felt Paul's fingers wrap themselves around his forearm and squeeze firmly. Minutes passed before his eyelids separated. Paul wasn't looking at him. His head was sunken, his eyes appeared to be shut.

"Paul, this is no joke, is it?"

The lack of response answered Chris's question.

"But this is insane."

"Chris, I wish I possessed the supernatural powers to turn events around. I'd snap my fingers and bring you back, you and Mr. Angstrom. Yes, you're both gone. This isn't going to be easy, Chris. For either of us. If there's something to hold onto, it's the one reality we have. You're alive."

Paul's fingers were still pressing like a vise around

Chris's forearm. Paul looked Chris in the eyes, seeing an empty disbelief. He realized that more words weren't going to alter the emotions that had been aroused. He pardoned himself, leaving the room. Outside, standing in the hallway, Paul heard the sound of sobbing coming from Chris's room.

For a while, it looked as if Chris had regressed back into his comatose state, and his vital signs were deteriorating. The team of doctors informed Paul that they were powerless, that they were witnessing a struggle of the will to live. Nearly a week had passed, when Chris's condition suddenly took a turn for the better. In fact, this time, he seemed fully recovered, his speech very clear, and his eyesight nearly perfect.

Chris again grilled Paul to tell him everything that had happened. Paul's greatest hesitation wasn't about the technical procedures that had been tried, but rather their intended purpose.

"Chris, something was telling me it wouldn't work. But it was a struggle between his intentions, which I still will not question, and the physical constraints of the concrete world. I have to take much of the blame. But you see, in my relationship with Mr. Angstrom, it was his intuition that was followed. I could not act on mine alone, and that's all I had, an intuitive feeling it wasn't going to be successful."

Chris wondered why he felt so little anger toward Paul. The emotion seemed appropriate. Chris blamed his lack of rage on the fact that Paul was being perfectly candid and forthright with him. It was also his growing awareness that Paul was an ally and perhaps his only friend.

Chris still didn't comprehend why Koan wanted to instill his soul into Chris's.

"What purpose would that have served? And how would anyone even recognize that one person's soul had been exchanged for another? I mean, how do you know, right now, that I don't have Koan Angstrom's soul in me, that the whole thing didn't work?"

There was again that baffled look on Paul's face that seemed so unfitting to him. "I don't know, Chris. No, I don't have an answer to that. But I have to presume that no transfer of souls took place, that the procedure didn't even get that far. I have to take that as a given."

"You mean, since cremating me once didn't work, we have to work on some other way to eliminate me?" Chris's words were meant in jest, but neither laughed.

"Chris, I see only one focus, one I hope you will choose to embrace. As you lie here before me, Koan Angstrom still exists, and the task will be to further that existence. It's that simple."

As Paul's words predicted, Chris found no conclusion other than to accept his new identity, no matter how reluctantly and with whatever bitterness, and it was equally clear that without Paul, he had no identity. This created a sudden craving in Chris to pepper Paul with questions.

Who was Koan Angstrom? Unfortunately, the answers to that weren't simple. He had been an immensely complex person. Each time Chris received some new explanation, it simply elicited dozens of new questions.

Aside from the personality of the man he was now supposed to be, Chris was also curious about more superficial matters, such as just how wealthy and powerful Koan Angstrom had really been? The truth that emerged was staggering. Chris realized he couldn't even think in such magnitudes, and again it underscored to him his utter dependence on Paul.

"Anyway the doctors, while they're still here, can install a tape player in me?"

"A tape player?"

"Yes, Paul. So you can record the business decisions I'm supposed to make and I can lip synch them as they come out. I'll try to avoid any dumb looks, look astute, and in control."

There was always a sober reality that came back to smash such levity like a giant black hammer. And Chris couldn't escape it. Whenever Chris's thoughts wandered back to his past, the numbing realization came to him that he no longer possessed a past, that there was nothing his life could connect back to, nothing familiar to use as reference points, only the script Paul was teaching him. That was when the most intense bouts of self-pity settled in, a mood that sometimes made Chris a juvenile monster to those around him.

The team of physicians strolled in and greeted Chris, who had finally agreed to adopt the name Koan. Their entrance triggered a barrage of verbal abuse. "Behind those cunning smiles of yours there's something you're withholding." The physicians reminded Koan of white gulls circling over a garbage dump, scavenging from discarded human waste.

Dr. Heilgott, the head physician, walked to the head of Koan's bed, raising a hand in appeasement. "There's no need to get upset. Especially not today. We have good news for you."

"More of your medical double-speak?"

"Please hear us out. We'll try to keep it simple. Koan, your body seems to have stabilized itself, completely, and we believe it's time to declare our endeavors successful."

Paul stepped forward. He too missed statements about immunological reactions and counter-destabilization measures, terms he had been hearing for months.

"Are you saying the recovery's complete?"

Dr. Heilgott leaned firmly against Koan's bed. "Yes, in fact, we've decided it's time for Koan to get out and about. Of course, you need to remember that you're no longer a young man. You need to drill that into your consciousness."

Dr. Heilgott stayed with Koan and Paul after the other physicians had left.

Koan was waving his fist defiantly. "You act as if I should be rejoicing."

Paul reminded him that everything had gone miraculously well.

"That's the hell. Something did go wrong. I didn't die."

Dr. Heilgott, a short, lean man with curly, pure white hair, walked around the edge of the bed and rested his hand on Koan's shoulder. "Koan, I understand. More deeply than you know. Much that has transpired and brought us to this point will haunt me."

"Am I supposed to feel sorry for you, Heilgott? It was greed, wasn't it?"

"Greed? Nonsense. It was a challenge. Perhaps the devil himself reaching out and daring me to try the unthinkable. But this never would have taken place if you hadn't demanded it."

"Who demanded it? The old man? I wasn't asked. The old man called it inevitable. Those were his words. But it wasn't. You could have refused."

Dr. Heilgott lost his professional composure. "Look, Koan, or Chris, whoever you are, I was against this. He pressured us. I said it was playing God. But we could talk forever. The person you were, that person insisted on it. He was possessed with the idea. Am I right, Paul?"

"Yes, that's correct. And we aren't going to reverse it by moralizing. You are Koan. Period. And it's you who has to stop feeling pity for yourself. You two get whatever you need out of your systems." With that, Paul left Koan and Dr. Heilgott alone.

Koan walked over to a window, looking out long and intently before drooping his head. Behind him Dr. Heilgott anguished in silence. Finally, Koan wheeled around, lifting his arms high and shook them. "How could a sane person believe in such a thing?! Two souls patched together! It's absurd!"

Dr. Heilgott didn't respond to Koan's outburst. Instead he confessed that he had panicked and had been tempted to flee after everything had gone awry. "But I was responsible for a life, your life."

"But isn't it my right to question whether it had been a life worth saving?"

"We don't stand in judgment over such things. We merely heal. You alone, Koan, must deal with that. And we don't heal souls." Koan sank back onto the bed, half-closing his eyes, but Dr. Heilgott was in no hurry to leave. "Koan, when the brain downloading procedures began malfunctioning, we assumed it was the untested technology. I no longer believe that. It was his soul. His soul was too powerful. It was stronger than the boundaries and limitations of his brain. We couldn't sedate that part of him. I believe his almighty soul raised itself in defiance. That's why you're here. I'm convinced of that. His soul lives on. I've felt it. And you will have to live with it, somehow. I don't believe you have a choice. Make peace with him, his soul, and yourself, Koan. It's the only way."

That night, Koan wandered in and out of sleep. His dreams were a jumble of noise, as they often were, since his transformation from Chris. In fact, Koan longed for dreams, the old kind, the nightmares, wet dreams, scenes of sadness or joy, but they remained absent.

During his tossing around in bed, Koan enjoyed a moment of amusement, an odd irony that flashed into his head. During one of those wonderful childhood nights on Windy Hill with Moss, they had grabbed a hold of one of those apparent absurdities they so loved to discuss until their minds were numb. That discussion had revolved around religion, a common theme, since church was so central to life in Shepherdstown. The specific object of their surmising had been a what if, what if Jesus Christ had not been the Son of God, but it had gotten mixed up and turned around; what if God had gotten trapped inside of Jesus Christ and were doomed to die with him? The easiest conclusion of their often lighthearted conjecture was that Jesus Christ probably would have lived forever, after his resurrection, and himself become immortal. Moss and Chris had laughed that there wouldn't have been any popes, that the existence of Jesus would have made them and the many denominations of Christian religion unnecessary. The different churches would have nothing to squabble about, like who was right or wrong about what the Bible meant. Jesus Christ would have stepped in and made a ruling.

Lying there in bed, Koan was, in part, amused by the wonderful naivety of those nights together with Moss, those nights on Windy Hill. What, however, brought the smile to his face was an irony that occurred to him, one he was living. Drawing an analogy to his discussion with Moss about God and Jesus Christ, Koan recalled how Paul liked to refer to the old man as nearly godlike. What if the intention had been to instill the soul of the old man into Chris's body, a temporary and limited vehicle for his purposes, fully analogous to God's appearance as Jesus Christ? Obviously, so it seemed to Koan, that had backfired. Did it follow that the old man was now doomed to die, rather than remain immortal? Or, as they had speculated way back then on Windy Hill, did it mean that Koan now would live on forever?

"Maybe I'd better start pacing myself? I could be in for a long haul." Koan laughed softly at his own words. "Yeah, and maybe that will give me time to finally figure out what the old man was all about. No, I doubt if an eternity would allow that."

"So, ready for another lesson?" Paul had entered Koan's office with a leather case of files. "Today, we're going to run through your companies again. Then we're going see how far you've gotten with Koan's idiosyncrasies."

Koan managed a smart grin. "I never had to study this much in college."

"This isn't for a degree, Koan, it's for survival. But give yourself credit. You're very intelligent. And more importantly, you have a sense of adaptation that will be the key to everything we're going to do."

"And I already respond to the name Koan. Right?"

"Yes, you do. That's who you are."

"And worth billions."

"Yes, that too. That's the carrot for you, isn't it?"

Koan folded his hands together and rubbed them. "I've finally gotten around to appreciating that. It motivates."

Paul smiled. "That's the attitude we need. There's a reward for playing the part. Let's get on with, and forget some of the little battles we've had."

Koan gave Paul a thumbs-up.

"And please drop that gesture. Koan never would have done that. He would have simply said, 'Let's move on, old man,' without so much as a glance at me."

Later, Koan retired to his den under the pretense of wanting to read. During the day, it occurred to him that it had been a year since he had last seen Freddie.

Life was good with Freddie. She was a woman. That's not part of the package here. Unbelievable, the old guy was celibate. I still get horny. That part of my body must still be mine. Not that Freddie was much of a lover. But beggars aren't choosers.

Freddie made me feel inadequate. I could never reach her ideals. She cheered me on, and I sucked up all that "Well done, Harry" stuff, but it was her way of being on top. Even in sex.

That fucking name, Hickory Harry. And dip-shit Manic Mouse. She was manic. Obsessive, compulsive.

What kind of fucked up world was that? People had the dumbest names, like Petty Poo and Dooly Dan. What the hell did Dooly mean? What were we, a bunch of juveniles or what?

Koan let out a deep sigh, closing his eyes tightly then opening them again.

I do miss her. She was good company. Good chemistry? Mom and Dad didn't talk about chemistry. People back in Shepherdstown married, stayed together, that was that. If anyone even joked about marital differences, they quickly added, "Times can be tough, but you make it through." Like there was some dutiful acceptance that transcended being truly happy. Thank God times changed. I don't think I did so bad with Freddie, but she was a lot like Dad, demanding a perfection I could never live up to.

Ah, Hope. She was so different. But that was one big confessional. I don't remember ever being able to look her straight in the eye after doing so much soul baring. I could have cheated on Freddie with her, but I never had the urge. Hope didn't appeal to my body, just my soul. Poor gal. Bet she would've loved to make the bed springs creak, but she never asked for things, not even apologies.

That's one helleva thought. Hell, with what I have now, I could impress the shit out of Freddie. I wonder what Freddie saw at the end of her rainbow? Geez, I never understood where she wanted to go. But you'd eat your heart out now, wouldn't you, Manic Mouse! I'm anything you could ever aspire to.

Is that a hateful thought? I don't know. In sex, nothing satisfied Freddie. She needed nothing to be satisfied. But she was a nympho when it came to pursuit and achievement. But maybe nothing ever could satisfy her. That was the madness of it all. The ad absurdum pursuit. Maybe that's what a nympho is?

Jesus, the old man must have had some fun. He couldn't have created all this without some amusement in mind. There had to be a bent or perverse side to the old guy. People like him always turn out to be real oddballs, kooks, eccentrics. Whatever it turns out to be, I hope it's something I can get into. With my luck it'll be something I hate.

And Paul, God, that guy's about as straight as they come. Never met anyone so totally in control. Not even Freddie. Really, he's just a bit weird. Once we get into a groove, maybe he'll loosen up. Sure. This is just his crisis mode. Maybe he'll turn out to be a good ole guy, and we'll raise a little hell together.

Chris, whoops, Koan, this may turn out to be the best damn trip in the world! Keep that chin up old boy. And fasten your seat belt.

8

Freddie could no longer say exactly how long it had been since Chris's disappearance. Her feelings toward him waned, and more and more she heeded the unsolicited but incessant advice of her mother.

"Freddie, abandonment happens every day. Sometimes you're really naive about such things."

"Your opinion, Mom."

"Then let's be more direct about it. Based on what you told me about Chris, it sounds as if he dwelled on things we best not think about. I bet with time some sort of radical would have stepped out and ruined everything you've worked so hard to achieve. Some things in life, darling, we give lip service to, because it's the proper thing to do, but getting involved is only asking for trouble. You have to know who you are at all times and not be questioning it. That's what made it so easy to raise you, Freddie."

"Mother's little robot."

"Why would you say a thing like that?"

"Oh, it's not important. I just recall being shuttled from cheerleading to Girl Scouts to dance lessons and day camps."

"Be glad you had parents who were willing to do so much to prepare you."

"I guess. And I guess there's a time to quit speculating about Chris."

"Right. I'm sure he made a choice, and that means there's no responsibility on your shoulders. Wipe the slate clean."

From friends, Freddie had also received lectures to the effect that people don't just totally disappear, not for such a long time.

"If they're not dead, they've usually made a conscious decision to turn their backs on their old existence, seeking a totally fresh beginning, without any old ties."

That had been the opinion of Jarrod Jeffers, a friend whom Freddie and Chris had first met at a networking get-together. Jarrod was a civil lawyer who specialized in pursuing ex-spouses who'd reneged on alimony or child support. "I can't look into Chris's mind, but I'd speculate he was either the victim of violence, or he just flipped out."

Freddie tended to agree with Jarrod's two possibilities. From what she had learned at the Burning Bridges bar, she could conceive how Chris might have been careless about where he went and been murdered, likely in that derelict section of Pontifica. Freddie preferred this theory, as the other left a bad taste in her mouth.

Recalling the writings she'd found in which Chris expressed cynicism and disdain for their lifestyle, that could have been the motive for a premeditated desertion, and if this were so, she hoped to never see him again.

One evening Freddie was sitting in her den, symbolically acknowledging the finality. She was pulling folders out of a filing cabinet and throwing away those that related to Chris. In front of her was a folder labeled "Misc. Income." Leafing through it, she stopped, picked up a sheet and studied it. It was a payment for two thousand dollars, and the ID for the payee was a cryptic "K-L H." Freddie leaned back, trying to recall the reason for the check. A conversation one evening with Chris, right there in the den, drifted into her mind.

Freddie had been sitting at the large, roll-top desk, opening mail and paying bills. Chris sat a few feet away in his big, overstuffed, leather reading chair, thumbing through a magazine. Freddie sealed an envelope, leaning back and taking a deep breath.

"I think that's the last bill. We're sitting very pretty this month." Chris only grunted, which irritated Freddie. "You didn't hear me, did you?"

"I'm sorry, Mouse. What'd you ask?"

Freddie turned toward Chris. "I simply said, we have quite a surplus this month, thanks to you."

Chris pointed his finger at his chest. "Moi?"

"Yeah."

"Well? Lift the veil of secrecy."

Freddie needled Chris about trying to make him more health-conscious. "I can put a thousand articles about diet and exercise under you nose, and you simply ignore them. Then, lo and behold, you volunteer for some health program, and, that's not all, you get paid for it?"

Chris asked how much it was and acted genuinely surprised at the amount.

"What'd you do, Chris, sell your soul?"

Chris sank back, grinning. "I hope not. Best I can remember, it was a study about the health risks young business executives are exposed to. Boy, were they thorough. You remember, the extra day I tacked onto the business trip, a month or so ago?"

"Well, whatever it was, it was definitely worth it."

"I guess so. Two thousand? Just for letting them poke around on me for a few hours. Wanta do something crazy with it?"

Freddie blew him a kiss. "I'm on!"

As it turned out, Freddie had used that money to pay the private investigator, who had searched in vain for some trace of Chris. Looking again at the check stub, something irritated her, but she couldn't nail it down. Finally, she wrote a note and attached it to the piece of paper, setting it aside.

In the ensuing weeks, Freddie's curiosity about Chris's mysterious health study developed into a welcome diversion. A little research and a few telephone calls uncovered that K-L H was K-Light Holding, and through interconnected companies belonged to Angstrom Unlimited. Through her regular diet of business publications, Freddie was knowledgeable about Angstrom Unlimited and fascinated by the mythical man at its head, Koan Angstrom. As it turned out, K-Light Holding, while listed as a health service company, appeared to be no more than a dummy corporation with no reported revenues or staff.

Tenacity was something Freddie didn't lack. She made several calls to Angstrom Unlimited, saying her husband was extremely interested in the outcome of their executive health study. Her stubbornness got her connected to various people, none of which knew anything about the study. Finally, dozens of calls later, she was talking to an icy-voiced man.

"I can appreciate your interest, but there's no information available for public dissemination. Give us your name and address, so we can contact you, if that changes."

Freddie wasn't gratified, but she was at a loss for any more threads to pull.

Putting the material she'd gathered into her desk, she let out a soft laugh. "See, Chris, I'm still in there plugging, trying to find out what they did with that gorgeous bod of yours. You're going to be proud of me and what I'm accomplishing."

But before we celebrate anything, I'm going to kick your butt good for the living hell you've put me through."

9

Well over a year had passed since Chris's recovery. Initially, he failed miserably in playing the role of Koan Angstrom. His only salvation was the reclusive lifestyle of the old man had led. Except for Paul, no one noticed a change. Still, Chris sought diligently to bring his thoughts and behavior closer to those of the old man, enough so that Paul allowed a few brief official appearances. For Koan it was a chance at the freedom and public exposure he was craving. He was obsessed with gaining an identity again, and for him self-identity depended on the feedback from others.

Koan was in his den, sitting in front of the big fireplace, staring pensively into the flickering flames. In the big leather winged-back chair next to him sat Paul. It was a rare quiet moment, one both were savoring. Nowhere, not even off in some distant room, was a telephone ringing.

"Paul, are we succeeding in our grand deception?"

Paul's response was delayed and measured. "I believe we've brought the ship safely into the harbor." Paul moved his sharp chin upward very slowly. At the top of the motion, his chin jutted forward, and his mouth tightened until his lips became a narrow, thin line. Koan recognized it as Paul's subconscious signal that he had mastered something.

"Paul, do you really think everyone's swallowed our hoax?"

"The predators of this world are a collection of species. Some were too blinded by greed to notice the transition. Others, at least intuitively, recognized something was wrong, but easy money bought them an illusion of normalcy."

A ripple of sarcastic laughter rolled out of Koan. "The old man's mannerisms changed, the aftermath of an accident, a brush with death. What a crock of shit. A grade B movie plot, don't you think?"

"Koan, it sold. When you boil it down, that's all that counts."

Koan arose from his big leather chair and walked over to the fireplace, where he poked at the logs until the fire became intense again. Leaning against the mantelpiece, he lifted his glass. "Here's to you, Paul."

"What gives me the honor?"

"I used to think I was a real hotshot, one of the best up and coming consultants around. Know what my wife used to call me? Hickory Harry. Good old Hickory Harry." Paul asked if the name had any special significance, causing Koan to laugh sarcastically. "I was tough as hickory."

Paul allowed a rare, tight smile, lifting his glass high to Koan. "Then to Hickory Harry. May his ghost still haunt the corridors of corporate America."

Koan drank with Paul. "You know, Paul, you've got the

class I aspired to, but never could've reached."

"That's flattering, but, without false modesty, all I do is what I do. It's my role, nothing more. If it weren't for you, I wouldn't be here. You're the key, a thing we best never forget."

"You mean we're ensnared in some kind of evil symbiosis? That's perverse."

"It's reality, Koan."

Koan sat back down. The flickering from the fire danced over his wrinkled face. "Paul, what if the doctors had been able to transfer the old man's mind back into my brain? Which would you have preferred, dealing with the old man, as he was, or with me?"

Like a touch-sensitive animal, Paul's arms jerked back from the armrests to his sides. "Too hypothetical to warrant speculation."

"It's a good night to talk about things that never get said. And there's no need for diplomacy."

Sinking back deeply behind the wings of his chair, Paul cleared his throat. "Koan, I understand your motives. Your self-loathing is often your strongest trait. But, good, I was in a groove with him. After years of working off the rough edges, it came automatically. He was a man of extremes, never satisfied with the mundane, and impeccable in his focus on the essential. Often it seemed he had no soul, that he was beyond human. Yes, I was in a groove with him. It worked, blindly."

"So you preferred him?"

"The routine animal in me did."

"I thought so. And then came all this shit, all the complications crashing down on your pleasant little world?"

Paul sank back so far that Koan couldn't see his face. Paul's voice became quieter, deeper, more intimate. "I don't care for conversations of this kind. I'm leery of the subjective, which is often irrational."

After minutes of silence, Paul again cleared his throat.

His legs uncrossed, his hands squeezed the armrests, like a death row prisoner waiting for the final surge of electricity. "I think it started when the surgeons said something had gone wrong. I felt a deep jolt of excitement. Not an overwhelming kind of excitement, just a short jolt, perhaps the way a stroke might feel. A better description escapes me. Somehow, I was becoming a stranger to myself, welcoming, uncharacteristically, signs of failure. That struck fear in my heart."

Paul paused, self-conscious about his openness. "Long ago, someone I cared for very much warned of this. She said my way of life would, in the end, be my self-destruction. She believed that. When the physicians said his brain had been destroyed, it was as if her prophecy was being fulfilled." Paul's body seemed to briefly shiver. "That evening, I sat right here, looking into that fireplace there, seeing the credits of a film roll upward into the chimney. That film, which was ending, was my life. I spent that whole night right here, praying."

Koan respected the silence that followed. It lasted long, but neither of them moved or broke the spell that had befallen them. As the silence lengthened, Koan got up to put logs on the fire, stoking it up before returning to his chair to wait.

"Koan, my eyes stared into the fire until it was just a yellow blur. Then I saw it, something so obvious I had to laugh. It was the challenge. That simple. That had been the jolt I felt when I realized the old man hadn't made it. At first, all I had seen was the empire crashing down, maggots gnawing into it and sucking the life out of it, leaving a gasping, dying hulk."

Paul leaned over toward Koan, his eyes wide and burning, devoid of their normal iciness, causing Koan to flinch. "You see, Koan, with the old man, it was all offensive, never defensive. His power was too supreme. There was never a thought given to whether the underpinnings might ever crumble out from under us. That night I saw this horrific, contourless form in the fire yelling, 'God is dead,' over and over again, and masses chanting back in agreement. Koan, you may wonder why I didn't run."

Koan nodded, his expression one of astonishment.

"Strangely enough, that option never occurred to me. Out of total despair came that one consuming emotion, the challenge, the ultimate test. And it was you, Koan. A summons to battle, to sell you as the old man, a new old man. You see, there were no choices, no preferences, as you put it. The only alternative was to embrace despair."

"Paul, that's incredible. I've never faced anything even close to that. It's amazing, humiliating. Yes, that's it. It makes me feel absolutely humble. Tiny."

"That's good, Koan. Humility was one of the old man's strongest characteristics. This empire, as some choose to call it, is not the product of a massive ego, or selfishness. It amused him to read such descriptions of himself by desperate journalists. He had unusual instincts and a powerful perception, but he also possessed infinite humility. He could enter into people he hadn't met, sense what made them tick.

"He never touched or interfered with people who had strength and substance. Maybe an occasional injection of capital to help them, however, he left them to flourish on their own. I'm sure all this surprises you and leaves you asking how he was able to accumulate such wealth?"

The trace of a smirk was on Paul's face.

"The old man was attracted to the weak and dark side of the human race, much like a cat toying with the mouse it's caught. It was a diabolical game to him, to set up such people, to allow them to swell up big and fat with their own self-importance only to swoop in and castrate them in the end. The money wasn't of any importance to him. It fell out of the corpses' pockets and landed on our doorstep. So much has been written about his business savvy, his brilliance in identifying a kill, but the substance was his absolute clarity about reality, and his values. Not the kind of thing you'll find in graduate school courses, or business journals. He even cursed the Bible, calling it a false portrayal, merely a self-indulgence of the human ego. He had this wonderful gesture, his thick index finger tapping on his broad chest, saying, 'This is where we must all look.' Yes, Koan, there was a humility about him, one I've never encountered in such purity. That, if I'm honest, was the source of my unwavering loyalty to him. Just being in his presence was a deliverance. That was also the supreme sense of loss I felt when he died."

Koan felt like a revelation had brushed him, one too ephemeral to grasp and hold onto. "Paul, I don't know how I'm supposed to react. How do I follow up on an act like that? I think you chose the wrong guy. Still, I'm flattered that insignificant me could trigger such a challenge in you."

"Remember, Koan, it's a challenge we share. I don't know if I should say this, I don't know if you can skim the significance from it, yet, but I'll say it. You're doing battle with your identity. That's obvious. Less evident to you is that the old man wrestled with his identity. It anguished him. In fact, it may someday turn out to be a blessing for you that you have less of a concrete identity to live up to than you think. He despised anyone and anything that sought to attach labels to him. He would've been perfectly happy to be absolutely and totally anonymous. But enough. Continue to come to terms with your new existence. Life is about moving forward and not looking back, except for brief glimpses to measure how far we've come."

The two men toasted each other.

"I suppose you're right, Paul. We have a beautiful scam going here. I've lost something in it all, but life's now, and not all that bad." Koan was ready to get up and call it a night. "Oh, Paul, one other thing. Did the old man use a word, something like 'holda'?"

"Yes, frequently."

"Well, what did it mean? I've looked through dictionaries in vain."

"You won't find it in any dictionaries. Nor can I give you

a precise meaning. Never did he say anything like, 'holda is.' It was a term he only used in association with other things. Like a punctuation. I'm sure there's a deeper definition. Perhaps like another word he was fond of using, elucidation. I'd venture to say, if you one day comprehend the meaning of holda, you will have come very close to becoming the old man."

Koan walked slowly around the car, his steely-blue eyes glowing, his thick hand sliding lovingly along the freshly lacquered surface, as if it were the tender skin of a newborn baby. The car's lines were those of a crouching cat, poised to leap forward and race with blinding speed. One of Chris's nocturnal wet dream was becoming reality. In a ritualistic act of love, Koan circled the impeccably restored car again, inspecting and caressing every detail of paint, chrome, leather.

Back in his childhood, there had been a magical summer seashore vacation with frequent evenings at a nearby boardwalk amusement park. He recalled smells; the tar in boardwalk planks, fresh pizza, french fries, cotton candy. Also the sounds; bells, buzzers, sirens, especially in the penny arcade. More than skee-ball or anything else, he remembered one machine. For an inserted nickel, a postcard-sized photo slid out, photos of exotic sports cars. When he got the one with the Aston Martin on it, that seemed the ultimate, but then, on another evening, a white Jaguar XK-130 roadster emerged. He never stuck another nickel into that machine. He had found his true love.

Koan stopped next to the sweeping front fender, where he planted a hand firmly on his hip.

"Everything all right, sir?" asked the sales manager.

"Yes, perfect. Absolutely perfect."

Koan entered the spacious hallway of his estate, where Paul was waiting for him, his mien serious "Yesterday, I left some papers on your desk, to be signed. The old man took care of things, as they happened, without reminders."

"Were they that important?"

"Transactions are a matter of timing. Two items were urgent, and marked as such."

Koan sighed, shrugging his shoulders. "All right. I'll go straight to my office. Okay?"

"There's one other thing, Koan. The old man never flaunted his wealth. More to the point, he didn't own sports cars."

"Hold on, Paul. Just a minute, here. Aren't there any kudos in this for me? How about if we chalk it up to late life eccentricities?"

"I'm not going to blow it out of proportion, but next time we talk about it up front, okay?"

"Gotcha."

"And please drop that expression."

Koan's foot bent forward against the accelerator, and a deep, rolling purr rose from under the low hood of the car. Twice more he revved up the engine. The rich, throaty roar was music to his ears. Next to him sat Geena, a rented woman.

"Hey, when ya gonna drive this thing?" Geena gazed around self-consciously, her thin legs crossed and jiggling. "Why you makin' all the fuss? Everybody's lookin' at us."

Koan slapped his thigh. "Let them eat their hearts out."

"Bullshit, man! They ain't jealous. Not of an old fart like you. They'd just love to steal dis car out from under yer ass. Let's git outa here!"

The words "old fart" snatched the smile off of Koan's face. Swallowing deeply, he shoved the gear shift forward, gunning the car away from the curb.

The strip of asphalt disappeared at a dizzying pace under the hood of the Jaguar. The road wound and turned over the hilly countryside, past woods, fields, and pastures.

"Where the hell we goin'?" Geena held her hands desperately to her heavily sprayed hair, trying to rescue it from the onslaught of the wind. "Why can't we find a place closer? You always ends up somewhere in the boonies. I's a city girl. I don't need this country stuff."

Koan reached forward and increased the volume on the stereo.

Stepping out of the low slung Jaguar, Koan stretched, pounding his chest.

"Smell that air!"

"I can't smell. Lost that a long time ago from snortin'."

Koan sorted through his key chain as he walked up the path to a log cottage.

"Come on, Geena, I have a surprise for you."

Geena walked after him on her high heels, a tight wiggle in her step, stopping to give her watch an exaggerated look.

Inside the cottage, Koan waved his arm around the room. "Look, Geena, I had these roses brought ahead. And there's champagne and caviar in the refrigerator."

With one hand cocked on her hip, Geena scanned the simple, but expensively furnished room. "This yer place, too?"

Koan nodded.

"Sure have a lotta money. My, my."

Koan retrieved the champagne and caviar, serving it on a low table in front of a huge, well-stuffed sofa. Geena flopped down onto sofa, snatching a look at her watch. "You know's I gotta be back by seven, dontcha?"

Geena wasn't enthused about the caviar, but quickly downed two glasses of the champagne. "Dis is classy stuff."

"The best." Koan refilled Geena's glass. "Geena, it would be nice if we could spend a little more time here, say until tomorrow. Money's no obstacle. Whatever you expect to make tonight, I'll give you tenfold."

Geena screwed up her face disdainfully. "Is that what you think? Dat all I think about is money? Damn. Money ain't everything. It sure is when times is tough, but it ain't all that makes this lady turn."

"Geena, it's good to hear you have values."

"'Cause you's savin' yer money?"

"No." Koan slid closer. "Look, I know you have feelings. What you have to do, you have to do. But that's just a well-trained act. Underneath's a sensitive person. Am I right?"

"Listen to those pretty words. You think puttin' a little sugar on me is gonna make me stay the night?"

Koan ran his meaty hand over his face, turning away from Geena.

"Hey, daddy, you's the one who said we should say it like it is. Don't get all screwed up just because I sez what I thinks."

Koan tried to smile, but it was an effort. "Can we talk? I'm sure you've known loneliness."

A brief flash of compassion in Geena's eyes quickly vanished. "Yer lonely? Wid your money? You can buy friends. Yer jus' wastin' yer breath on me. I was left on my own as soon as my mom quit nursin' me. She had ta git out and hustle. I ain't complainin' or nothin'. I'm still here. Could've been dead, long time ago."

Koan just stared at Geena. Whatever he wanted to say got stuck inside of him.

"Hey, when we gonna do somethin'? That's what I'm good at. You don't seem to wanna know. Like I could bite yer thing off, or somethin'. Ain't gonna do that. No, sir. I'm sweet and nice. How about a li'l trip to heaven?"

Koan got up and began to pace around the room.

"Hey, wud I say now?"

Koan stopped and turned to Geena. A tear had traced a path down his cheek.

"What is this for a hell? Doesn't anyone want to know who I am? Geez, I'm just trying to be a human being to you. Is that so incredibly difficult to comprehend? And all you want to be is some common whore. I can't even say I care about you. You flinch like I've cut you with a knife. Are words so threatening? You'd probably rather be beaten than carry on a conversation."

Geena got up and backed up toward the door. "Hey, man, yer gettin' weird on me. I come along to please you, but none of that crazy stuff. I think we better go. Keep the bread. Find another who wants to chew the fat with you."

Koan reached for the champagne bottle, rearing back and letting it fly. It smashed against the fireplace, sending Geena dashing out of the house screaming.

Koan sat in the house a half-hour, alone, grasping for thoughts, tearing and shredding them again in his mind.

Hope's the only woman I've ever held with any sense of passion. Mom, she scared me. Dad wouldn't talk about sex, let alone the birds and the bees, not even when two dogs screwed right at our feet. Mom said I was a 'gift from heaven,' but she didn't say that the way most people did. It was if she and Dad never had intercourse, like I'd been immaculately conceived. That's probably why I never dated in high school, and not really even through college. I felt horny, and that seemed the wrong reason to be close to someone.

God, being an old man, I'm lonelier...yeah, I was that, a loner, with a ton-plus-one friends. Like painted-on masks, all around me, those glued-on smiles, pretentious preppiness, strutting peacocks, baseless bravado. And married to one of those phony friends too.

With God as my witness, I'm going to bust out of that mold. I've got the means now, and sooner or later I'm going to find the right tricks, the buttons to push, and it's all going to fall together. No one's going to say, "Chris, you're not living up to what you could be." Hang in there, Hickory Harry, don't let a few slaps in the face deter you. As Paul would say, concentrate on the power you now have. I'm going to use that power, and one day the sun's going to rise, as beautiful as it was those mornings up on Windy Hill.

Koan finally decided to go out and take Geena home. Without exchanging a word with her, he started up the car and drove it away in a billow of dust.

• • •

Paul clenched his fists at his sides until the knuckles were white. "Just when I think you comprehend the gravity of our situation, you pull one of your stunts."

Koan shrugged his shoulders.

"This goddamned joyride with a whore! How often have you done that?"

"Every once in awhile. I have to get out. I'm going insane."

"Insane? I'm the one who's going insane, hellbent on believing we're going to make this work. Look, if it's a woman you need, that can be arranged. But discretely. Not this jack-assed tendency of yours to go out and make a public spectacle. Don't you understand, Koan, we're hanging on a thread, and the heart of that thread is consistency and self-discipline?"

"You sound like my father."

"What the hell does your father have to do with this?"

"Jesus Christ, Paul, give me a break! All I was looking for was a little company, someone to talk to."

"And it had to be some two-bit whore?"

"Look, the old man may've been able to live in this monastery, but I'm not him. I need interaction."

"Again, Koan, it's not your needs as much as your style."

"Okay. So I wasn't cool. But, really, this is worse than prison." Paul's face showed a trace of compassion, and Koan jumped on it. "Paul, maybe we could make a deal? I'll promise to be out in the open about what I want, and we can discuss how."

Paul eyed Koan skeptically, then agreed. With the tension abated, Paul brought up a new subject. "I don't know yet whether it's cause for alarm, but we've got someone sniffing."

"Sniffing? Who? What?"

"That's insignificant. I believe it'll blow over. Someone satisfying their curiosity, and when they run into enough dead ends, they'll desist. At least, that's what I expect."

"Tell me this much, was it someone who's noticed a change in Koan, or someone trying to find Chris?"

When Paul said it was the latter, Koan got more insistent about knowing who it was, but he hit a brick wall. Finally, he asked Paul if he would consider eliminating such a person? "I'm not yet sure how to deal with it. But enough. A completely different subject. You've never talked about your ex-wife. I can call her that, can't I?"

"Yes, I guess. I assume we're no longer married."

Paul observed that Koan hadn't exhibited any emotions concerning her, no less any great urge to talk about her.

Koan smiled. "You catch everything, don't you? No, we weren't exactly soul mates. We respected, yeah, admired each other, but it was more a marriage of convenience."

Paul's focus moved to Freddie and what kind of person she was. After nearly a half hour, it dawned on Koan that Paul never inquired about anything without a motive. The feeling of being flattered by Paul's interest gave way to a sense of being manipulated, which killed his enthusiasm for the conversation.

Later that evening, and the next day, Koan found himself wondering whether Freddie might be the mystery person Paul was referring to, the one seeking Chris. It had been awhile since Koan had dwelled much on Freddie, but suddenly his thoughts were preoccupied with her. He tried to imagine what she might be doing, how she had taken his disappearance, whether she might recognize his personality, despite his new appearance? Playing through a reunion with Freddie, even if it was only a fantasy, provided a welcomed amusement and diversion.

Hey, at least she isn't a whore. Paul might even consent to that, my happening to run into Freddie again. A cheap thrill. And if she's the one on my trail...why?

10

Despite the blue sky and glaring sun, the day was a transitional one, lacking the warmth of summer, a creeping chill of autumn in the air. Freddie walked toward a park with a plastic bag dangling from her hand. A while later, she was sitting on a park bench perched on the bank of a lake, fishing bits of stale bread and rolls out of the bag next to her. The ducks on the lake recognized the ritual and swam toward Freddie, loudly quacking and vying for the first blobs of bread.

A voice behind Freddie startled her. She turned to find an older, well-dressed man.

"You scared me."

The man apologized. "I saw you feeding the ducks. In fact, I've seen you here before."

To Freddie, the older man didn't appear threatening. "Yes, I guess this has become something of ritual. The fresh air does me good. And the poor things always seem to be starving." Freddie tossed another handful of bread pieces into the water, watching the ducks squawk and nip at each other.

"The ducks probably find enough to eat on their own. I'd say it's less hunger than greed."

Freddie looked at the man more intently. His tone was more provocative than jesting. She didn't recognize him. "Greed? That's a strange observation."

"I simply noticed that before you came the ducks were swimming around peacefully foraging on the bottom of the lake. They weren't fighting."

Irritated, Freddie started to throw another handful of bread, then stopped

"Maybe you're right, but aren't you over dramatizing it just a bit? Greed?"

The old man gazed out over the lake, then turned his eyes back to Freddie. "I thought the word greed would catch your attention."

"Greed's a part of human nature. Besides, where's there a sign saying 'Don't feed the ducks'?"

The old man smiled. "Of course, you're right. It's your choice whether you want to feed the ducks. Perhaps it only bothers me to see greed being incited in nature, where survival stops short of such a human trait."

Freddie found her discussion partner a bit too heavy, but he dispersed the tenseness by grabbing a handful of bread and tossing it to a ducks with a loud laugh.

After that, the exchange drifted into small talk, and a half-hour later the two parted, wishing each other a good day.

A couple weeks later, Freddie called Hope to see if she wanted to get together on the weekend and take a ride to the beach. Hope was delighted. After a sumptuous seafood dinner on Freddie's credit card, they decided to take a walk on the beach.

Far out on the straight horizon of the sea, towering, mushroom-shaped thunderheads illuminated at irregular intervals. Freddie and Hope interrupted their leisurely walk to observe the natural light show.

"Boy, that must be quite a storm." Freddie stared intently at the jagged pulses of lightning that intermittently snaked out of the clouds. "That's spectacular! A storm's beautiful. From a distance. Do you think it's coming our way?"

"Who cares." Hope pulled her long hair back from her face, twisting it into a knot in the back. "A good storm cleanses."

The friendship between Hope and Freddie was a curious one. Its seed had been planted at the Burning Bridges bar. That traumatic humiliation might have caused any other person to leave well enough alone, but not Freddie. It left blemishes that Freddie was dead intent on eradicating.

One bruise she'd suffered was a mysterious woman whom her husband had more highly regarded than her, the nurse named Hope. Laboriously, Freddie had called and inquired at clinics and hospitals until she found her. Her next step was to lure the woman into a meeting at an upscale restaurant, familiar turf for Freddie, which she assumed would put the lowly nurse at a distinct disadvantage. Posing as an insurance investigator, Freddie grilled Hope, bent on demonstrating her superiority while generously insinuating her competitor was little more than a cheap slut.

If Freddie had hoped to humiliate Hope, it was because she had underestimated the woman's toughness. In the end, Hope had turned Freddie's thrusts back at her. She denied Freddie's accusations that she had enticed Chris into an intimate relationship, and finally, when Freddie's attack only escalated, Hope lashed back saying, "It's the coldness of a wife that chases a husband to a warmer nest." Hope had gone on to portray Chris as a troubled person who simply had no place he could spill out his hurt. As the confrontation came to a conclusion, it was clear that Freddie's attempt to assassinate Hope had left a bullet in her own chest.

Despite the series of lessons in humility, outwardly, particularly in her professional guise, Freddie hadn't missed a beat. Privately, however, the aftermath of Chris's disappearance and uncovering of his secret life caused Freddie to turn more frequently to an old crutch, her secret stockpile of prescription drugs. One desperate evening, she feasted on a large collection of pills, tablets, and capsules. She overdosed. Though desperate and scared she might die, Freddie was unable to bring herself to call her mother, friends, or even an emergency number. She feared her actions would expose her as weak and vulnerable. Approaching panic and unconsciousness, she reached for the number of a person who was only an unpleasant footnote in her life, but it was someone fully apart from the mainstream of Freddie's world, and by some twist of logic in Freddie's hazed thoughts, Hope offered the blessing of discretion. Hope, being a nurse, quickly recognized the situation and got Freddie to a hospital.

After that incident, Freddie, with Hope's assistance, secretly entered a rehabilitation program. This shared crisis became the foundation for their friendship, a fragile and tentative bond between two very dissimilar people.

Further down the beach, the bright lights of a small carousel beckoned welcomingly, inspiring Freddie and Hope to resume their walk in that direction. As they gradually approached the lights and calliope music, Freddie yelled out, "How about a ride on the merry-go-round?"

Hope waved her off.

"Come on, Hope. You're not afraid of the child in you, are you?"

"I'm not sure I ever was one."

Freddie laughed, but then noticed Hope was serious. "You've never talked much about your youth, except that there was alcohol abuse."

"Try this. When I was about seven, one of our neighbors took me aside and said to me, 'Hope, your parents are the children in your family. You're what holds the family together. Be strong.' That says it all. But don't believe a child makes a good caretaker for its parents. My parents wound up killing themselves in a chaos of alcohol and violence. I survived because I didn't know what it meant to be fragile. I've often thought that was the intention behind my name, a thread of hope in a swirling storm. Like out there." Hope sighed deeply. "Old baggage."

Freddie's smile was awkward. "Well, yeah. I guess we've all got a little of that. Do you mind if I take a ride? It looks too neat."

"Go for it."

Freddie climbed aboard a unicorn that was much too small for her, but whooped it up as the half-drunk operator pushed the lever to start the carousel.

After several rides, Freddie climbed off. "Whew, that was a ball!"

"Even though it was just going around in circles?"

"Hope, the real fun in life is mostly pure fantasy. I sometimes get the impression you haven't recognized that yet, that we live in an age of illusion. I, for example, was riding off to find my Prince Charming."

"Did you find him?"

"Hell, what would I do if I did? Besides, the quest is everything."

The two walked over to a big rock and sat down. Hope lit a cigarette and stared again at the stormy light show out at sea. "Chris could be out there."

"Huh?"

"I don't mean literally. Chris had a storm of emotions churning around inside of him. I've often wondered whether he ever got a chance to resolve them."

Freddie looked at Hope's eyes. "Hope, did you have a crush on him?"

"Hand on heart, I have no idea. What I perceived in Chris was someone seeking a soft shoulder, and I offered him one. Anything more than that was fantasy."

"I thought so."

"No, I don't think you know what I mean, Freddie. My fantasies were about a Chris who was genuinely happy. I didn't harbor any illusions about the other possibilities."

"See, that's what I said before, you don't know how to enjoy illusions." Freddie stretched an arm around Hope. "Look, old friend, I have no hard feelings about Chris. I'm not sure it would've been any different if you'd been his lover. He never really made my knees weak, honest, but he was a great buddy."

Hope stared out at the blinking thunderheads. "I hope the hell he's not out there."

Freddie ignored Hope's comment and bent her head back to look up at the sky.

"It's clear above us. The stars are beautiful." Then Freddie laughed. "There's something I've been meaning to tell you."

"Sounds mysterious."

Freddie giggled girlishly. "Someone seems to have a crush on me."

"That's interesting! Who is he?"

"You're gonna freak out. I know you will."

"Why, is it some juicy beefcake?"

"Promise, no opinions, no words of wisdom?"

"Oh, no, a client? Okay. I promise to keep my opinions to myself."

"Do you remember the old man who talked to me in the park?"

"Yeah, I remember you telling me. Not him?"

"Uh huh. And he's asked me out to dinner. Can you believe that? Hope, what should I do?"

"First of all, there's the age difference, then the manner in which he approached you. That's already two strikes against him."

"Maybe you're right. He seemed rather hung up on things."

"Weird?"

"No. Not really weird. I'd say lonely."

"But why you, Freddie? I mean, there're plenty of people his age around. You said he seems well off. He's got the pick of the old biddies."

Freddie cackled. "Hey, I've got a big decision to make."

"Yeah, whether to show interest in the hunk, or play coy."

Laughing, they decided it was time to head home.

Arriving back at Freddie's house, Hope fired up the coffee maker, and a while later they were lounging at the kitchen table, feet up, mugs in their hands.

"You know, Freddie, there's nothing wrong with you going out with the old codger. It might be educational. Old people get a bad rap. He's probably got a daughter who never calls or visits. See, that's a possibility. His paternal instincts." Hope took a long sip of coffee. "You said you found him a little weird. What'd you mean by that?"

Freddie recounted the episode in the park and the discussion about the ducks and greed.

Hope laughed. "Maybe he had a point. When you said weird, I thought maybe he was a flasher. Go for it, Freddie. The distraction would do you good. Besides, he sounds as if he might be wise enough to straighten you out."

For over an hour, Koan Angstrom had been following Freddie's car from place to place, assuming she would eventually return home. Her parents were with her.

Freddie's car turned in to a parking lot, one Koan immediately recognized. The restaurant, Anthony's, had been one of Chris and Freddie's favorite. Koan waited a few minutes to give Freddie and her parents time enough to be seated. As he entered the restaurant, he was greeted by Anthony. Koan enthusiastically asked how he was.

"*Benissimo*! Who can complain?"

"Geez, it's been a long time. How's Celia?"

Anthony's smile faded, his hands rising in a prayerlike position. "Dear Celia. It's been nearly a year now. You didn't know?" Anthony made the cruciform, then his brown eyes moved upward toward the ceiling. "I'm sure God has a good place for her in His kitchen." Anthony chuckled warmly. "So, what'll it be?"

Koan's blunder reminded him that Anthony wouldn't recognized him. "I wanted to ask you for a special favor."

"You know Anthony. Just ask. A special dish? A special wine?"

"Well, no. Actually, what I would like is, uh...a special table."

"A special table? One you've reserved?"

"No, I'm afraid I came in rather spontaneously." Koan explained that he wanted to be seated near Freddie and her parents, but not too close, at least out of their line of sight.

One of Anthony's eyebrows raised, followed by an impish smile. "I see. You are detective." He laughed. "Should I whisper?"

A half-hour later, Koan was seated at a table close to Freddie and her parents, a planter situated between them and himself. What Koan overheard from their table revolved around the usual subjects a family discussed; ailments, trips, relatives. It updated and refreshed old memories, but Koan's ears perked up when Freddie and her mother began arguing.

"If you ask me, find another man, Freddie. Someone like Chris. Someone who would straighten your life up again."

"Mom, I'm happy! What is happiness for you, anyway? My definitions may not match yours...oh, let's stop this."

For a while, silence fell over their table. Finally, Freddie talked. "I have news to share with you."

Freddie's mother chirped in, "You did meet a guy!?"

"No, Mom. I think I'm onto something about Chris."

"And?"

"Well, it's not a whole lot. He was involved with a rather

strange organization, right before he disappeared. Something tells me the two are connected."

"Freddie, when will you ever accept he's dead?"

"Mom, they never found him. How do we know he's dead?"

"So what? You're hanging onto illusions. But for the sake of discussion, let's say he's alive. He left you, Freddie, and he would've had a reason. If he made that choice, why in the world would you want him back?"

"Mom, you're so callous. Why can't you show one ounce of compassion?"

Freddie's father broke in. "Freddie, please! Show a little more respect!"

"I'm sorry, Dad. Really. But can I finish?" There was dead silence before Freddie continued. "Only after Chris was gone did I find out who he really was. I didn't know he had to go half-across town to find someone to listen to him."

"Freddie, I've heard this. Spare me the details."

"Mom, just let me talk. Well, there I was, thinking Chris was having an affair, while all the time, all he was needing was…," Freddie cleared her throat, "…all he needed was someone to listen to him."

"Freddie, your melodramatics are breaking me up."

Freddie's father got angry. "My God, let her talk. She's our daughter. Go on, Freddie. It seems important to you."

"Where was I? I guess, yes, I guess I realized that…that Chris must've known, somewhere down inside himself, who he really was, or who he really wanted to be."

Freddie stopped to blow her nose. "When I discovered Chris had been sharing that with others, it made me bitter, betrayed. But maybe it was my fault?"

Freddie's father broke in. "Hey, Kitten, don't be so hard on yourself. Life doesn't expect that much of you. Keep it in perspective."

Freddie's mother resented the camaraderie between Freddie and her father.

"Freddie, dear, I hear what you're saying. Fine and good. But look where it got Chris. He risked this, whatever you call it, a search for his true self, and where did it put him, in the grave?"

"Mom, if you think I want a happy ending, that's bullshit."

Her father broke in. "Freddie, you know we don't like that kind of talk."

"Sorry. Look, all I want is to meet Chris again. Just so."

There was a minute of silence that tortured Koan. Finally, Freddie continued. "You know, I can't even imagine what he would have done with his life. He had a side I didn't know. Maybe he's out there going for it. Who knows? And it doesn't really matter."

"Freddie, it's your mother again. I'm listening. I hope you appreciate that. Assuming he's alive, then why would you want to see Chris? What purpose would it serve? You've said it yourself, that you two were so different."

"Mom, I have feelings. It never seemed important to talk about such things when we were together. But, you know, it's worse to know you no longer have the chance." Freddie paused again. "All I want is to tell him. Tell him I loved him."

Anthony approached Koan's table, personally bringing him his entree. Koan raised his sunken head, startling Anthony.

"Are you okay, sir?"

"Yes, I'm just fine. It was just one of those sentimental thoughts. About someone who's gone." Koan wiped the dampness from his cheeks.

Freddie and her parents had in the meantime found their way into the parking lot of Anthony's.

"Mom, I'm sorry I lost it. Who knows, you may be right. Chris and I came from completely different backgrounds. Forget the scene from earlier. Maybe I've just been seeing too many movies, or the soap opera I tape. A little sappy, I know. It seemed appropriate."

Freddie's mother wrapped her arm around her daughter.

"It's best that it's all behind you. And if you allow me the suggestion, I don't think hanging around with his old girlfriend helps you move forward. She isn't your class."

"She saved my life."

"So? I'm not chummy with the doctor who took out my gallstones. It's their job. You show people too much gratitude, and they get sticky. But enough's enough. We've beaten the past around too much. You've got opportunities ahead of you, ones you deserve."

Freddie shook her head, grinning. "Mother knows best. By the way, I do have something cooking."

"What?! Out with it."

"Not yet. Give me some time."

Freddie's mother pointed her finger sharply upward. "One thing. Does he have money?"

"Mom, you're impossible."

"No, a realist."

"Okay, he seems well off. No, I'd say very well off, but more importantly, he's got connections. There's been no movement in my firm, everything's blocked up to the top. I'm stagnating. I'd love a new challenge."

"Continue, please. Who is he?"

"No, that's enough, Mom. I'm really glad we've gotten together. It's been nice. I'll tell you more, but when I'm ready."

11

Koan was lying in bed, in the dark, wide awake, thinking. *That's the phrase I'm looking for. A frame of reference. The Jaguar, the car I always wanted. One drive and the thrill was gone. Who'd it impress? I have no peers anymore. Who cares that I own that car? The frame of reference is gone.*

Koan climbed out of bed and put on his robe. Though it was deep in the night, he needed a walk. He made his way out to the back of his mansion, across the large verandah to the gazebo, where he sat in the inky darkness, gazing up at the stars.

I've been robbed of anything to attain. And even if there was something to strive for, I'm too old to start anything.

Koan reached out and tore off a stem of jasmine vine, drawing the flowers to his nose, savoring its sweetness.

I can count on one hand the number of times Freddie said she loved me. And when she did, it was empty of emotion. And all of the sudden, there in the restaurant she says she loves me? And she sounded all choked up. Does she really believe her fantasy of a young, idealistic Chris out there somewhere chasing after some cause, depriving her of her chance to tell him she loves him? Why do I find that obscene?

Koan tossed the jasmine vine away. The sound of the crickets and other nocturnal insects ushered in a feeling of sentimentality.

Those summer evenings were somehow different, sitting there on our front porch, Mom and Dad inside, watching TV, or reading. I loved the sounds of the night. Now I fear them.

Koan sucked in a deep breath and yelled loudly, "Oh, Chris, why won't you die?!" Koan looked back at the estate to see if any lights went on, but apparently no one heard his shout.

This half-god I'm supposed to be, the great Koan Angstrom, his soul's gone, and mine's empty. But oh does he fascinate me. There's something enlightening, no, what's the word I'm looking for, it raises my spirit. But it's only emulation. How could any one suppose it's more?

Every mirror shouts back how inadequate I am to be him. If only it didn't feel like a replay of my youth back in Shepherdstown. I hear my father in the hallways, echoes of his disdain for me. He would've gotten some satisfaction from this, seeing his pony trying to be a thoroughbred. Well, Dad, the old man didn't run in a pack either. He was a lone fox. So much for your pet theory.

Koan broke out in cynical laughter. "Dad, is this the scourge of a father on his son? My punishment?"

Koan cursed into the blackness of the night, then plodded back to the estate.

• • •

Paul and Koan were in Koan's private jet, returning from an obligatory contract signing ceremony. It was dark in the plane's cabin except for the light above Paul, who was reading. Koan was stretched out on a day bed trying to nap, without success.

"Paul, you've talked about someone delving into my disappearance. Is that still acute?"

Dropping the reports he was reading, Paul rubbed his eyes and stretched. "It's still a nuisance."

"Only a nuisance?"

"Yes. Just an unusually strong show of persistence."

"Who is it? Not the police?"

Paul yawned. "There might be a better time to talk about this. Staging the signing today required a pretty heavy smoke screen. You screwed up several times. But no one even flinched. They want you to be Koan, even more than you do." Paul revealed a rare smile. "It breeds cynicism, doesn't it?"

Koan agreed but returned to his question. "Paul, who's our bloodhound?"

"Look, it's just an obsessive personality fighting a bad case of boredom."

"Does that mean you aren't going to act on it?"

"If the stakes get high enough, maybe."

"Would you consider snuffing them out?" Koan put his finger to his temple.

"Does a cornered rat bite?"

Thinking of Freddie, Koan dropped the conversation and tried to sleep.

A few days later, Koan invited Freddie to have lunch with him. She had turned down several previous invitations, but this time accepted. Koan had suggested a small, rustic restaurant up in the Escapany mountains. It was an area Chris used to enjoy visiting, on his own, to enjoy its natural beauty. Koan had hoped that association would entice Freddie, and it worked.

Freddie gazed out over the tree tops down to the azure

lake waters at the base of the mountain. "My husband used to tell me how gorgeous it is up here."

"It's still relatively undiscovered. No hotels or condos cluttering the landscape. This view is damned close to how God created it."

"You like nature, don't you?"

"Yes. Down deep I'm a naturalist, but I don't often admit it. It exposes too much sentimentality."

"That had a cynical ring. But look who's talking. My only involvement in nature is my annual membership check to the Sierra Club. That despite my conviction that they're a bunch of Chicken Littles."

After their salads were served, Freddie asked if their meeting in the park had been coincidental. "Somehow it seemed you already knew me."

"Yes, and no."

"That's too evasive." Freddie poked at her salad. "Do you mind me getting extremely personal, like asking your last name?"

"Is that so important?"

"Oh, it's just a little quirk of mine. Usually I don't even ask for the first names of my dates."

Koan chuckled. "Okay. It's Angstrom."

Freddie dropped her fork. "Not Smith, or Jones?"

"No. Koan Angstrom sounds a bit heavy, but you learn to live with it."

Freddie took on a cute, girlish tone, which grated Koan, who'd always wondered why grown women felt compelled to project a teenagish image half their lives, as if feminine maturity threatened male egos.

"So, so. You're Koan Angstrom?" Freddie rested her chin on her upturned hand, grinning sweetly. "How dumb of me. I didn't make the association. Koan Angstrom. Who would've thought? This is interesting. It brings things into perspective."

Koan played dumb. "I'm afraid you've lost me."

Freddie's eyes narrowed as she peered across the table, trying to read Koan's emotions. "Hand on heart, are you aware that I've been inquiring into your organization."

"No. Why? Are you considering a business association?"

"No, that's not the reason. Maybe I'm paranoid, but the talk we had in the park now seems suspiciously less than purely coincidental."

"Much of life is just coincidence."

Freddie twisted her napkin in her hands. "I'm sure I'm being irrational, but somehow I feel, how does one say it, threatened. It's like I'm expecting the other shoe to drop."

"It won't be mine. They're laced." Koan tried to steer the conversation onto other subjects, but Freddie was no longer into it. She only toyed with her entree, and turned down coffee and dessert.

"Mr. Angstrom, I'm sorry. I really am. It's been awfully nice of you to invite me up here, but I hope you'll excuse me. I'd feel a lot better if we could continue this conversation some other time. I need to be heading home."

Their parting was courteous but cool, leaving Koan wondering even more what Freddie knew.

The lunch fiasco hardly cooled Koan's interest in Freddie. His fear that her inquisitiveness might be putting her in danger nagged at him. After a number of unreturned calls, Freddie was finally on the other end of the telephone line.

"Mr. Angstrom."

"Please, I insist on you calling me Koan."

"Okay, Koan, I apologize for my shortness at our lunch meeting. In reflecting on it, I may've been making too many assumptions."

"How's that?"

"I told you I'd been involved with your organization. Well, it had nothing to do with business, but rather my husband. He had once participated in a medical study conducted by one of your firms and never gotten any response, or a copy of the study's conclusions."

"I'm very sorry to hear that. And considering what you were going through, I'm sure you didn't need the extra aggravation."

There was a pause on the other end of the line. "How do you mean that?"

"After what happened to your husband." Suddenly, Koan recognized his slip-up. Why should Koan Angstrom know anything about Chris Folkstone's disappearance? "Look, it shouldn't be that difficult to get someone to provide you with information about the study. I'll look into it right away. And I hope we can set a make-up date for lunch or dinner."

There was a long pause before Freddie responded. From her guarded tone, Koan suspected she'd caught his veiled admission. After their conversation ended, he sat long in thought.

Hell, if she figures this out, there might be a golden lining in it. She could become a wedge between Paul and me to neutralize him and his control over me. But that assumes she'd recognize me? Freddie who detests science fiction? Fat chance. No, if anything, she'd probably perceive it as another maneuver in some high-stakes game. The kind she's convinced she's masterful at.

But maybe she wouldn't have to know I'm Chris. My wealth's got to impress the shit out of her. That's a big hook for Freddie. The prospect of a partnership with the great Koan Angstrom? That's all we had in our marriage anyway. I'm sure that's what's behind all this schmooze and playing up to me.

Paul underestimates her. I don't like treating her as a pawn. She's too obsessive, too assertive. Ultimately, she's got to see herself at the top, and creating an illusion to satisfy that craving would be a real challenge, one she'd relish. But, in the end, it may be the only safe way to deal with her.

12

Over time, another key person from Koan's past crept into his thoughts. Hope.

He missed her grit and down-to-earth manner. And more than that, she was the straightest person he'd ever met. He trusted what she said to be real, regardless of how much pain that could inflict upon him. The more he focused on her, the stronger was his urge to search her out.

Koan stood in the hallway of an older, yellow-brick apartment house, his eyes scanning the row of doorbell buttons on the turquoise wall. He'd stood there often enough to know which button was Hope's, but he wanted to enjoy a sense that some things remained constant.

Answering her buzzer, Hope was caught by surprise and begged for a few minutes to "tidy up." Finally the door latch buzzed, allowing Koan to enter the main hallway and climb the familiar steps, much slower than earlier. He paused to catch his breath in front of Hope's doorway. Before he had recovered, the door opened, and Hope eyed Koan inquisitively. It was all he could do to keep from reaching out and embracing her.

Without any great explanation as to who he was or why he was there, Koan asked if he could come in. Perhaps it was the beads of sweat on his brow from climbing the stairs or his age that spawned passion in Hope's heart. In any case, she beckoned him into her living room, where the two sat a short time later.

"So, how did you know Chris?" Hope sat pressed into the far corner of her sofa. Koan was perched, equally stiff, in an armchair on the other side of the coffee table.

"He was an associate."

"In your company?"

"Well, not exactly."

Hope's expression was taunt, her eyes intense and studying. "You said you wanted to talk about Chris?"

"Yes, when he disappeared, you wondered, I'm sure, what happened to him."

"I suppose everyone did. There was no trace. It was eerie."

"Do you think he's still alive?"

"Why does that matter? Look, I don't want to seem rude, but I don't know who you are, or why you're here. You said you're not from the police, or an investigator, but you sound like one."

Koan rubbed his palms to evaporate the moistness on them. He'd set out to see Hope with a soul full of warmness, but sitting there across from her, there seemed no tactile thread between the present and a fondly remembered past.

"I don't know quite how to tell you this, Hope. What…what if I told you Chris is still alive?"

"I'd be skeptical. Very skeptical." Hope wasn't responding with the show of emotions Koan expected. "For quite a while, I went through too many games of why, where, and how. It left me drained."

"I understand. Fine. But if he were alive, would you want to see him?"

Hope crossed her arms across her chest. "Let me warn you, I don't care for games. Also, I still haven't heard how you're connected to him?"

Koan eyed a pack of cigarettes on Hope's coffee table. He wasn't allowed to smoke, because the old man hadn't, but he couldn't resist taking one. The first drag made him cough. He said insistently that he was close to Chris, asking if that sufficed, and Hope nodded, still eyeing him with distrust.

"Good. First of all, I can say with certainty that Chris isn't dead. He underwent a transition in his life, more precisely, surgery, drastic surgery."

"He never mentioned any illnesses. Was it an accident?"

"Neither. It was cosmetic surgery. In fact, if he were sitting here right now, you wouldn't recognize him."

Hope grabbed a cigarette. "Hold on. Chris wasn't exactly a happy camper, but a change of identity? He was very good-looking. That sounds a bit preposterous."

"It wasn't voluntary."

"I see." Hope inhaled deeply, blowing a billow of blue smoke toward Koan. "I'm not by nature a mistrusting person, but you're barging in here with such revelations, it doesn't sit right. Why hasn't Chris gotten in touch with me, or, better yet, his wife?"

Koan leaned forward with a pleading look. "It wasn't possible."

Hope pulled her arms close to her sides and bit on her lower lip. "I still don't have the foggiest idea who you are, and you're expecting me to swallow your story?"

Frustrated, Koan said he knew Hope was a nurse, that she and Chris had met at the time of his father's death, but Hope wasn't impressed. "That scares me, but, then, if you were close to Chris, he could've told you that."

Koan massaged his face, questioning why he had come there. "Look, I wouldn't blame you for thinking I'm full of shit."

"I wouldn't be quite so blunt, but I keep looking for the reason why you're here. For a while I thought it might be to aggravate me, for whatever reasons I can't imagine, but, no, I sense you have better intentions than that. I really think you should contact his wife, Freddie."

Koan said Chris didn't trust her.

"I'll give you credit for that observation. Apparently you know her." Hope's smile disappeared again quickly. "Look, even if you're telling me the truth, what are you expecting of me? That I should be feeling overjoyed that he's out there somewhere getting on with his life, under some new identity no one would recognize?"

Koan closed his eyes, leaning his head back. The conversation wasn't gratifying either one of them, but the prospect of simply leaving triggered a sense of desperation.

"Look, Hope, what if I, sitting right here in front of you, were Chris?"

"That's enough! You may not realize it, but you're jacking around with my feelings. Big time."

"I'm sorry, really, but I have to ask. What if I were Chris? Would you be able to accept that?"

Hope got up abruptly, her body facing the front hallway. "My patience is running low. May I ask you to leave?"

"Then I have to say it. I am Chris."

Hope's eyes shut. "Enough." Hope started toward the door, but Koan moved to stop her.

"What have you got to lose by testing me? If I really am Chris, wouldn't that be okay with you?"

Hope's expression was that of a trapped and fearful child

questioning whether the situation might be dangerous. Warily, she sank back down onto the sofa, her whole body tensed.

"Okay, let me tell you how we met, what we talked about, even the kind of beer you drank. For starters, we met at the All Saints Hospital. It was night, late at night, and I was sitting in my father's room. He was dying."

The explicitness of Koan's description got Hope's attention. "That's all true. But what did we talk about?"

"Nothing. Neither of us spoke."

Hope looked baffled. "Go on, why didn't we talk?"

"Because I was crying."

Hope got up and walked to a window, taking a deep breath, avoiding eye contact with Koan. "How do you know all that?"

"I've said why."

"But I don't believe you." Hope turned around, her eyes fixed on Koan's. "I don't know what kind of friends Chris had. Maybe he was able to talk to someone about all that. No, I don't want this. Let see how much he told you. I don't think Chris would've told even his best friend such a thing. It would've embarrassed him too much. What was the kinkiest thing he and I ever did?"

"The kinkiest thing?" Koan's eyes narrowed. "Lying on your bed and hugging. Or maybe crying in your arms."

Hope's face reflected her fright. She stumbled to the sofa falling down onto it, looking faint. Koan wanted to tell her it was all right but didn't know how. A confused silence hung in the room awhile, then was broken by Hope's crying.

Koan was sitting on the sofa next to Hope, squeezing her hand in his. He'd gone through the tale of his abduction, captivity, the operations, and his recovery as the old man. Hope questioned him, continuing to resist a reality that was gradually settling in.

"Why didn't you go to the police?"

"And done what? Had myself arrested? I, Koan, instigated the abduction."

For the first time since her bout of crying, Hope smiled, then backed off from Koan. "I feel you. You are Chris." Hope reached out and ran her palm across Koan's jaw. "You know, it was so much easier to believe you'd run away, or were dead. Such illusions were digestible." She reached out and gave Koan a warm hug, then laughed softly. "My cue used to be, 'It's time you get back to your wife.' But now I don't know you well enough to say anything like that. Do you have a wife?"

"No."

"I can't use that one to kick you out, can I?" Together they enjoyed a tension purging laugh.

Hope insisted on fixing something to eat, and for the first time in a long time, Koan enjoyed a sensation of being at home. He and Paul had a meeting scheduled, but Koan ignored the time. Even while busy cooking, Hope would stop, step over to Koan, touch him, look questioningly into his eyes, tell him she was still trying to convince herself he was really Chris.

"You know, if Freddie finds out you came here first, heaven help me."

"How would she know?"

"We're friends."

Seeing Koan's surprise, Hope explained. "There's a lot you don't know. Freddie tracked me down." Hope recounted how Freddie had invited her to a restaurant, posing as an insurance inspector. "She tried to make me feel like some slut panting after her husband. You know me. There's only so much I can take from anybody, then I blast back. Well, later she needed me. Did you know she had a drug problem?"

Koan shook his head.

"Prescriptions. Dozens of them. One night, real late, she called me, totally strung out. She'd overdosed."

"Freddie, Miss Self-Control?"

"Drug abuse is as often as not about maintaining control,

at all costs. She had it well organized. Multiple prescriptions, pills for ups and downs. No moods, no off days. A case of wanting to be so perfect, it kills." Hope elaborated on the rehab program she'd helped Freddie through. "Along the way we became friends."

Koan smiled wryly. "Not a likely pair. And you're still good friends?"

"Until recently. Freddie's become distant. I wrote it off as a passing mood, but it seems more." Hope looked at Koan with a soft smile. "You know, there's a lot of Chris in you. It feels right. And you've mellowed out. That's nice. Real nice."

Finally it occurred to Koan that he'd have to get home and deal with Paul. As he was ready to leave, Hope threw her arms around him, tears streaming down her smiling face. "Welcome home, stranger. And don't take so long to come back again. Please."

"Paul, I'm sorry I'm late. I was taking care of an insurance policy."

"An insurance policy?" Letting the papers in his hand fall on the table, Paul's eyes narrowed. "You let me wait for over an hour, then come in here talking nonsense. If it's a joke, out with the punch line, so we can get on with business."

"I'm dead serious, Paul. I needed extra insurance."

"Is the angry young man breaking through again? Let's talk in whole sentences. Okay?"

Koan sat down, folding his hands in front of him, saying he felt like a laboratory animal, that as long as the experiment went well, he was safe, but if things went wrong, the experiment might end, without him, and he would be the last to be told it was over. "No one had any hesitation about fucking around with my life back then. What guarantees do I have it won't happen again?"

"That's rubbish, paranoid fantasy."

"Paul, I've listened to your logical mind, and you always

make sense, but logic is its own end. Don't forget, I used to use that same crap manipulation. This is one big game for you. I'm not standing in judgment, just looking out for my ass."

Paul pounded his hand on the table. "Koan, this insults me! When it comes to loyalty, my life speaks for itself! Sometimes your little flights of fancy are hard to swallow. Do you know what real loyalty is?"

"Loyalty to what?"

"Oh, enough. Could you just tell me where you were, what happened, and leave out the emotional frills?"

Without mentioning Hope's name, Koan said he had confided in someone, and he considered that a security against anything happening to him.

"Koan, did you hear about the guy who went to get insurance, took the medical exam, and upon discovering that he had a chronic ailment, no one wanted to insure him? Your best insurance has been secrecy. With your paranoia, I'm surprised you found someone you could trust. Your ex-wife?"

"Why should I tell you? So you can consider whether to eliminate them? No thanks."

Paul was as mad as Koan had every experienced him. Paul took a real deep breath. "Let's just change the subject. Okay? For now. You recall, I'm sure, that someone's been searching around in our organization. I underestimated them. They've leveled a veiled but clear accusation."

Paul's revelation swung Koan's mood. He wanted to know more.

"There's an old-fashioned word for it, blackmail. Silence for a price."

Koan couldn't envision Freddie going that far. "How much do they know?"

"I want to believe it's just a hunch. I've asked myself a thousand times, and there's no plausible way they could know more. That is, not unless you've talked about it."

"Me? I don't even know who it is? You've refused to tell me. If I told anyone, they'd probably consider me nuts."

"You haven't told anyone?"

"I said no. Only the one person today, and they certainly didn't suspect anything. They were convinced I was dead."

"And you're sure no one would have picked up on nuances, mannerisms, or expressions Chris would've used?"

"You programmed me too well."

"Koan, you're an astute observer. Are you sure there wasn't a little reaction, a flash in her eyes, a pause, a shared remembrance, some small sign of recognition?"

"No, I would've noticed. I know her too well." Koan slammed his eyes shut, realizing Paul had trapped him. "Damn it."

"And how was she? The same?"

Koan pounded the armrests of his chair. "Your games make me feel like a simple assed schoolboy."

"My apologies. And I compliment you on figuring out who our blackmailer was. Good. Now we can talk straight. Number one, why didn't I reveal her identity? I feared sentimental emotions. And I was right. Your instincts were to warn her."

Paul walked around Koan and patted him on the shoulder. "I guess that explains the escalation. Koan Angstrom doesn't go around making personal appearances like that. Fortunately for us, she values money more than justice."

"What does she want?"

Freddie had suggested to Paul that she'd always had a pet dream, her own advertising agency, but never possessed the necessary start-up money. "Interesting, isn't it? She placed the solution in our hands. A venture capital partnership, something Angstrom Industries is involved in on a routine basis. It makes no waves, creates no questions. And she gets the power she dreams of. Very tidy."

"All she wants is money?"

Paul squeezed Koan's shoulder. "I understand your emotions. She is far less interested in Chris than her own personal ambitions. But, really, Koan, her actions are consistent with how you described her to me. You knew her very well."

"Yes, I thought I did."

13

Koan Angstrom had an immense estate. The new Koan had viewed most of it, its many rooms, including the one in which he had been held captive, but it had taken him much longer to familiarize himself with how the old man had lived. The far eastern wing of the estate had been his real inner sanctum. One room was lined with massive bookshelves containing the finest editions of books on philosophy and religion. Unlike his predecessor, the new Koan rarely read, preferring the more immediate, audio-visual experience. Fortunately, there was also a film library and screening room.

At first, Koan found few of the film titles of interest to him. Many were foreign films with subtitles or dubbing.

Often out of simple boredom he had pushed himself to view such films and in time discovered a growing fascination. His earlier friends used to joke that anyone who watched such films, like those of Ingmar Bergman, couldn't be a whole lot of fun. Koan, however, found himself watching them over and over again. They took him back to simple, fantastic childhood speculations about existence, mortality and immortality; a further tie back to his previous existence, a tie he couldn't relinquish.

Koan picked a video cassette and slipped it into the projector, but in a few minutes his thoughts were elsewhere.

These films are fine, thought provoking, inspiring, but I still haven't uncovered what could have sustained the old man? It's Paul who's had the exciting role, the heroics. What was the old man's game? What gratified him? He must've been more than a passive bookworm, connoisseur of films, the arts. Sure, there had to be genius there to accumulate so much wealth, but, according to Paul, he invested very little time in that. What did he get so involved in? There's something here somewhere so incredibly subtle that I can't find it. And it burns me to know. God, why am I here, if there was no greater purpose than to be a shadow of the man?

Was it that damned word holda? While Paul professes to be in the dark about that word's meaning, he makes comments that make me wonder if he knows the secret. Like when I was arguing that Native Americans might be closer in their beliefs to the real meaning of communing with God. Paul shot right back that the old man used the word when talking about some tribes of Native Americans. But in what sense? Paul's only answer to that was that the old man used the word holda like a punctuation.

The film rolling on the screen in front of him caught Koan's attention again, but just for a few minutes.

If it were my film, my script, I'd have Freddie discovering who I am. Yes, there'd be tears. But how does a filmmaker project the saltiness of tears, really burning ones, not that dribbly, sniffily stuff? But then again, why tears? There would be joy, passion, a spontaneous embrace, the kind we never had in our marriage, a desperate need to draw closer and know each other. When the camera zoomed in on Freddie's eyes, I'd have a reflection in them, the reflection of an old man's sad face coming alive. Yes, genuine emotions, not staged directions from Paul.

What was that in that film the other day on photojournalism? The power of a camera to record the naked, unadulterated truth? How presumptuous of me. How would I know what the camera would capture in Freddie's eyes? Probably her endless hunger for achievement and recognition, not emotions like love. That's if I sought to portray realism, and not illusion like dear old Freddie.

I used to be so damned cynical about people who compulsively watched their soap operas, but I feel like I'm caught up in one. That scene at Anthony's, Freddie's declaration of love, and there I was crying. Why? Was it my loneliness rather than Freddie?

Could some whore have said those words, and offered a warm embrace, and I could have drowned myself in it? What were her words? Really love, or was it nothing more than a twinge of guilt, or worse, a heartless, calculating parroting of emotions she felt were expected? I'm going nuts.

Koan looked across the table at Freddie, admiring her. She had always valued a plain, inconspicuous, unintimidating look, one that wouldn't make her male counterparts squirm or overlook her professional qualifications. For Koan, she broke her own rules. For their dinner date she had on a sparkling sequin gown, dazzling jewelry, and had invested in a sophisticated hairdo.

"I'm honored to share the company of such a lovely woman."

Freddie started to drop her eyes, but caught her show of emotion and raised her chin, smiling with pride. "Let's say,

I felt inspired to look especially good tonight."

"Wherever that inspiration came from, I'm enjoying it. Freddie, does it bore you that I'm so curious about you and your life?"

Freddie brushed her wine glass across her chin. "Your interest is a compliment, but, to be honest, you still intimidate me."

"Then pretend I'm someone else. Maybe your ex-husband, looking for subtle changes that've taken place since he last saw you."

Koan's words broke the spell. "Can we just concentrate on us?"

As Koan continued to delve into Freddie's past, it amused him how she over embellished everything, which teased a desire in him to correct her. The conversation had progressed to where she had made her decision on a career. Freddie explained how it began with a psychology course in college. "It totally blew my mind. The professor used a phrase that really bit me. He called it the 'science of manipulation.' He went on to explain how one took a desired response, then built a pattern of signals designed to elicit that response. That seemed so awesomely powerful."

Koan leaned back, scratching his head. "Just a thought, but a desired response can be almost anything, good or evil. Take a totalitarian government and its propaganda. Does it matter, to you personally, whether the message has redeeming value?"

"It's a business. Even your TV evangelists recruit advertising professionals. Some of the best. The pattern's perfect. Create self-guilt, a sense of incompleteness, inadequacy, and isolation, then offer something they can belong to, as children to parents, who can forgive them. Equate financial contributions with redemption, forgiveness. It's like pushing consumer goods, except the product's a pat on the head. Nothing's immune to advertising. Not religion, politics, or anything else of significance in our world. It's who can manipulate the best.

Advertising keeps the whole system moving. But listen to me. Here I'm sitting across from Koan Angstrom, pretending to be an expert. What I wouldn't give for insight into your mind."

"I doubt that. My good fortune has been little more than pure chance."

"Such modesty. You know, it embarrasses me to tell you how I envisioned you. Ruthless, ice-cold, a hackneyed stereotype. Wrong." Freddie smiled coquettishly. "You're not a mythical monster, as someone portrayed you, but a very charming gentleman."

"Thank you, but isn't it a basic advertising principle to create a perception that may or may not be congruent with the truth?"

"You've done your homework."

Awhile later, Koan mentioned he'd learned that Freddie would be setting up her own business. Freddie toyed with her wine glass, hesitating with her response. "I hope you understand how I mean this, Koan, but do you believe in paying a person back for something you caused them to lose?"

Koan smiled. "If you don't, you usually find yourself in litigation."

Freddie tapped her wine glass against Koan's. "We can leave out the lawyers. As far as I'm concerned, it's been a fair trade. And I can assure you, I can let bygones be bygones."

"If offered the right compensation."

Freddie grinned, shaking her head slowly from side to side. "Look, there's no satisfaction in getting bent out of shape about things that can't be changed. I'm satisfied with this new association. I feel it's appropriate to say thank you."

Koan shrugged.

"One more thing, Koan. I hope the association might expand beyond the business arena."

Hearing Koan had dined with Freddie, Paul asked whether his ex-wife appeared satisfied with their offer.

"She's a person who lives for the striving."

Paul raised his chin smugly. "Strivers wind up buried twelve feet under. Even when digging their own grave, they can't recognize when it's time to stop. Ironically, our organization thrives on such people. Given the right direction, they are extremely effective."

"You're a manipulative bastard, Paul."

"Pragmatic, Koan, nothing more. I feel we've effectively neutralized Freddie. With her new company, she's now got a major distraction on her hands, and chances are she'll flail around with that for quite a while. We're probably in for a bailout or two. But we'll gladly pay. My only real concern, Koan, is you."

"Me?"

"Yes. Her obsession to find you has waned. She appears satisfied to let Chris fade away. That must be tough for you. Or have you found a philosophical balm?"

Koan argued that his relationship with Freddie was never one of great emotions, that Freddie's appetite for self-perpetuation hadn't surprised him in the least.

"Still, it would only be natural that it hurt." Paul stroked his finger over his lips. "Do you mind my asking whether there was another woman?"

Koan's reflex was to deny it, but Paul read through him. He asked if Koan had gotten back in touch with the other woman, and whether she was what Koan had termed his insurance, the person who could uncover everything, if anything happened to him.

"Does this mean you're going to search for her?"

"No, Koan. That would alarm her. And it would provide credence to your paranoia. I have to assume she loves you, that she would be protective, that she would sense that any indiscretions on her part could lead you into big trouble."

Koan shook his head from side to side. "Paul, your mind amazes me."

"Save the compliments. If I'm right, this old relationship is very timely. You crave someone's company, and this is a lot easier to deal with than some two-bit call girls. It may also explains why you aren't embittered by your ex-wife's behavior. The other woman isn't like her, is she?"

"Hardly."

Paul folded his hands together. "Just go about it in a confidential and discreet manner."

It was well past midnight. Koan was in his bedroom, reclining on the chaise lounge next to his bed, feeling too agitated to sleep.

Hope knows I'm still there, but it was tough slipping back into being Chris. I lost less than I thought. No more bitter tears. Yes, I do want to hold onto the child I was. I need that reference point to direct me. I can't ever become Koan, but I can become that which I once wanted to be. Hope knew that part of me. Oh, yes, he did too, old Father Nick.

I wonder what happened to him? I remember the day I went in there, pissed off as hell about Sam getting the promotion, the one I thought I deserved. Freddie gave me hell, accusing me of not promoting myself enough. That did it. I think I wanted to get mugged, or beaten up. That's why I went to that part of town.

I met Nick. The ultimate confessional priest. Reminded me of the old men who used to hang around at Stanley's filling station, back in Shepherdstown. Moss and I loved to sit there sipping soda pop and listening to their stories.

I'd love to chew the fat with Father Nick again. With Moss, too. Paul'd have a heart attack. Or maybe not. He gave his blessings to the thing with Hope. Why not? From his perspective it pacifies me. And me? It gives me back some identity. What little I want of the old life.

14

"Your car, sir."

Koan slipped behind the wheel of the old black Packard that as a child had reminded him of an inverted bathtub. He'd taken over an odd collection of cars from the old man, among them older models of an army jeep, a sleek Citreon sedan, and a stodgy Rolls Royce. The possibility that the Packard might get stolen put a evil smile on Koan's face.

For an hour or so, Koan zipped along the interstate, humming happily to Beethoven's *Eroica*. Earlier he had only listened to classical music out of pretense. Having inherited an incredible library of recordings, grudgingly, classical music had grown on him.

Gradually, the rural landscape gave way to the urban sprawl of Pontifica with its ten-lane freeways and endless billboards. It's wasn't long before Koan approached a section of the city Chris had known well, an area most people sped by on the elevated freeway. Koan exited down a litter-strewn ramp, and soon he found the object of his search, the Burning Bridges bar.

Koan didn't know whether he was disappointed or relieved. The front of the building was boarded up. Still, the longer he sat there, the more he longed for a reunion with Father Nick.

Driving slowly, Koan stopped a few times to ask where Father Nick might be found. Finally, a sorry-looking, toothless man wearing a dirty, ill-fitting overcoat said he knew Father Nick and gave Koan sketchy directions to a community center where Father Nick supposedly worked.

Finally Koan spotted an arrow painted on the side of a building, under it written, "Community Center." Rounding the next corner, his eyes were met by an incongruous sight. A brightly painted building, appearing like an oasis amidst a desolate blight, sported a large sign saying it was the Southside Community Center.

Many of the surrounding buildings had been renovated, and the people on the street seemed surprisingly energetic, and decently dressed.

Koan parked his car, contemplating what he might say to Father Nick. A young boy walked along the sidewalk toward him with a cheerful bounce in his step, whistling with all his heart. Koan recalled how he'd won a few whistling contests during his youth. Koan attempted to whistle, but his lips were too puffy and stiff. Cursing under his breath, Koan climbed out of the car and headed for the community center. Above the steps he stopped to read a crudely-written banner, "From Despair to Rebirth."

Inside, Koan was greeted by friendly faces and directed to a room upstairs. Sitting around a large table in the room was a group of men engrossed in lively discussion. Koan identified Father Nick. Even though his face was thinner and freshly shaven, his body was still round, if a little less weighty. Father Nick acknowledged him with a curt smile.

"Can ah help ya, sir?"

"Yes…uh, actually, I was looking for you." Koan introduced himself and pardoned his interruption, stepping back out into the hall to allow them to finish.

Father Nick was obviously the leader, and the discussion was about organizing people and materials for a building they intended to renovate.

"Sorry to keep ya waitin'." Father Nick scrutinized Koan. "Weez gotta keep dees people lined up, or day wander off perty fast. So, wadya wanta ask me?"

"It has to do with a man named Chris. He used to visit a bar, the Burning Bridges bar. Do you remember him?"

"Da guy dat disappeared?"

"You knew that?"

"His wife came by and wanted to know all about 'im. She gave me some line, but ah could tell id was da wife. Ya smell doze things. Ah don't know anything 'bout dat boy disappearin', bud ah can tell ya fer sure, wadever happened to 'im, id didn't happen here. Ah asked around a lot. Didn't hear a thing."

Koan explained he wasn't from the police, but simply an acquaintance of Chris.

Father Nick chuckled. "Dat's wad 'is wife said. Anyway, dat boy seemed lost or sumptin'. Some people're like dat. Don't know where day fit. Got plenty of 'em round here."

"So, you're fixing up buildings?"

"Da people who own 'em would just as well tear 'em down and chase deez people out. Day don't care dat someone's livin' in 'em. Dat ain't no life fer any creature, runnin' 'round lookin' fer a place to sleep each night. People need ta belong somewheres." Father Nick scratched his head, peering at

Koan as if concerned he'd said too much. "'Scuse me, but ah haven't seen you before, have ah?"

"No, I only came to ask about Chris. And to talk to you. Frankly, I'm impressed with what you're doing here."

"Wouldn't have some extra lumber, bricks and things, would ya? We sure could use 'em."

"We can talk about that too. I think I can help."

Father Nick gave Koan a slap on the shoulder and invited him to see some of the buildings they were working on. Hours later, Koan climbed back into his car, suppressing a desire to shout for joy. And he laughed, too. "Damn. I was hoping someone would steal this damned old Packard. Feels more like something my father would've driven."

"Quite honestly, Paul, I expected one of your speeches."

"No, Koan, I like the idea."

"You do?"

"Yes. It's got potential. It would reflect on your image in a way that's difficult to transform into any negatives."

"That's just posturing. What about the specifics?"

"Oh, I can recall numerous conversation with the old man about center city revitalization. He believed it had to come. He dwelled a lot on the concept of community, that clear definitions of communities reflected the basic pack instinct in man, blaming many of our contemporary social problems on the deterioration and decay of communities through mass urbanization. But he could say that with a whimsical smile. There was an appropriate expression he was fond of, 'Nothing lasts forever, only the forces of renewal.'"

"Interesting." Koan repeated the phrase. "I'll have to remember that. But look, there's no profit motive in this. It's just charity."

"Fine, but don't label it charity. The old man didn't care for that term. He believed in sparking the forces of human potential, while he saw charity as an opiate. But let's not get lost in semantics. Is this Father Nick a priest?"

"Yes, a holy man." Koan couldn't suppress a grin. "Apparently the landlords want to tear down the buildings they're renovating. Maybe we could buy them out?"

Paul smiled. "That didn't take long. We're coming together. We may be able to cloak this in an investment venture after all. But allow me to change the subject."

Paul got up and walked over to get a drink. Leaning against the bar, he toasted Koan. "As I expected, you impressed Freddie."

"I did?"

"Yes. We were discussing the framework for her new firm, and she repeatedly talked about the dinner with you. With stars in her eyes. Good show. She feels she's arrived."

Koan laughed cynically. "That's insane."

"What about you? Did you enjoy it?"

"Mixed emotions. I am beginning to enjoy this little game of having two identities, knowing she doesn't know one of them."

"Well, enjoy it, but don't push it too hard. She's clever. As long as she worships the ground you walk on, she's out of commission."

Koan had truckloads of building material sent to Father Nick and his crew and was anxious to get some feedback, so he invited Father Nick to dinner at a dive called the Midway Diner. Earlier it had been an in yuppie place, hailed as a half-hour in the twilight zone, a little battle ribbon to say you had rubbed elbows with the salt of the earth.

The conversation with Father Nick was a delight. He was lively as ever, full of trouser-pocket wisdoms. Nick also took a liking to their waitress, a full-figured, middle-aged shuffler. "She reminds me a lot of Nellie. We were kinda close, 'fore ah got muself in trouble. Nice gal she was." Nick's eyes followed the waitress's generous hips as she sauntered away.

"Nick, I'd like to do more."

"If ya mean more stuff, we could always use more. Der's

more buildings dare dan ya can shake a stick at. And lotsa of more people needin' a roof over der heads. Seems der's new ones every day."

"Good. I'll make sure you have everything you need."

"Mighty generous of ya, Mr. Angstrom."

"It's Koan, okay."

"Den thank ya, Mr. Koan."

The waitress brought them their coffee. Father Nick winked at her, shaking his head slowly. "Ah say. Ya sure is a sight for deez old eyes."

The waitress planted a hand on her hip, gayly barking, "You got old eyes."

"Ah knows a classy lady when ah see 'em."

She thrust her heavy hip at him, laughed, then shuffled away.

"Nick, I've been meaning to ask you something."

"Wud's dat?"

"It's about the buildings you're restoring. It concerns me that, one day, out of nowhere, the owners could come and tear them down. There's a way to prevent that. I'm considering buying as many building as we can get ahold of. If we make it lucrative enough, they'll sell."

"Lucrative?"

"Offer them a price they wouldn't turn down."

"You'd do dat?"

"Yes, I would." Koan looked proudly over at Nick, whose eyes moved quickly away in search of the waitress. His sense of timing was good. The waitress was rounding the corner of the counter with Nick's bowl of chili and Koan's platter of stew. Nick yelled at her. "Yer about to make dis old man real happy."

The waitress shoved the chili in front of Nick with a big smile. "It ain't no prize recipe, darling, but it'll fill ya up."

Nick beamed at the waitress, asking if she had any crackers, sending her off with a hint of speed in her step. Nick chuckled as he sank his spoon into his chili.

"She'd make a good woman."
"You ever been married, Nick?"
"Wud fer?"
"I don't know. To have a family."
"Didn't have one muself."

The waitress brought Nick crackers and a few slices of white bread. Nick thanked her, waving a big hand at her bottom and receiving a gentle slap accompanied by a high-pitched giggle.

"Yah know, Mr. Koan, id's not like ah doesn't think highly 'bout wud ya said, wid da buildings, but ah don't think id's so good."

"Why not? It would secure your projects."

Nick leaned back, aimlessly scratching the top of his hairless head. "Sir, don't misunderstand me, bud some wonders why ya wansta help us."

"I understand, Nick. But I can assure you, my reasons are personal, not business-related. I see injustices that need to be rectified. There shouldn't be people sleeping on the streets at night."

"Yer intentions seem all right ta me. May sound a liddle crazy, but ya see, we kinda hope one of doze people will come and tear one of da buildin's down. One wid people in it. Ah appreciate what ya wanna do fer us, bud ya see, der is lotsa people out dare. Id's worse dan day say in the news. Ya see, if a buncha us gits killed, den people gonna know we're dare. Dat's ma point. A lotta dem wants ta fight."

"Fight?"

"Yes, sir. Day don't mind to die. Life's cheap fer dem. Day don't even get berried. Death ain't no different than bein' alive. Day see someone dead, day say goodbye to 'em, like they say goodbye every day."

"A bunch of you will just wind up in jail." His comment got laughter.

"Dat ain't so bad. Dare they has sumptin' ta eat, a place to sleep, and id's warm. Ya see ma point?" Nick took a drink of water, looking around to see whether anyone was listening. "Sir, when day comes to tear a buildin' down, we'd stay right dare, and maybe day'd be fool enough to let doze machines kill one of us. Ya see, dat would get in da television or sumptin'. Den maybe day'd come and talk wid us."

"So, you want a confrontation?"

"Weez talked a lot about it, sir. Ah hope ya understand. Yer a mighty generous man. Ah know that."

Koan's face was tense and twisted. "Nick, I'm trying to understand. I'm trying."

"We'd still like da stuff ya offered us."

"Yeah, we can still do that."

"Thank ya, sir. We're all mighty thankful fer dat."

"I'm glad."

Driving home from his meeting with Father Nick, Koan fought back self-pity and rejection. His mind sought a distraction, wandering back, as it so often did, to his childhood.

When I told Dad about the treehouse Moss and I had built, I thought he would hit me. There was rage in his eyes. But then only silence followed, that silence that was worse than a scream.

Moss and I took the wood from that empty, three-story orange brick house, the Babler spookhouse that never got built to completion. We carried those boards all the way back to Turtle Hollow, where the big oak leaned out over the creek. It took us all summer to build that treehouse. And when it was finally done, we stood up there, high up in that oak, and we screamed, screamed at the tops of our lungs. We were proud.

Moss and I loved that treehouse. We would sit up there and talk about things, like going out into the world and doing things we couldn't do in Shepherdstown. I already knew then I'd be leaving there.

I told Dad about our treehouse, because I was hoping he'd want to see it. He didn't. Instead, he went silent. And when weeks later he finally said something about it, he preached about why we should join the Scouts, that we didn't spend enough time at church. He never understood why we wanted to be on our own.

That's when I screamed I was going as far away as I could. He hardly acknowledged that. Instead, he turned away and didn't look back at me.

That silence. I never learned who Dad was, or whether he knew me. Or liked me.

Sometimes I thought he had no real identity. Just that dead silence. And caring for others. No, I never could have been like him. Nor remained in Shepherdstown. I had to find out who I was, not what that world wanted me to be.

15

Hope, sitting on her sofa, swung her head back, combing her fingers through her long, straight hair. "Koan, I haven't been able to come up with any good way to tell Freddie."

Koan was lying on the carpet and gazing up at the ceiling, just as he had done, years before as Chris, mostly in silence, listening to Hope.

"Koan, why can't Chris just remain dead? What's his life got to do with you being here now?" Hope looked down at Koan to see if he was awake. "It's no secret that I didn't care for Chris's lifestyle. Or attitudes. I've asked myself what's different about you. Your wealth has the potential to be an escalation of what I despised in Chris. In other words, I'm usually not particularly fond of your kind."

Koan put his hand over his face. "And how do you think I feel? For awhile I was bananas about what all I could have. Now it all repulses me."

"There's a tone in that that sounds like Chris." Getting no response from Koan, Hope lit up a cigarette. "You know, when I finally got it into this little brain of mine that it really was you, I prayed that you'd grown out of that old self-pity of yours." Hope expelled a billowing cloud of blue smoke. "Have you ever once tried to see things from my side? Do you know what I was for you, and may still be? A confessional booth. Not that that is all I wanted."

"I know, Hope."

"No, you don't know! There's always been this egotistical tone that implied I wanted to flick your switch, get you in bed with me. Freddie was obsessed with the same notion. Yes, I wanted to flick a switch in you, but what I hoped is that it would turn you on to your potentials to make a difference. No, I was even less than a confessional booth. I was a compost heap for you to toss all your whining and crying into."

Hope stomped out her cigarette in the ashtray, then leaned back and broke out laughing. Her laughter continued, getting louder, nearly hysterical, then stopped, tears suddenly cascading down her cheeks. She slid down to the carpet next to Koan, wrapping her arm around him.

"Do you know, I cried when I heard you were gone. I cared that much about you. I felt a deep loss."

Koan drew his arm around Hope and squeezed her to him. "I cried too. I didn't appreciate how much you meant to me." Their close, quiet embrace lasted awhile, then Hope drew back.

"It's funny how a loss can have two sides to it. I missed you, but there was another sense of loss, a lost chance to tell you who I am." Hope ruffled Koan's hair. "You and Freddie were so much alike. Neither of you entertained the possibility that someone could really care for you. Not in the loving sense. Friendships were strategies without emotions. And you both loved yourselves too much to love others."

Hope's statement caused Koan to cringe. "Maybe I shouldn't have come back here? I needed, yeah, desperately, I needed a thread back to myself."

"And you knew there'd be a sea of compassion to spread out and engulf you. Right? I'll never change." Hope bent down and kissed Koan." I have one hope."

"What's that?"

"In following that thread back to whoever you were, it turns your head around toward the future."

Hope climbed up to her feet to get something to drink, and when she returned, Koan told her about his involvement with the Southside Community Center.

"I'm hearing something I never heard from Chris. Altruism. Compassion."

Koan smiled, enjoying Hope's show of admiration. "I'm planning on throwing a big holiday dinner at the community center."

Hope twisted up her lips. "Koan, be careful how you package it. There's a fine line between charity and being patronizing. Okay. I'd hate to see your good intentions come back to smack you in the face." Hope rolled over on top of Koan, running her fingers over his chest. "Hey. Maybe you are changing. Maybe it's more than just your new appearance. I'm sorry if it sounded like I was bad-mouthing you earlier." Hope gave Koan a soft kiss. "Never let go of hopes." Hope pointed to herself. "At least not this Hope."

Overwhelmed by a feeling of goodness, Koan walked from room to room, greeting the many people who'd come to the Southside Community Center for Thanksgiving dinner. Several hundred had already eaten, and outside there was still a long line, waiting to get in.

Seeing the hungered faces chomping on turkey, yams, biscuits, and green beans reminded Koan of a principle practiced by his family. His parents never used the terms vagrant or bum. People who wandered into their area with little more than a duffle bag over their shoulder were called the "less fortunate." They were offered odd jobs and fed. As he grew older, Chris became ashamed of his parent's altruism, viewing them as backward and naive. Koan felt a rare flash of kinship with his father, sharing this day with the "less fortunate" of the Southside ward.

"Dare he is! Mr. Koan!" Father Nick was sitting at a group of tables arranged in a hexagonal form. Koan pulled a chair up next to him, commenting on how many people were there.

"Der's only one thing louder dan da growl of empty stomachs. Dat's the word der's chow to be had."

"It'll be the first good shit we've had in a long time." The comment came from a very thin, hollowed-eyed man sitting several chairs down from Father Nick. The man had long, stringy hair and wasn't smiling. "Most people offer us little more than self-righteous food for thought. Tasty wisdoms, like how we should get off our lazy asses and work."

The man's fine articulation captured Koan's attention. Father Nick poked his elbow into Koan's ribs. "This is Old Cornelius, our man wid words. Corny, ya know we don't understand yer shit."

"But that man does. He knows exactly what I'm talking about."

"C'mon, Corny, Mr. Koan's been real generous to us."

"That's as hard to swallow as food, when your stomach's not used to any. Why's he here, maybe checking out how many of us are still around?"

To Koan's surprise, Nick made no attempt to downplay the remarks. Instead, he nodded, rubbing his chin, seemingly encouraging Cornelius to continue.

"Wealthy man, do you know what real desperation's like? No, how could you? It's the willingness to toss mortality to the wind. Like revolutions. It's having something to die for, and nothing to live for. You say, revolutions only happen somewhere else far away? Those twenty-second flashes in the evening news, abstractions summarized in thirty words or less. Take a good look. We're not abstractions."

The haggard man scooted his chair toward Koan, making him feel threatened.

"That's right. For most, we're just statistics in the news. 'Authorities estimate there are ten thousand homeless in Pontifica.' It doesn't make the news that another building was torn down, or torched for insurance, depriving another dozen people of a roof over their heads. No problem, right, we're resourceful people. We'll simply find a cardboard carton to sleep in tonight. That's quaint, and cozy."

Koan considered leaving the room to remove the reason for the man's tirade, but Nick wanted him to stay. "Old Corny's got a few things to say, ain't he?"

Koan cleared his tensed throat. "There's some truth in what he's saying." Koan's tentative statement initiated another round from Cornelius. "Just look how many of us have come out of the woodwork. And a whole lot more didn't show up because they suspected it was a trap. Maybe to record them, so the authorities can get them out of the city. Do you have any idea who these people are, or why they're here? Me, for example?"

It was a question Koan had been dying to ask. "Why are you here?"

"Fear."

"Fear of what?"

"AIDS. I was on the fast track, in the media, then it was determined that I was HIV positive. I thought I could talk about it, openly, but under all the sympathy and compassion rose a fear, a fear strong enough to shunt me aside. I got less and less work, lost my health insurance, and, after that? In time, there'll be millions more like me. Along with the ex-criminals, who can't get jobs. And the discards of mental health programs, addictions. And what do we all have in common? Hah! We strike fear in the hearts of 'nice' people like you."

For the first time the man grinned, but it was a diabolical look. "Actually, I'm surprised you're here. The public would rather believe we've been disenfranchised from any identity, disconnected fully from society, but, as you see, we're here."

Cornelius pressed a finger to his head. "We're there in your nightmares, those nagging dreams that one day we'll reappear, the lost masses, and we'll come back to choke the system that abandoned us, like the adult child who despises the parents who deserted it."

Koan was churning. He didn't know how much the others in the room understood, or whether they respected Cornelius or considered him a kook. Koan opted for a bland statement, saying he was there to better understand the problems Cornelius was addressing, but he got a sneer.

"I was curious what kind of do-gooder you are. You can buy out tired old men, but take a good look around at the numbers of young people. They'll slap the hand that offers them charity, because they still have pride. It's their territory, and those outside are the enemy. It's your kind who're creating these bitter people, and one day they'll topple your self-indulgent lives."

Father Nick broke in. "Enough, Corny. Ah don't like ya callin' me a tired old man wid no fire in ma guts. Ah could sit on ya and snuff ya out in a second, ya old bag a' bones." Nick's remarks got a round of laughter. "Besides, it takes a dumb dog to chase da hand dat feeds 'em. Mr. Angstrom here ain't askin' nuthin' in return fer dis. Til he does, ah say we be nice to 'im."

Voices raised in support of Koan. It quieted Cornelius, and gave Koan the opportunity to move on. A half-hour later, Koan decided it was time to head home.

As he was headed for the door, Father Nick spotted him.

"Sir, ah'm sorry 'bout da thing wid Corny. Ya shoulda spoken up. Corny woulda listened to ya. Ah think he's lonely fer someone to talk to. Sorry id kinda spoiled da day. Der a lotta happy folks 'round here."

Koan gave Father Nick a pat on the back. "It was good for me too, Nick. I would have eaten my Thanksgiving dinner alone. I had great company."

"Thank ya, sir."

As Koan drove away from the Southside Community Center, he switched on the radio. They were already playing an occasional Christmas song. When Bing Crosby's "Silver Bells" came on, Koan hummed along, thinking back on his childhood, singing the line about city stoplights flashing bright reds and greens.

He had been in grade school, when the first and only traffic light was installed in Shepherdstown. The colors of that traffic light had fascinated him, even when no cars were around to follow the signals. He couldn't remember the occasion, only that he was standing under that traffic light, one stone-quiet evening, and heavy snowflakes were falling out of the black sky, dancing past the tireless sequences of green, yellow, and red up above him. It was as if the deep, oppressing mystery of the heavens was being joyously illuminated, and he felt a disappointment that no angels were singing, only that monotonous click of the traffic light. For a moment Koan recalled the exact thought he had had, standing there under that light.

Did God dislike colors, preferring to live in the blackest of darknesses, sending away the bits of light that invaded his realm in the pure white flakes that fell to earth?

Koan cursed. "A part of me will never leave that place."

Freddie was on the telephone with Hope. It had been months since they'd last talked. After a few pleasantries, Freddie plowed enthusiastically into the news about her new business. She asked if Hope weren't curious about how she'd gotten the start-up capital, but, disappointingly for Freddie, Hope's interest was lukewarm.

"Hope, Mr. Angstrom and I've been seeing quite a lot of

each other. I like him. A lot more than I thought. In fact, I'm playing around with the idea of spending the holidays with him."

That piqued Hope's curiosity. "That sounds like more than a business partnership." Enjoying that Hope had taken the bait and hook, Freddie deliberately didn't respond. "You know, Freddie, giving you that much money might get people's imaginations going. Like what you might be doing to please Mr. Angstrom? By the way, do you still think about Chris, with the holidays coming and all that?"

"A little, I suppose, but at some point you've got to move on. Weren't those your words?"

"I guess. But, then again, miracles happen. Especially this time of year."

Freddie's laugh was sarcastic. "Well, if such a miracle occurs, along with the jolly little man and reindeer, and angels descending out of the heavens, be sure to let me know. By the way, maybe I'll get a chance to introduce you to the hunk. Remember, you used to call him that?"

"Why in the world would he want to meet me?"

"See, that's the trouble with you, Hope. You don't aspire to enough. I'm not the one to be giving advice, but life's about going for it."

"Thanks, Freddie. Your success should remind me of that. You do sound very happy."

"I am, Hope. I'm real close to having it all."

Two weeks before Christmas, Freddie called Koan, asking him if he was booked up for the holidays.

Koan found himself in an awkward position. Christmas and its many meanings had faded toward the end of his youth. He had no plans, but he also didn't wish to spend Christmas with Freddie. He resorted to lying about important commitments and politely listened to her rationalizations that she had asked him much too late.

After their conversation, Koan thought about his cynicism toward Christmas.

Christmas back in Shepherdstown had had a Currier and Ives touch, truly magical, approaching each year with gushing anticipation, parting again as a deep sense of loss and loneliness. It was a rockhard landmark for each year, a resounding reminder of something constant he missed.

An idea popped into his head, at first just a playful one. *Why not a little pilgrimage back to Shepherdstown? Maybe just a drive through, yeah, maybe after dark, to see the lights. I haven't been back there since college. I doubt if much has changed. Except Mom and Dad no longer being around.*

The more Koan thought about it, the more this idea appealed to him.

16

The asphalt highway wound its way up a steady grade at the top of which was a sign, "Summit—Unincorporated." It was familiar territory for Koan. Kids from there had been bussed to his school in Shepherdstown. Not much had changed. There was only one almost-new house among the self-built, tar-papered structures. It struck Koan that Summit and the southside section of Pontifica had a similar mood to them, only Summit wasn't an island in a sea of affluence.

Another five miles of driving through a narrow, creek-carved valley and Koan reached Shepherdstown. Slowing down, he recalled familiar houses, some with colors that had changed, or new siding, others abandoned and decaying.

Here and there were Christmas lights, cheery in their simplicity and contrast to the murky, gray sky. Koan imagined how much nicer everything would look with a blanket of white snow over it. Finally, his car approached the old traffic light at the intersection of Main Street and Route 21, still the only traffic light in town. The light turned green, but Koan's foot remained on the brakes. He stared at the light as it changed several times. Nothing compelled him to drive on. His car was the only one on the streets.

Why am I here? To sit under this old light and watch it, like then, not knowing which color I liked more? That light seemed to regulate life itself. Everyone stopped and waited, like God was in that light, even when there wasn't another car in sight. Reliable consistency. Is that what breeds religious respect?

Shepherdstown had shut down for Christmas. The only building lit from within was a convenience store gasoline station that stood where Stanley's General Store and Texaco filling station used to be. Koan pulled his car in and went inside.

"Hi, how ya doin'?"

The man wearing a plaid shirt, perhaps in his mid-thirties, was sitting in a wooden chair, tilted backward, his feet up under the checkout counter, an opened magazine on his lap. He was too young to be Red Stanley, who, back then, owned the Texaco filling station, where the men in town met to trade stories and local news.

"I was surprised to see you open."

"It's hardly worth it. People 'round here stay home at Christmas. What can I do for ya?"

Koan decided the man might be Red Stanley's son, Jerry, who had been younger than he and Moss. They'd been jealous of Jerry, because he could take candy bars and pop from his father's store any time he wanted, while they had to save their pennies to indulge themselves only every week or so.

"I might be able to use a little gas. But that's not why I'm here. Maybe you can tell me whether Moss Tripp still lives around here?"

"Moss? Sure. He lives up at his father's place. Ya know 'im?"

"Actually, uh...his father."

"When were ya last up there?" Koan said it had been years. "Moss's father done passed away, I guess, yeah, maybe a couple years now. Ya plannin' on goin' up there?"

"Well, no, I hadn't planned on it. That would be imposing."

The man grinned and scratched his head. "I know darned well, Moss'd chew my ass out, if I didn't tell 'em you was here."

Koan regretted having said anything. Having opened the door, Koan knew he'd be breaching local custom if he refused to at least talk to Moss. The man, who turned out to be Jerry Stanley, as Koan speculated, called Moss, and Moss insisted Koan drive by their place.

Koan found the gravel road he'd walked up so often as a kid. Talking on the phone with Moss hadn't been easy. It had evoked too many distant memories, connections that seemed from another lifetime.

As Koan got out of his car, which he parked in front of the old, weatherworn barn, a silhouette appeared on the front porch of the house, a man with a child next to him. A woman came out and stood behind the solid silhouette, an infant in her arms.

"Howdy. I see ya found yer way up here."

Koan shook Moss's hand, apologizing for disturbing them on a holiday. The woman on the porch asked shyly if he wouldn't come in for bite to eat.

"I wouldn't want to put you through the bother." Koan studied Moss, whom he hadn't seen since high school. His face was ruddy with a deep furrows from working outdoors, and his upper lip was covered by a dark, bushy mustache. The intense but friendly blue eyes were still there, his voice, though, was much huskier than earlier, but still with a simple, gentle edge.

"We'd like you to come on in, Mr. Angstrom. Bonnie Sue, she's made all kinds of goodies for Christmas, more than we'll ever eat ourselves. Ya certainly ain't imposing. Not in the least."

They went inside, Moss taking Koan into the small but warm and cozy living room, while Bonnie Sue went to make tea. The first quarter-hour or so of conversation was stiff and tentative, Moss searching for where Koan fit into the scheme of things.

"By the way, Mr. Angstrom, did you know the Folkstones?"

"Yes, I recall the name."

"Chris Folkstone was my best friend. His dad's also passed on."

From the kitchen, Bonnie Sue chimed in, "The way Moss speaks of 'im, you'd think him and Chris were blood brothers." Her laugh was beautifully melodic.

Moss grinned. "Yeah, Chris and I did most everything together. Got into a peck a' trouble too. But it was a good kind a' trouble. Yeah, we sure had some good times." Moss was looking down at the floor as he talked, smiling contentedly. "Didja ever hear what happened to Chris? We never heard much around these parts. He never once came back. Don't know if Dad woulda told ya, but Chris's daddy and him had a real big fallin' out, and after that Chris's daddy never talked much about 'em. Not ever."

Koan hesitated. "I believe Chris became a business consultant."

Bonnie Sue yelled in, asking if Chris had ever married and had any kids. Koan said he hadn't. "That's a real shame," Bonnie Sue said lamentfully as she walked into the room with a tray loaded up with tea, cookies and cake. "It sounded like he would a' made a fine daddy." Bonnie Sue then excused herself to get the kids ready for bed.

Moss and Koan set forth their conversation about his father, letting it expand to what Koan knew of Shepherdstown. Gradually, Koan relaxed, immersing himself in an old but familiar situation from his childhood. Soon he'd lost track of the story he had fabricated, not noticing the subtle signs of skepticism coming from Moss.

Koan grinned and let out a small chuckle. "And what how about Windy Hill? I assume it's still there?"

Moss's eyes narrowed. "Who told you about Windy Hill?"

"I guess your father did."

"I never told Daddy that name. Ya see, Chris and I made up names for all kinds of places 'round these parts, but they were our secret. Folks 'round here've always called Windy Hill Bald Ridge, 'cause no trees grow up there, but Chris and I liked Windy Hill a whole lot better. I wonder how Daddy would a' known that name…"

Koan felt the heat rising in his face. He excused himself to go to the bathroom, trying to think of a way to repair the damage.

"Moss, there's something I have to tell you." Moss's eyes had a sad look of distrust in them. "Moss, Chris is dead. And everything I know is from Chris. Windy Hill, Turtle Hollow, all that. I don't know why I couldn't tell you. Maybe I thought it'd be too painful?"

Moss peered intensely at Koan. "Chris's dead?"

"Yes, it's been more than two years now."

Moss shook his head slowly. "I had a sense there was somethin' like that."

Koan thought he detected wetness forming in Moss's eyes, who cleared his throat then got up abruptly, walking to the hallway.

"Bonnie Sue, we're gonna go out and take a walk."

Moss and Koan took a long walk, a couple miles into the center of Shepherdstown and back. In bits and pieces and with more caution, Koan told Moss what he knew about Chris, but Moss kept coming with more questions. Finally, chilled and weary, they returned to the house.

From Moss's demeanor, Bonnie Sue sensed something was wrong. She sat down next to him on the sofa, putting her arm around his waist.

"Bonnie Sue, Koan knows somethin' 'bout Chris you should know."

Koan didn't want to be the one to tell her about Chris's death. Tears welled up in Bonnie Sue's eyes, but her inner strength reigned back an urge to cry. "Moss and Chris were like family. Brothers."

Moss covered Bonnie Sue's hand with his. "I understand why you didn't wanna come out with it, but I appreciate that ya did. We wish ya could stay longer, but I know ya gotta get goin'. Still, we'd be mighty happy if you came by again."

Koan didn't know quite the proper way to say goodbye. The handshakes were tentative and in stark contrast to the firm ones he'd been greeted with earlier. At his car, Koan turned to wave again, and it seemed the shoulders of Moss and Bonnie Sue weren't as square and solid but rather somewhat sunken.

On the drive home, Koan's emotions swirled. He had driven to Shepherdstown for some voyeuristic reminiscing, but it had gone far beyond that.

Goddamn it all! How many identities can I deal with? Paul guides one, Freddie tugs at another, and Moss revived a third. I'm beyond schizoid. I need to get away. Far, far away. And if it were my choice, I'd stay away, disappear, search for a new identity. Or the total lack of one? No. No. That's death. And I'm not ready for that. I'm going to have my one last, great hurrah. One way or the other.

17

After the Christmas holidays, Koan and Paul left for Europe. There were no compelling reasons why Koan needed to accompany Paul, who was going to negotiate financial restructuring with British and German organizations in which Angstrom Industries had controlling interests. Koan had argued that he needed a vacation from the estate and Pontifica, and Paul raised no objections.

Their first stop was London, where they stayed in The Dorchester, and there was a small irony in that. Chris and Freddie had only been to Europe once. In London, they had stayed in a small, non-descript hotel in Kensington, despite Freddie's pleading they spend one night at The Dorchester.

Why had Freddie wanted that, even though it would've busted their tight travel budget? Actually, there had been two reasons. The first related to her mother, who idolized Elizabeth Taylor, who obstensibly stayed in The Dorchester when in London. The second reason was more devious. Freddie's firm had opened an office in London, and that had been celebrated with a gala held at The Dorchester. Freddie hadn't been among those chosen to fly over to attend. By staying there overnight, she said she'd be able to say she had been there, and make it sound believable by throwing out little details of the place to prove it. Freddie was quite capable of fabricating realities to bolster the image she wanted of herself.

Koan wasn't overly impressed with what he had missed on that trip. If anything, the atmosphere of the hotel was subdued, and the rooms quite austere in their old-fashioned ambience. Still, despite anticipated jet lag, Koan sleep very well.

Following breakfast the next morning, Koan and Paul went to the lobby to meet their driver, who turned out to be an American.

"Mr. Angstrom, boy, am I impressed to meet you. You're an absolute legend. I just started up my own limousine business. Maybe you can give me a few tips while we're driving?"

Koan took Paul aside, whispering to him, "Would you mind if we take a taxi?"

Paul gave the chauffeur a generous tip, explaining there'd been a change of plans.

"Maybe the next time, Mr. Angstrom. Go give 'em hell."

Outside, the London air was brisk, the winter sun emasculated by a soupy haze. Their taxi sped off past Hyde Park toward Knightsbridge, but was soon ensnared in the grinding traffic, causing their taxi driver to throw up his hands in disgust.

"It's all them bloody foreigners."

"You mean us?" Paul shot back.

"No offense, pal, but if you shipped out the whole lot of them, it'd be a more civil place. They say foreign interests are essential for the economy, but you'd be hard put to find an Englishman in these parts anymore." The driver adjusted his rear-view mirror to make eye contact with Koan. "Maybe we should just kill the whole bloody lot. It's in us, you know. We're the bloodthirstiest folk on earth."

Koan smiled, asking him to elaborate.

"If you're much into history, you'd know all this rubbish, the blasted monuments, statues, they're all glorious tributes to a bloody past. The sweet old ladies from America would rather hear some smart old gentlemen tellin' 'em charmin' tales about how civilized we are. There's nothing terribly civilized 'bout a real Englishman. He'd just as well bash ya as have a civilized discussion."

In any other tone, the speech would have been offensive, but Koan and Paul were chuckling.

"I say, damn the friggin' economy. Half of us are already on the dole, watching you foreigners take it all with ya. God didn't intend for us to wind up like yer Indians, sittin' around on reservations waitin' fer the bloody tourists, the little old ladies to come by and throw a few quid at us."

Koan interrupted, "Do you really feel it's gone that far?"

"I know one thing. A lotta folks're playin' god, and the world's not a bit better off for it. If Jesus Christ stepped out in front of us, right here, who'd recognize the bloke? You'd probably think he's one of those Hari Krishna fellas and run over 'em. Picture what I mean? To be important today, ya've got to have a particular image. No one's goin' to get a fair shake who's walkin' about spouting off the godly truth. No, if you were to ask me what I think, I reckon Jesus would come again as a lowly commoner, and not even the Pope would give 'im the time of day. He'd be down in the underground shakin' a cup at people fer a few bob."

Paul had gotten edgy about the lack of movement in the

traffic, but Koan was enjoying himself, animating the driver to continue.

"Ya see, people's gotten too damned nice to say the truth. Ya know rubbish is comin' out as soon as they open their mouths. But I can't drive wherever I bloody please. I go where ya tell me. Ya see my point?"

"Just out of curiosity, where would you go, if you had your choice?"

The driver smiled into his rear view mirror. "Thinks ya have me, dontcha? Well, I'd take off and find that Jesus fella, and kiss his fuckin' ass."

Paul interrupted the driver's chuckling, asking if he thought the traffic were going to break.

"Hate to give up the fare, but you'd be better off with the underground."

Paul didn't seem pleased, but Koan jumped in. "That's fine. I'd be curious to see if we run into Jesus down there, with his tin cup."

Paul and Koan got out, and after Paul had paid him, the driver gave Koan a tip of the hat, yelling out, "I hope you find that Jesus fellow. God knows, we sure as hell need 'im."

Three days later, Koan and Paul flew on to Hamburg. Jet lag was finally catching up with Koan. Paul had suggested an excellent seafood restaurant with local north German specialties, but Koan passed, preferring to turn in early. Around eight o'clock the phone rang.

"Freddie. You of all people."

"Surprised?" Freddie explained she had used a few tricks to locate Koan. She asked about his trip, but Koan was too tired to get into specifics.

"What about tomorrow night? Can you slip away?"

Koan got peeved at what he perceived was cute game playing. "So, where shall we meet? Your place? Or maybe Paris? I can have Paul check out whether a Concorde's available."

Freddie laughed, saying she was much closer than that. "I'm just up the street, at the Intercontinental. That Hotel Vierjahreszeiten you're in's too stiff and stodgy for me. Besides, there's a casino over here. You are a gambling man, aren't you?"

Koan said he wasn't. He asked Freddie if she weren't pulling his leg, but she really was in Hamburg.

"Okay, if I can't entice you with gambling, what about a certain young woman who might be interested in more than just a business relationship? Or is that gambling too?"

Freddie's aggressiveness caught Koan by surprise, and more out of weariness he accepted her invitation. "I guess I have to admire the effort you've made?"

"And I hope I can make it worth your while."

The short taxi ride the next evening to Freddie's hotel hardly gave Koan a chance to look out at the city lights reflecting on the half-frozen waters of the Alster Lake. There seemed to be life in the city after dark, a contrast to downtown Pontifica, which was hardly more than a collection of purposeful skyscrapers, which every evening voided themselves of people fleeing out to their suburban homes. Koan corrected himself. There were people remaining in Pontifica nights, but they avoided lights, preferring to lurk in the shadows.

Freddie arrived in the hotel lobby looking absolutely gorgeous. Ten minutes later, they were at an old Weinkeller with a lively but rather intimate atmosphere. Their reserved booth was in a far, half-darkened corner, the hurricane lamp on their table softly illuminating their faces. Koan complimented Freddie on her choice, and her appearance.

"Thank you. You're sweet. It exposes a side of me I'm not accustomed to. Vulnerability. And it scares the hell out of me."

Koan laughed. "I had an old high school football coach, who liked to say, 'If you're not scared before a game, you'll get hurt.'"

"Is tonight a big game?"

Freddie's exaggerated coyness annoyed Koan. She had indeed dressed up in a most unaccustomed way. Freddie believed in functionality, also in being unobtrusive in appearance. Her usual wardrobe was sober, her makeup minimal. She had once explained this as being strategic, to avoid creating discomfort in others and thereby make them more accessible. Accessible didn't relate to personal sharing but rather doing business. There was Freddie, looking quite beautiful, the makeup almost exaggerated to bring out her best feminine features. Koan couldn't help surmising that was probably also strategic and less an expression of endearment or desire to please him in a more intimate way.

Leading the conversation aggressively, Freddie tried to delve into Koan's personal life, and past, but Koan fluffed over it as lightly as possible.

"What about your name? I've never met another Koan."

"It's just a name."

"Does it have a special meaning?"

"Yes, but that creates even more questions."

"Try me. Freddie cupped her chin in her upturned hand, leaning forward with a demure but smartish smile.

"Fine. The name relates to the Buddhist religion, more specifically, to the belief that enlightenment is arrived at through intuition, rather than logic or reason."

"Like your intuition for business deals."

Koan chuckled. "Perhaps. But there's a paradox in that. I'm wealthy, but reluctantly so, yet being so disinclined and withdrawn has, as much as anything else, empowered me. But back to my name. If enlightenment comes via intuition, then the intuition must be nurtured and developed. And how is that accomplished? That's the key. By concentrating on paradoxes. Anyway, in a nutshell, that's the meaning behind the name Koan."

"Are you Buddhist?"

Koan's old face took on a look of boyish innocence. "Possibly. But religions, per se, don't gratify me. Some are too complex, too mystical, as if their creators didn't intend for anyone to comprehend them. Others are as simplistic as a Disney cartoon, playing on the naive nostalgia of childhood dreams and fantasies. Finally, there are all those charismatic leaders, wonderfully charming snakes who'll say anything to get the donations coming in."

"Koan, you amaze me. But I have to admit, religion and philosophy have never been my cup of tea. Does that make me a bimbo in your eyes?"

"No, just unenlightened."

That got a hearty laugh from Freddie, who abruptly switched gears. "Have you ever wondered about my name? I'm sure you've guessed Freddie's not my real name."

"It could've been. Traditional names aren't in vogue anymore."

"They were with my parents! They named me Florence. Can you imagine? Worse yet, they shortened it to Flo. I felt like a walking toilet joke. Self-preservation gave rise to the name Fay. I created it back in junior high. Well, actually I borrowed it from a character in a book. But I made my girlfriends use it until it stuck, to the great disappointment of my parents."

"Doesn't Fay mean something like fairy?"

"Wow. How'd you know that? Hold on, though, that's only one meaning. Do you happen to know the other?" Koan admitted he was stumped. "At least there's something you don't know. It means a close pact between two parties. Who knows, maybe us?" Freddie leaned forward and extended her hand toward Koan's. "Do you believe names can be predestining?"

"One can't rule out anything."

Freddie squeezed Koan's hand. "Sounds corny, I know, but who knows, maybe we will become the bond my name implies."

Koan wanted off the path the conversation was taking. "Let's back up just a little. Why'd you drop the name Fay?"

"Pretty straightforward, actually. I wanted to make it in a man's world. Fay didn't sound tough enough."

"Even if it that meant dropping Fay's predestining possibilities?"

Freddie laughed. "Got me, didn't you? Okay. How about Freddie Fay?"

The nonsensical banter was getting Koan edgy. He flagged down the waiter, asking him to bring tea for Freddie and coffee for him.

"How'd you know I'm a tea drinker?"

"Lucky guess."

Freddie toyed with her earring, smiling demurely. "I've been dying to ask you something, but I haven't had the right lead in. Have you ever been married?"

"Not really."

"Does that mean almost?"

Koan shifted his posture. "Let's say I was in such a relationship, once, but to call it a marriage would be exaggerating."

The answer pleased Freddie. "Have I told you I'm here for three more days?"

"I wish I could give you tips on what to see. Hamburg's a terribly commercial city. Not exactly a tourist magnet."

"You know, I really can't tell when you're putting me on. Shall I be more direct? I was hoping we'd share more than this one evening." Freddie studied Koan's eyes. "You're not biting, are you? Well, tell me if I'm wrong, but I'm sensing a hint of condescension. Is it just our ages, or something else?"

It pleased Koan that Freddie was getting the message. "Freddie, you were saying something earlier about perspectives. You said something like the two of us are coming from two different perspectives, but in reality they might be very much the same."

"That's right."

"Well, I had to think of the old cliché about a journey not

being merely to get somewhere but to be enjoyed along the way. You seem very focused on a destination. And perhaps impatient to get there. I happen to feel, when we move too fast, the price for the journey may be our soul, and no amount of wealth or power can ever buy back a soul."

Freddie planted her elbows on the table, cradling her chin in both hands. "I think you just put me down, and I should be pissed, but you defuse such feelings. And, strangely, you seem to know me better than even my deceased husband did."

"What kind of relationship did the two of you have?"

"How specific do you want it?"

Koan didn't bite. "You were talking about knowing someone."

"Yes, knowing someone, or each other. No, we didn't care to know each other. Not that well. Sure, we knew all the details of what went on…stop, I'll correct that. Most things. But that was the level we operated on. Our professions, functions, obligatory friends. We shared it all. But heart to heart? No, it was total avoidance. Big time."

"Did he know everything going on in your life?"

"Sure."

"I'm impressed. Most of us have a skeleton or two in the closet."

Freddie took a purposely long sip of tea, which had been served without the two noticing it. "Okay. Maybe a skeleton or two. I'm human. Little things I didn't believe he had to know, or cared to know. But I don't think that could be the case with you."

"Why?"

"Because you intimidate the hell out of me. You really do. What's this feeling I get from you? Like, 'tell me everything, lady, or get the hell out of my life.'"

Koan stretched his body, complaining that his age was creeping up on him. "It's an irony, or one of those good old paradoxes, that you find me intimidating. I've reached a point where I'm searching for simplicity, the basic fundamentals.

It's a humbling experience, with little excitement or heroics. Rather than intimidating, I would expect to be rather boring."

Freddie shook her head from side to side, her eyes trained on Koan's. "I can't tell you how fascinating you are. Here I've imagined this enormously complex man with a Midas touch, and you call it simplicity. Your humility is very endearing."

Koan found nothing to add, suggesting they call it an evening.

Koan decided to walk back to his hotel, along the bank of the Alster Lake in the cold, moonless, night air.

For the first time ever, it seemed she might want to know who I am, but that last statement about me having "a Midas touch," that was vintage Freddie, always going for the gold.

Koan stopped at edge of the lake to see how far out the ice extended from the shore.

I'm still treated like some two-bit actor. Father Nick liked the goodies, but slapped my face when I offered a solution. And Paul? To him I'm just a game piece to move around on a board. Freddie? I imagine she fantasizes about the association with me and the doors it might open for her. I wonder how thick that ice is?

Koan pressed one foot out onto the frozen surface of the lake. It held. He lifted the other foot and moved it forward. More steps later, he looked back at the shore.

"Look at me, world. I'm Jesus Christ walking on water." Koan took a few more steps before a dull crackling sound somewhere down deep in the ice stopped him.

Jesus Christ would keep walking. What went through his mind? Doubts about whether the water would hold him up? What faith! Or was it desperation? I wonder which it was?

Back in church they always said he was a man like all of us. He must've sensed that coming. All that wisdom he spouted getting so fucked up later on. If he was human, and not totally naive, he must have anticipated that too, that those who followed him would be tempted to capitalize on his mystique? So what great gift is wisdom? Just one more thing to be exploited?

Another deep, sighing noise rolled through the ice, but Koan made no attempt to turn back to the shore.

Jesus, people have killed in your name. Back in church, they sang "Onward Christian Soldiers" with such a gusto. I did too. What a release. Crusaders slaying Moslems in the name of Christ. Jesus, is that blood splattered over your white tunic? There was also something I learned in church, "Thou shalt not kill."

Koan made several more daring steps out onto the ice.

So, Christ, I'd really like to know, why did you walk across water? Wasn't the gospel truth from your lips enough leverage? It must have depressed you, knowing your words alone weren't hacking it. You must've felt like the rare politician who possesses real integrity, wanting to tell the truth, knowing, though, to get elected he has to promise miracles. But maybe you didn't really want a miracle. Maybe you were as depressed as I get, and drowning would've cured your depression.

What happened? Did your old man step in, like mine used to do? 'Hey, boy, you aren't going to make it in this world that way.' He didn't let you drown. He humiliated you for your weakness, and at the same time your miracle got everyone's attention back, made them listen to you again. I can sympathize with you, inheriting an obligation that's way over your head. Too big to be drowned in water.

Koan ignored numerous threatening moaning and popping sounds near his feet. "Hey, world! I just met Jesus Christ! He had the guts to walk on water, but I chose to walk on ice. He had more faith in his old man."

The heavy, chilled air deadened Koan's yells into the dark. Koan dropped his head in a prayerful posture, debating whether to walk further out onto the ice. He then turned and slowly retreated. Walking back to his hotel, he felt purged of the stressing dinner with Freddie, but more aware than ever of an emptiness at the core of his being.

As his plane crossed Ireland on its westward path back to America from Europe, Koan fell into a deep sleep. Hours later when he awoke, they were over the southern tip of Greenland. He looked out the window at the ocean below that was speckled with white icebergs and recalled something he had once written.

"How close is the next ice age? Or unpatchable cracks in the egg shell called our atmosphere? Is it misguided religious faith or simply myopia that lulls us into believing in immortality, ours and this world's?"

Koan picked up a folder of papers that Paul had prepared for his reading, but he didn't open it. Instead he leaned his head back and shut his eyes.

Is it the disintegration of my self, or a deliverance, that I'm becoming more and more the old man? Why do I carry around with me these scribbled notes from him like they're words from God, pages out of some undiscovered supplement to the Bible?

Each living species, a piece in the great puzzle, nodes in a vast, integrated, ever-evolving matrix. How brash and grotesquely over inflated of man to believe he's the center piece, the keystone that holds it all together. Solitary, man will one day recognize his one piece is inconsequential against the beauty of the puzzle's entirety.

The old guy really had a low opinion of the human race. But he was a human. Or was he? Sometimes I'm not so sure.

He talked about rewards, some great kudos I was going to enjoy, and I saw only his wealth and power. It's like he knew after a period of giddiness all that would become meaningless to me, a scourge, a weight on me I can't rid myself of. You've made your point, old man. I was happier sitting on Windy Hill, with empty pockets and holes in my jeans.

No, his greatness wasn't his wealth. But I still don't see it. What secrets did he hold within him that put him so above it all? I remember asking Paul if there was much written about the old man, maybe a good biography. I was hoping to find a script, something I could emulate. Paul just laughed, saying, "Mortals have only managed to write myths about him." So? I said to Paul, if the world perceives Koan Angstrom as a myth, then acting out that mythical character would be good enough. Paul scared the hell out of me. With ice in his eyes he told me to go ahead and play the myth, alone, without him. No, without Paul, I'd one day wind up in the Southside ward, or in the gutter.

But that too gives me this tentative sense about my existence. I often think Paul's doing the same, turning me into a myth, but a myth of his choosing. Maybe so. He believes I'd screw it up, trying to be the myth of Koan the world perceives. Probably right. Paul's masterful.

Old man, you talked so much about elucidation. Elucidate me! Why did you want me? I was supposed to represent you, be accepted by the masses as one of their own, something you could never be. Wasn't that it? But therein lies the great paradox I have to live with. How can I represent you when I don't understand you? What image is it you wish me to portray? Or is it values? Am I doing the right thing with the people at the Southside Community Center? Is that what you want me doing? You haven't snuck up behind me, whispered into my ear and said, "More of that, keep it up."

Hey, if you don't start cluing me in, what am I? I'm nothing more than an ordinary guy, a mere mortal, searching for his own identity. And I'm finding nothing so terribly elucidating in that.

18

"Where've you been, stranger?"

Koan brushed his fingers across Hope's cheek, kissing the tip of her nose. "Nowhere special. Consumed by the world. And trying to change my identity."

Hope's head snapped back. "Oh, boy. The lost son's still searching."

"Maybe not."

Hope pulled Koan into her apartment, helping him out of his coat. "Is this a break from solving the world's problems? Ready for some basic creature comforts?"

Koan smiled and hugged Hope, settling himself down onto the sofa. After Hope had brought some hot tea, he told her about his trip to Europe, including Freddie's surprise showing in Hamburg.

"Do you think she has any clue who you really are?"

"I don't know, but it's been hard to resist the temptation to throw in hints."

"She hasn't hooked into anything?"

"No. Maybe she's just not capable of tuning into such subtleties?"

"How does that make you feel?"

Koan brushed his hand over his mouth. "Well, that's Freddie. Her eyes only see as far as what can be of use to her. I should probably be happy that she sees only Koan Angstrom in front of her."

"But, God, Koan, don't you see the perversity in that? You're the man who took her husband's life."

"Obviously she's made that connection, in the past, but quickly chose to ignore it. I've said it a thousand times, Freddie tunes into what might put her ahead, and blocks out any associated value issues. I've always considered her absolutely amoral."

Hope shook her head. "That's the hardest part for me, trying to comprehend how she could forgive you for her husband's disappearance. Without even a whimper. I mean, she's falling all over her husband's executioner. That's beyond amoral. That's plain sick." Hope's hands jerked up to her cheeks, pressing on them.

"What's wrong, Hope?"

"I'm not sure I want to say." Koan prodded her. "Okay. But you're going to label me paranoid. My mind just made one of those sudden leaps. I said Freddie has cozied up to her husband's executioner. Well, why wouldn't she do the same with your executioner?"

"Who's going to execute me? I've considered it a possibility with Paul, but no more. He needs me. Talk about identity problems. I thought I had a corner on them. No, Paul's identity is totally defined by who I am. If he destroyed me, he'd destroy himself."

"How should I know anything about that, Koan? And I wasn't thinking of anyone specific. I just don't think Freddie would have any problems with you being done away with. She'd find some new opportunity for herself in it."

"I'm not sure Freddie sees me as just an opportunity."

"You mean she's developing emotional attachments?" Hope's tone was cynical.

"Does that disturb you, Hope?"

Hope's face screwed up into a deep frown. "If you're implying jealousy, Koan, you wandered into the wrong apartment. Besides, I've never ever entertained any claims on you." Hope detected a hint of disappointment in Koan's eyes. "Don't misunderstand me. Our closeness is bread that nourishes me. But you eat the bread when it's there, not stick it away somewhere and let it get stale and moldy. You've let me care about you, Koan, and that fulfills me. Unlike our lady friend, it's not glorious outcomes that count for this woman. It's the modest little moments I savor."

Koan spontaneously embrace Hope, giving her a warm kiss. "How easily I forget that you're sobriety itself. Look, enough of this. There's something else I want to tell you, something a lot more important. And I think you might even like it."

Hope was smiling, a genuine smile, a happy one. "I'm impressed, Koan. I really am. Sounds like you've finally decided to face the sun and quit looking back at the shadows of your past. That earns a little celebration. I can't offer you champagne, but you've always enjoyed a good can of beer."

Koan continued rolling out more details of his plan.

"Koan, please don't take this as a flinch by the other woman, but you again mentioned Freddie."

"Why not harness those boundless energies of hers?"

"I was the one who fell asleep in physics class, but I recall something about energies having direction."

Koan responded with a smartish smile. "I'm impressed. And I get what you're saying. Maybe I have confidence I can bend those energies in the right direction?"

"And that takes us back to an old thorn, manipulation, something you and Freddie never seem to stray far from. But I'm not going to deliver any sermons. Another question is bothering me too much."

"That is?"

"Correct me if I'm wrong, but all that you've told has dangling on the end of it a, uh, yes, a planned exit."

"An exit? Maybe? Haven't I done that before, and magically reappeared."

Hope ignored Koan's joking, peering intensely at him. "You once had a deep vein of self-destruction in you. Is it possible it's still there?"

Koan smiled tenderly, shaking his head. Hope wrapped her arm around him, burying her face in his neck, and in a few moments Koan felt the warmth of tears.

"Koan, I want so badly to shout with joy and celebrate what you intend to do. I also have this deep sense…a deep sense it's dangerous. I know the old wisdoms about risks and gains. A nurse often chooses to ignore the odds, the futility of offering comfort to someone declared terminal. One has to believe in the impossible. But what I feel isn't about wisdoms. It's cold, barren. It feels like death. And it scares me. I hope it's only a lingering chill from a late winter, physical and nothing more."

Increasingly, Freddie had little time for the friendship with Hope. Freddie's advertising firm had limped into existence, requiring long hours and several infusions of additional capital before a significant client base began to come together. When Hope answered her phone, she was very surprised to hear Freddie's voice. Freddie not only wanted to see her, but invited Hope to her new home.

Hope recalled that Freddie had been effusive about the

new house during the planning and constructing stages, so she wasn't astonished by its size or the plushness of the furnishings. Still, it was far beyond anything she had ever personally experienced. After a grand tour, the two of them settled down on the couch in the spacious living room.

"I'm blown away, Freddie. This is a change. I admit I kind of liked your old house, but I guess there were too many memories?"

"And not enough class. You won't find another house like this. I made sure of that. It put me in a hole of major proportions, but I love it. I can even bring prospective clients here. Face it, people want to identify with a winner, and that was the theme that went into the design of this home. It has that image, don't you think?"

Their conversation drifted from the house to the more personal. Hope asked if Freddie had finally put Chris behind her.

"Yes. But since you won't let the topic die, I take it you still think about him?"

Hope lowered her eyes. "Yes, I do. He has a way of being resurrected. At least in my thoughts. That reminds me, I met a dear friend of yours."

"Who's that?"

"I think I once called him an old fart or something. He's a fascinating man, your Koan Angstrom."

As Hope anticipated, her revelation snapped Freddie to attention. She wanted to know how Hope had met him, but Hope's response was intentionally vague. That irritated Freddie.

"Just out of curiosity, Hope, how'd you find the man you just loved to put down?"

"Oh, I did have my fun ribbing you about him. Didn't I call him the hunk too? Yeah, the hunk. Funny, but I now better appreciate why you were so interested in him. He's quite a man."

Hope's soulful sigh didn't sit right with Freddie. "Yes,

he's definitely a fascinating person. Maybe a little too remote or esoteric at times. I'm generally not attracted to people who have to find significance in everything. Then again, maybe you haven't spent enough time with him to pick up on such nuances."

Hope brushed back her long, straight hair. "Actually, we've had some pretty intense conversations. Quite challenging for this little mind of mine. But I decided I could use some stimulation for my gray cells."

An uncomfortable silence followed, which Hope finally broke. "Sorry to be digging into the past again, but Koan seems to know a lot about Chris. In fact, I've learned things about Chris I didn't know."

"Chris? That's easy to explain. There was a loose association between the two of them." Freddie fought back a blatant show of interest in Hope's remark, disguising it instead with cynicism. "So tell me, what all did you learn about Chris? That he came from a hick town in the middle of nowhere?"

"No, I already knew that from Chris. Shepherdstown? Sure, he talked often about that. Also about the strained relationship with his father."

"He told you that? Frankly, Hope, I never quite understood why that was so. But I'm not sure I need to know either."

"Oh, that was simple, Freddie. He and his father butted heads on values, and it was symbolized in the contrast between Chris's roots and the lifestyle he chose for himself. I think you could also call it tensions between his spiritual self and the striver for fame and fortune he later became. But listen to me talk." Hope laughed. "Like I'm the expert."

"Hope, Chris was fucked up. Pure and simple. I don't know if I ever told you, but I found writings of his, little secret things he'd written and stashed away. What he wrote made me conclude he was a real asshole, a total SOB. It was typical Chris. He didn't have the courage to say such things to my face."

"Didn't you just say a moment ago that you didn't enjoy such, what'd you call it, esoteric discussions with Koan? It's possible Chris recognized that wasn't one of your favorite things and spared you the pain? He had it in him to be considerate. But what are we doing here? Chris is dead, and here we are speculating about who he was. All I wanted to say, I guess, was that I found comfort in knowing he had substance."

"Substance?" Freddie laughed, shaking her head. "Hope, looking back on that dreadful marriage of ours, I think that's the thing I resented the most. Chris couldn't focus on the real world. That's where the substance is, my dear friend. Want to hear something insane? It's utterly ridiculous to put the two in the same category, Chris and Koan, but sometimes I think the two of them may've enjoyed each other. In fact, that might explain why my interest in Koan has waned?" Freddie leaned toward Hope. "Hey, a little bit of advice from a friend. Wasn't that little arrangement you had with Chris enough? I don't know how chummy you imagine you could get with Koan Angstrom, but I'd ask myself, whether I might not be setting myself up again? Do you get what I mean?"

"No, I don't, Freddie."

"Take a good look at yourself, Hope. I think the world of you, but the mental image of you and Koan Angstrom, sorry, that's two different worlds. Maybe you could be an amusement for him. Who knows? I don't pretend to understand him. But why waste your time, Hope? It's a ticket to loneliness. My advice? Latch onto a doctor or an orderly, someone on your level."

Koan had chosen a late hour to call Paul to his den, laying down strict orders not to be disturbed. Since the subject matter hadn't been preannounced, Paul sat and listened attentively as Koan went through a long, logically developed plan for a conversion of his holdings. When Koan was done, Paul didn't respond immediately. Instead, he got up and walked around the room several times, massaging his jaw, gazing upward, sometimes with his eyes closed. Koan began to fidget, his eyes following Paul as if he were begging for a reply.

"Koan, any definitive feedback will have to wait for a run through the details. You've obviously put a great deal of work into your ideas. One matter, however, bothers me."

"What's that?"

"One could interpret your motives in different ways, but one possibility, certainly, is that it's a backing out. Said differently, your proposal might offer an elegant vehicle for relieving yourself of responsibilities."

"I was prepared for that, Paul. No, that wasn't a driving force."

Paul sat back down, his eyes, at first lowered, rose and studied Koan, as if they wanted to confirm it was him. "Koan, if you've really done your homework, I'm sure you've recognized the magnitude of such an endeavor. And even more ominous is its all-or-nothing character. Once we've backed out of our holdings and channeled everything into a trust, there's no turning back."

Koan nodded, inwardly bursting with gratification that Paul was taking his ideas earnestly.

"There's another consideration here, an important one. How consistent might this be with the intentions of the old man?" Koan didn't know whether that was a question directed at him, or simply the jumping off point for what Paul wanted to say. It was the latter. "Koan, I can say this much. The old man flirted, numerous times, with the idea of directing his financial accumulations into philanthropy."

Koan flinched at the intonation on "flirted with," anticipating reasons why the idea had been discarded.

"Koan, I never presumed to be capable of anticipating his conclusions, and that subject never came to a clear resolution. He did express doubts as to whether such gestures could bring any permanent or decisive changes. It goes back to his belief that anything using money as a lubricant, his term, was inherently divisive. And there's that word you sometimes seem so fascinated with, holda. He used it in the same breath with another word, unifying, as an antonym to divisive. You see the dilemma, I'm sure."

"Yes, I do, Paul."

"I'm sure you're also aware, Koan, that philanthropies often carry the name of their benefactor. His ego didn't desire mass admiration. Quite the opposite. He had an aversion to publicity. Although I had ample opportunities and urges to do so, I never praised him, knowing that would violate his perfect countenance of humility. But I'm digressing."

Paul took a deep breath, and twisted his neck a few times. "You understand I'm not condemning your idea, Koan, but simply performing the role I know best."

"Yes, I've come to respect, sometimes grudgingly, that you're world champion at playing devil's advocate."

As always, Paul ignored the compliment. "One of the challenges we face is to explore how such a philanthropy would be perceived. I remember him laughingly saying, 'Wouldn't it be ideal, if such a movement could spring up magically from nowhere, like mushrooms after a soaking rain?'"

"Okay, Paul, I know we still have plenty of homework to do, but tell me, do your instincts say we could pull this off?"

"I'll only say this much: it would be a momentous challenge."

"The kind you like?"

Paul allowed himself a faint smile as his reply.

"Thanks, Paul. You've been forthright with me. I admit, at the bottom of this are some selfish motives. For starters, I have a track record of playing roles miserably. I can't go back and sort out the web of identities Chris tried to keep in balance, nor do I harbor any hopes of ever duplicating the stature of the old Koan Angstrom. I guess that could leave me with no identity to turn to, but, no, I feel it presents an incredible opportunity, a flight into the future, a chance, maybe my last, to establish who I really am. Certainly, that's at the crux of my motivation, to be recognized as someone unique, someone with real substance."

Paul nodded, then sank into his chair and went silent. Minutes passed, and Koan became impatient. "What are you wrestling with, Paul?"

Paul shook his head like he had cobwebs in it. "I'm not sure you want to hear it." Paul looked for the right words. "Koan, back then, when that so-called 'soul-merging' was going awry, I felt something escaping, and I nearly panicked, like everyone else, but for different reasons, ones I don't believe anyone could have comprehended…" Paul stopped, clenching his fists together, flexing his fingers vigorously. "It was the old man's immortality. I feel no shame or embarrassment when I say, he was, in my eyes, a supreme being." Paul broke out in unguarded laughter. Koan couldn't discern whether the edge was cynicism or mere relief.

"Koan, the irony of that disaster was overwhelming. The utter failure of a team of experts to play around with the human soul, yes, that humanized Koan Angstrom. It struck at his one vulnerability, his temptation to see the human race as capable of operating on the same level as he did. Why did he succumb to that? The only explanation I've found was intense loneliness, the absolute and crushing solitude of being above it all. There must have been a desperation there that drove his imagination to construct a bridge between himself and mankind, or the common man, as he chose to say it. And, as we know, it led to his demise."

Paul squeezed his eyes tightly shut. "Koan, I often wondered if that ever occurred to you. I hoped not, during your recovery phase, when you needed to be pumped up with optimism. You see, I was so intimately linked to him that for all practical purposes I died with him, and I did consider ending my life. It would've been so easy. What prevented it? There was something deep within me protesting vehemently.

The best term I find for it was a sense of obligation. No, I didn't feel obliged to die with him. The answer was in the purpose I served in his world, and that was to carry out his will. It had never been so profoundly clear that he had instilled something in me I could never rid myself of, a belief that there's a purpose in all this, that every new challenge that arises, even his passing, that it's all part of a great inevitability."

"Amazing, Paul. Do you know, those were his very words, right before the operation."

Paul's eyes barely acknowledged Koan's comment. His head sagged, but then he looked up and at Koan with his bold chin jutted out. "Koan, does it surprise you to hear me confess that I've questioned my role, my role without him?"

Koan got up and walked behind Paul, putting his hand on his shoulder. "No, I guess not. But there's something I've never understood clearly, Paul. Did you create your role, or was it created for you?"

"Unequivocally, it was he who defined my role. You probably see in that an apparent contradiction, Koan. That is, with him I carried out his will, and with you I've had to create and improvise to make you who you are. That seems like opposites, doesn't it? You see, Koan, whether the image in front of me is that of the old man or a young man implanted into his body, I made my code of honor servitude to him, a dimension of him I can't see with my eyes. That awareness snapped me out of the despondency that settled over me after that fateful operation." Paul twisted his neck like he needed to find something lighter. "You know, Koan, in this an interesting question arises."

"What's that, Paul?"

"Perhaps it's just a speculative game, but when I imagine you one day rising to his stature, I feel at that moment I will be compelled to disappear."

"Why the hell that, Paul?"

Paul looked at Koan searchingly. "How could one who

has doubted you so often be expected to turn around and serve you?"

Koan squeezed Paul's shoulder. "How can any person have so much integrity? You simply amaze me, Paul. What can I say?" Koan took a step back. "Can we get back to my plan. We don't need to beat it to death right now, but I'd like to think we're on the threshold of a great new venture. Honestly, Paul, isn't that turning on the adrenaline in you?"

Paul got up, clamping his hand around the binder with Koan's plan in it. "I'll give it a thorough going over, Koan. Tomorrow's good. We can sink our teeth into it again, and if it doesn't bleed to death, maybe it will be worth pumping life into it."

Paul started to leave, then stopped. "Koan, in all your concerns about whether I have enough to challenge me, have you thought seriously about all the mine fields this will put in front of you? You'll wonder at how many people hate a do-gooder."

19

Koan carried an embarrassment around with him. He thought often about his visit to Moss in Shepherdstown and how he had betrayed his closest boyhood friend. It became a regret he could not shake loose of, one that became a shame that stained his conscience.

Actually, there were only a few people Koan would have felt guilty about deceiving. Certainly, Hope was one of them, the other Moss. Moss had only been a distant memory, but talking with him again revived something long buried. Chris and Moss had shared everything with each other, even their souls, an inner sanctum of Koan not even Hope was ever privy to.

Koan was drawn back to Shepherdstown. He was drawn back by a sense of obligation. He wanted somehow to repair the damage. There was no plan as to how he would do that, but he felt it had to be done..

On his way to visit Moss again, Koan wondered how Moss viewed those boyhood days he and Chris spent together; with a smile at their naivety, or with a sense of regret that their searching came to an irrevocable end? Within Koan, a repressed hurt had been released, the image of something lost, a child that had remained in Shepherdstown, a child he wanted to find, a child he'd never understood or really known, his childhood self.

The lunch at the Tripp family table was overwhelmingly familiar. All that was missing were Mr. and Mrs. Tripp, Moss's parents. And the food was almost as simple as back then: cured ham, black-eyed peas, and cornbread. And it tasted wonderful to Koan.

When they were done with lunch, Bonnie Sue cleared the table, and Koan and Moss stepped out onto the porch.

"Koan, it's amazin' how much ya know about Chris. I swear, about all that's missing is thatcha ran around with us."

"Those must've been great times."

"They sure were." Moss gazed out beyond the far fences of his front pasture.

"Funny, but we weren't really part of all this, yet we understood it a whole lot better than most of 'em."

"Was that just the sweet innocence of youth, Moss?"

Koan didn't get an immediate reply. Moss massaged his jaw thoughtfully, then let out a muted chuckle. "Ya got me on that one. I've never stopped thinkin' about a lotta things we used to talk about, Chris and me. Ya know, it took the two of us to see things real clear. Thoughts by themselves don't change a whole lot. I've missed him." Moss turned and slapped Koan on the shoulder. "Maybe Chris had you come by so I could get to talkin' again? How'd ya like to git out and learn some of the places Chris and I use ta go?"

"I thought you'd never ask."

From inside, Bonnie Sue had kept an ear trained on their conversation.

"Where you two plannin' on goin'?"

"We're thinkin' of makin' our way up ta Devil's Gardens."

"You guys sure had names for places. If it's far, remember it gets dark early."

Moss and Koan had been trudging along for more than an hour. Koan wished it were late fall, when the leaves of the maples and oaks displayed their colors, rather than lying brown and faded on the forest floor. Moss suggested they take a break, pointing to a pool of water, a spring. Moss scooped up a handful of water. Koan did the same, exhilarated by the purity of its soft taste.

As Koan raised his head, he heard a familiar sound that gradually increased in volume. It was the honking of geese. His eyes finally located the great V moving across the gray sky.

"Are they heading north already?"

"Yeah, it seems mighty early, doesn't it. I'm sure, though, they know what they're doin'."

"Frankly, I'm envious."

"Why do ya say that, Koan?"

"They know where they're going, a place that's always been theirs, from the moment they hatched until the ends of their lives. That's permanence."

"Yeah, Nature takes care of itself, without God havin' to worry a lot about it."

"Ever wonder if God's regretted having gotten so carried away by what he created, adding mankind?"

Moss chuckled. "No. And you know why? Without us, He wouldn't have a dang blasted thing to do."

Koan and Moss pushed on, reaching the Devil's Garden a while later. Their trek had taken them up along the ridge of a hill, then down the far side to a small, narrow valley. Most of the rock in the area around Shepherdstown was sandstone, but in the Devil's Gardens large outcroppings of granitelike stone containing pockets of quartz jutted out of the earth. Koan recalled how the rocks sparkled when the sunlight hit them, but he couldn't remember why they had called it Devil's Gardens.

"What's the secret behind the name?"

"I don't recollect now. Maybe 'cause they tried to scare the dickens out of us in church, ya know, about ole Satan, and maybe we thought this was an entrance ta hell."

"Do you believe in Satan, Moss?"

"Naw. That's just pushin' blame off on someone else. That ain't takin' no responsibility fer ourselves. I also don't believe in demons and gettin' possessed. People jus' make bad judgments, that's all I believe in."

Koan grinned. "I have to agree with you. Besides, there's plenty of hell in this life without worrying about more afterward."

"Ain't that the truth. Butcha know, I'm bad as any of 'em."

"How's that?"

"Oh, I tell my kids about little demons that wanta nest in 'em, if they let 'em. I tell 'em what those little demons don't like is when a person talks about 'em so everyone knows they're there. One word about 'em, and they're up and gone. Damned stupid story, but it gets ma kids talkin' about what's botherin' or worryin' 'em, you know, their little demons."

"Whatever works."

Koan climbed up onto one of the large outcroppings and draped his body across it, sighing deeply, enjoying the stillness of the late winter day.

Koan rubbed his eyes, wondering how long he'd been dozing. He looked over and saw Moss perched on an adjacent boulder busy trying to scrape out a quartz crystal with his pocketknife.

"Moss, I was wondering about Chris and his father. Why do you think they never came to an understanding?"

Moss kept scraping with his knife. "Chris's daddy was a hard man, a good man, but mighty principled. Hardly anyone 'round these parts was more community-minded, but he didn't like anyone makin' a big fuss outta that. It was just his way of livin'. I think that's what broke his heart. Chris didn't wanta bother with all that stuff, you know, the church, the scouts, all that. I didn't either, but my Pa was different. He said that'd all come in its own time. But Mr. Folkstone, it pert near ate him up. Ya could see it in 'im. He never forgave Chris. I heard him say that to my Pa, just before he died, that he thought Chris only cared about himself and no one else."

Moss blew on the rock where he had been digging with his knife. "I sure wish I had a chisel along. Got a nice crystal here. You know, Chris's daddy had a good heart for those sufferin', but his own flesh and blood…guess he just couldn't see the hurt it put on his son."

"Moss, how'd you feel about Chris leaving? Was it courage or betrayal?"

"Interestin' question. I think it took a lot more courage than goin' in the church." Moss chuckled. "That's still sufferin' for me. Truth is, I envied Chris."

"You did?"

"Sure. Pa liked to say that sufferin' built character, and I think that's what Chris set out to do. He was after something, and doin' a whole lot of sufferin' to find it." Moss went back to digging at his crystal. "Bonnie Sue says Chris was lucky to know you."

"I guess that's good?" Koan laid back, looking out toward the gray, darkening horizon, watching a thin ray of sunlight knife down through a hole in the clouds.

"Moss, have you ever been back up on Windy Hill?"

"Yes. That's where I go to talk with God. Ya know what Chris and I'd say? When God made somethin' real clear to us, we'd say it shook us. That's what's so special about Windy Hill. You could almost be sure, when you went up there, that God would shake you."

"Those shakes must have felt good."

"Yeah, like the shake they give a newborn baby."

For a few brief moments, Koan felt as if his inner self had escaped his body, risen upward above him. He'd forgotten that expression, God shaking them.

That's it! That's the fucking elucidation the old man spoke of. I'm sure. We'd get so lightheaded, not really dizzy, but it was as if we were no longer thinking but rather what was in our heads came from somewhere else. And later we always agreed we understood something that had confused us. My God, it's like the old man and I share something. Finally!

"Moss, I'd love to go up to Windy Hill."

"Sure. Jus let me know, and I'll take ya there sometime."

Koan then told Moss about the taxi driver in London, and how he'd said if Jesus were to reappear on Earth, few of us would recognize him. "He thought Jesus would be something like the beggars on the streets. What do you think of that?"

"Why'd God even want 'im here? We've already got too many people preachin' their heads off, and ya can't trust a one of 'em. God don't need anyone else to speak for him. Not if he can shake us."

Koan laughed. "Now there's a good paradox."

"What's that, a paradox?"

"Oh, a stupid word."

Moss finally snapped the quartz crystal free and tossed it over to Koan.

"Thanks." Koan looked at it from all sides. "You know, it's a lot like life with its many sides, yet unlike life, it's perfectly clear."

"I like that. Maybe God's in such crystals? Well, it's about time we get goin'. Bonnie Sue'll be a fussin' if we get back after dark. She don't mind me wanderin' if she knows when I'm comin' back. And I always do."

For the first time since he as Chris had left for college, Koan was genuinely glad he'd come back, not so much to Shepherdstown as to his soul brother, Moss.

20

Under Paul's masterful leadership, the conversion of the Angstrom Industries to a trust ran smoothly. Koan more often than not stood back in awe of the whirlwind of activities. People were working around the clock, negotiating, unraveling complex capital transfers, ploughing through the red tape of innumerable laws and regulations. Amazingly, though, the process required only months.

"Paul, I won't even pretend to understand what's been happening. I stand in reverence before your talents."

Paul didn't allow himself any self-satisfaction. "I was led by a vision. No, actually it was a dream, a very concrete dream. In it I was trying to see the image of the old man, and whenever I looked directly at him, the light was too intense. It blinded me. I woke up in a sweat, terribly agitated, wondering what the significance of the dream might have been? I anguished over it a long time, but then it came to me. The old man was trying to tell me something, to not look back at him."

"Not look back at him?"

"Yes, Koan. He was telling me I was being blinded by my fixation on the past, as if it had been an ideal lost. An aura overcame me, that this dream was his blessing, that he was verifying, legitimating this, the challenge facing us, the future. What you've been witnessing, Koan, had been nothing more than the inspiration that came from that dream."

"So everything's whole again?"

"Yes, even if we lost millions in the liquidation of many of our assets."

"Paul, perhaps your dream was something like my first visit to the Southside Community Center? It felt like a knot snapping inside of me. It was like I'd finally found a rhyme or reason for being Koan. You haven't been there, have you, Paul, to the Southside ward? How about it, would you care to go there with me?"

"Certainly, Koan. I feel like I've been in a pressure cooker here, and things have settled down now. Yes, I'd like to experience your inspiration."

"Oh, yeah, Paul, there's one other thing. It's occurred to me that we've left Freddie in the dark about all this. I realize you've carved out her business and signed it completely over to her, and that might satisfy her, but I can't shake the feeling that we're letting all that obsessive energy of hers go to waste. Why don't we invite her along on our little excursion? We can use the opportunity to fill her in on the changes. Who knows, maybe she has a few ideas?"

"I don't know, Koan, from what you've told me, that's no place for a woman."

"That sounds sexist, Paul. Besides, Freddie's nurtured a tough-girl image. Did you know she created her name

Freddie?"

"No, but I did find it unusual, hardly very feminine."

"She deliberately sought to neutralize male attitudes toward women by taking on an asexual image." Koan chuckled. "Her ambition was also to be a virgin neuter."

Paul didn't smile. "To each their own."

"In any case, Paul, I'm certain she can handle it."

When Freddie recognized into which part of Pontifica they were headed, she guessed it had to do with real estate speculation and urban redevelopment, but Koan and Paul remained mum. Koan did make a point of having their driver cruise slowly down the street where the remains of the Burning Bridges bar stood, hoping to get a reaction from Freddie, but she showed none.

"Well, here we are. I called ahead to assure a guided tour."

Scanning the buildings around the Southside Community Center, Freddie ventured a show of optimism. "I never realized anyone was attempting to rebuild this area. These buildings must be from around the turn of the century. Some classy restoration, and, who knows, it might become a camp inner city residential area?"

Inside the center, Koan asked for Father Nick, and again Freddie showed no reaction. Moments later, a loud voice yelled from behind them, "So dare ya are, ma old friend, Mr. Koan!"

Koan introduced Freddie and Paul.

"Ah don't believe ma eyes. Ah remember ya, ma'am." That Father Nick recognized her visibly embarrassed Freddie. "Ma'am, ya look a whole lot better dan ya did dat night. Did ya ever find out wad happened to yer husband?"

"No…no. But I appreciate your asking." Koan tried to make eye contact with Freddie, but her eyes avoided his.

Father Nick invited them upstairs to show them their renovation plans. Paul, who had been momentarily taken aback by Father Nick's connection to Freddie, gradually developed an interest in the entrepreneurial spirit of Nick and his people, but Freddie remained tentative, as if working on why she was there. Nick then took them on a tour of the buildings, and afterward let other people explain programs they were running, such as drug rehabs, literacy, and family planning. Finally, Koan thanked Father Nick.

"Mr. Koan, you've become wonna us here. And ah sure enjoyed seein' yah again, ma'am. Ya wurn't so happy last time our paths crossed."

Walking to their car, Koan suggested lunch to Paul and Freddie. Suddenly, a scraggly figure appeared. Koan tensed up, recognizing it was Cornelius, the man who had so aggressively attacked him during the Thanksgiving dinner.

"Ah hah, the great man appears again."

Koan wanted to ignore Cornelius, but the next sentence stunned him.

"And what do we have here, the infamous Freddie Folkstone?" Freddie's body jerked upward stiffly, as if Cornelius had pointed a gun at her. "Old man, I've done my research on you, listened around. I've come to the conclusion you are here for more admirable reasons than I gave you credit for."

Koan was preparing himself for another of Cornelius's tirades. "I guess I should say thank you."

A smart smile came over Cornelius's tight, haggard face. "Sounds rather strange, you saying thank you to this sorry soul standing in front of you. Takes guts to do that. Look, I buy into what you're doing. In fact, for having chewed you out, perhaps undeservedly, I feel I owe you one. As if I have much to offer." Cornelius let out a grating laugh that went over into a bout of deep coughing. "Sorry. Probably pneumonia. And the beginning of the end for me. Anyhow, remember, if you should need me, no more trash talk, I'll help you in any way I can."

Still skeptical, Koan was also touched. "I appreciate that. I really do."

Cornelius's hollow eyes again focused on Freddie. "I must say, you do keep strange company. Freddie Folkstone. When was the last time we two saw each other?"

Koan was sure he hadn't known Cornelius back when he was Chris, and he couldn't recall Freddie ever mentioning such a name. Freddie's expression was one of 'let's get our asses out of here.'

"Obviously you don't remember me. My most vivid recollections of you were at a symposium titled 'Selling with Ethics.' Inherently contradictory, that title, but what stands out in my mind was the stubborn little girl chiding a whole roomful of accomplished advertising professionals. Wasn't your position something like advertising is merely fulfilling basic human wants and by nature a most ethical thing?"

Cornelius couldn't suppress a sarcastic snigger. "It was so strange, because the whole purpose of the gathering was an attempt at self-scrutiny and self-criticism, a very refreshing act of soul searching about whether the driving motivations of advertising were getting away from any code of human values, and there you were, dead obsessed with refuting the very intention of our being there, as if our questioning was going to beschmudge our lily white vests. You just didn't get it. And the intensity with which you admonished us. A woman possessed. For your sake, I hope you've mellowed out."

Absolute despise contorted Freddie's face. "Look, I don't have the foggiest idea who you are, and, frankly, I don't give a damn. Your great wisdom obviously got you what you deserved." With that, Freddie climbed resolutely into the car.

As they drove to the restaurant for lunch, everyone was quiet. The scene with Cornelius still hung in the air, and no one dared touch it. Only after they were seated at their table did anyone say anything of any significance. It was Paul explaining how impressed he'd been with the Southside project.

"I want to thank you, Koan. I was myopic about what's

going on in places like that." In a rare gesture, Paul shook Koan's hand.

Freddie lifted her neck as if seeking attention. "I still haven't figured out what interest you have in that area. It was really sad to witness the enthusiasm of those people, knowing from a broader perspective how futile their efforts are."

Koan ignored Freddie's cynicism, asking Paul to explain why they'd been there.

Paul cleared his throat and straightened his back, more than was customary. "Freddie, Koan has made some decisions that have drastically changed the nature of our endeavors." Paul's lead-in got Freddie visibly uptight. Paul spelled out how most of Koan's holdings had been liquidated and the funds converted into a trust. "Of course, you will be retaining your company, but with a slight change. We have transferred complete ownership over to you."

Seeing Freddie was stunned, Koan broke in. "Freddie, one could view this as an end to our relationship, but I'm not sure that's necessarily the case." Warily, Freddie asked what Koan meant. Paul was also eyeing Koan with skepticism. "Freddie, I don't need to tell a widow how finite life can be. I accept that I won't be around forever. What we're embarking upon is an enormous challenge, one that may fall completely into Paul's hands one day. And I'm sure he will lean on a lot of great talents."

Freddie's eyes went back and forth between Koan and Paul. "The light's coming on. This trip today has to do with your trust, and not some development scheme. Obviously there's a lot I'm not aware of."

Koan smiled. "I couldn't begin to describe the activities that've taken place in the past months. It suffices to say we've moved from a profit motive to something more idealistic."

Paul nodded. "Actually, Koan's been involved with the people at the Southside Community Center for some time now. I think you can view it as a category of projects the trust will be addressing."

"That's quite a surprise. No, a real stunner." Freddie took a very deep breath.

"Whew. It's really hard for me to envision the worldwide financial power brokering of Angstrom Industries suddenly going underground. And what a way to break it to me."

Koan sensed the undertone of anger in Freddie's words. "Freddie, I'm sorry, it didn't occur to me that this might be a reunion for you and Father Nick. I knew of the connection."

"You did?"

"Yes. He was one of the puzzle pieces that led you to us, wasn't he?"

Freddie managed a strained smile. "You're right. I did feel like I'd been set up, even though I couldn't imagine you knowing that person. And did you also arrange for that nut to jump in our faces out at the car?"

"No, I had no idea you and he were in any way associated."

"Associated? Me with him?"

"I wasn't implying. I only know he was also in the advertising trade before he contracted AIDS. His name is Cornelius."

Freddie's face went briefly pale. "Cornelius Vonderende? I can't believe that. He was once one of my idols. Obviously he's gone off the deep end. C'est la vie. But back to Father Nick, yes, I did meet him, once, and I can't say I regret it. As much as that little episode disgusted me, it led me along a path that's put me where I am today. So I guess I should have hugged him. Sorry, though, that would have been asking too much."

"Again, Freddie, I'll assure you that wasn't a set-up. The purpose of our trip today was to give Paul a firsthand look at the Southside project, and as a sidelight, I thought it would present a good opportunity to fill you in on our new direction."

"I appreciate that. So, this trust of yours is going to be some kind of big charity?"

"Not a charity, closer to what you might call a philanthropy. Even better, its mission will be to provide seeds for good, humanitarian causes. I'm curious whether all this inspires any thoughts in you?"

"That sounds a bit like a loaded question." Freddie narrowed her eyes, rubbing her jaw. "Something that big is going to require plenty of promotion." Freddie laughed. "Did I say plenty? When I think of the dollars you'll be throwing into this, that's a mega-account for any agency. Several agencies, in fact. Are you in any way implying that you'd even consider me, or is it just one of your teases?"

"I suggest, at the very least, that you and Paul have a good talk. Who knows?"

"Paul, what do you think about Freddie?"

The two men were back in Koan's office. Paul held a crooked finger over his lips, but didn't ponder long. "How bittersweet that things can twist like a vine and come right back at you. I thought we'd be celebrating her departure. Especially you, Koan. But, yes, of course, she could be utilitarian, if that's really your will?"

"Maybe you're right, Paul. She's been, how do I say it nicely, more often than not an irritant. But she was also my wife. I can't deny I've enjoyed being a rung above her."

"An old vendetta?"

"I don't know. Airing out some old resentments, perhaps. But, Paul, didn't you once lecture me about bridling good people, that that was a trademark of Angstrom Industries?"

"Yes, I probably did, and that included compulsive people. But I hope I also said people who can accept guidance."

"Are you implying that Freddie can't?"

"Maybe I'm being too harsh in my judgments, but I'm not sure she's capable of seeing beyond her own self-promotion."

"Isn't self-promotion only human? I can't profess to be immune from it myself. For example, our trust, I'm sure, it's to some extent an ego trip for me."

"To a minor extent, I hope."

"Whatever, Paul. I'd like to have another talk with Freddie about this."

"So be it. But respect the striking distance of a viper, Koan."

Koan had wanted to keep his talk with Freddie less personal, but she insisted he come to her home for dinner. Koan left early so that he could drive at an easy pace. Winter was relinquishing its repressing hold and giving way to spring. Rather than take the interstate highway, Koan opted for back roads until he neared the outskirts of the Pontifica. He enjoyed the splashes of blooms and fresh greens, which mirrored his inner feeling of renewal.

Koan was given a royal greeting by his hostess. Her new home was very impressive. While on a tour of the rooms, a sense of grieving seeped into Koan's otherwise buoyant mood. Nowhere was there a trace of Chris. With her usual obsessiveness, Freddie had meticulously erased that chapter from her life.

Asked what he'd like to drink, Koan inquired whether Freddie had Drambuie.

"Why, yes. It's not a favorite of mine, but for my husband, it was the ultimate. A little boarish, but he liked it straight in a shot glass."

"I share his good taste."

"But not in a shot glass?"

"Yes, of course."

"Sometimes I find you spooky."

During dinner, Freddie announced her interest in working for Koan's new trust. Koan asked whether she was already formulating strategies.

"One thing has occurred to me. We're not talking about competing products, rather it's a case of establishing faith in a promised reward. There's a ploy for that called the mythological embellishment."

"That's Greek to me."

"Very funny." Freddie set forth her explanation with chilling efficiency. "You're perfect for that, Koan. I mean, who really knows you? We've spent time together, and you're still a mystery to me." Freddie's laugh sounded hollow. "That circumstance, that you have no well-defined identity, offers tremendous latitude. We could elevate you to almost any level, a mythological god, if you like. Am I getting too carried away?"

"I suppose I'd be provided a script?"

"You aren't taking me seriously, are you?" Freddie was gazing beyond Koan. "If you're into morbid thoughts, the perfect situation would be your death. I mean, don't take that seriously, but if you think about it, that would make your image untouchable."

"You have a point. If I were dead, I couldn't foul up the perfect image. There are parallels." Koan crossed his knife and fork demonstratively on his plate. "Where would the Christian religion be if Christ had hung around until he was geriatric? Imagine those people busting their butts to establish the early Christian Church, and there's Christ staggering around babbling senile nonsense. And there's another one for you, Freddie. His early death left the things he said pretty nebulous, fully open to interpretation. Perfect, according to your little theory."

Freddie impatiently acknowledged the similarities, then plowed on. "Koan, you mentioned you were backing out. What exactly did you mean?"

Koan shrugged his shoulders. "I don't yet exactly know. I'm putting my faith in enlightenment."

"You're sometimes as smart-assed as he was," Freddie snapped back. "My husband was always trying to be so clever, as if we were in some sort of competition."

"Maybe he thought it was the game you wanted to play."

"That's exactly it. He thought of it as play, while I took it dead seriously. To get ahead, you use every weapon you have. But forget him. He's the last thing on my mind."

"Good. At the risk of being a party pooper at what was supposed to be a nice, relaxed evening, there's one question I have to ask you."

"Go ahead, shoot."

"I listened to your ideas about a promotional scheme to elevate my image, or the trust, whichever, to a movement of faith. Isn't that what you called it?"

"Yes, that'll do."

"Well, I can see promoting some organized religion, a televangelist, or whatever that way, but the word faith, at least for me, goes far beyond religion or any thing institutionalized. Isn't faith a very personal thing, something like a belief that spans across eternal time, yes, I'd even equate it with one's relationship to God?"

"Look, Koan, to me those things are all one and the same. Personally, I have a very simple belief, that I'll somehow be immortal, and that's that. I don't need the religions or philosophies. But lots of people do need a crutch, and why not capitalize on that?"

Koan scratched vigorously the side of his head. "Okay, let me phrase it a little differently. Isn't it the birthright of every person to search their soul for the meaning of existence?"

"Sure, so?"

"Isn't such a scheme a premeditated luring of people away from their own personal soul searching? I guess what I'm trying to ask, in a diplomatic way, is whether or not you sense any discomfort about proposing an opiate rather than an inspiration?"

"You know, Koan, I will never comprehend how someone with your sentimentalities was ever cold-blooded enough to amass your wealth. In my dictionary, exploitation isn't a dirty word. It's synonymous with opportunity. Look, my mind focuses on what the masses want and tries to give it to them. Period."

"So there's no struggle of conscience?"

"None whatsoever."

After she had cleared the table and made coffee, Freddie brought in a Grand Marinier soufflé. Freddie waved off Koan's compliments, admitting she had had it prepared. "I never would have gotten it to rise."

"And you want to elevate me to a god?" After they laughed, Koan continued, "So, Freddie, you've really been bitten?"

"Why shouldn't I be? It's the biggest thing I've ever touched. Looking back, it's strange how I wandered into this, searching for my husband. Fate has its ways. To think that Chris and I'd still be grinding away in our numb, dumb little world."

"Aren't you glad he's not here to hear that?"

The question disturbed Freddie. "It's amazing how often you bring him up. Like he could still mean that much to me."

"No, I think it's me who's so attached to him. I can't deny being somehow involved with his disappearance. Call it a sense of responsibility for him, if you like."

"Well, I, as his widow, should feel worse, but for me, life goes on."

"But, you know, Freddie, you've gotten closer to him than you could ever imagine."

"Is this another one of your riddle games?" Freddie's tight smile expressed hope that Koan would get off the subject, but he didn't.

"Freddie, when you happened onto Angstrom Industries, you had essentially found Chris."

Freddie laid down her fork. "I see. I'm finally going to learn what happened to him."

"Will a fairy tale do?"

"If that's easier for you, fine. Shoot."

"Good." Koan settled back in his chair. "Well, there once was this godlike person, powerful but very lonely. His only fault was a fear, a fear of no longer being held in reverence.

He was godlike, because he was terribly wise, but despite all his wisdom, he couldn't find a way to dispel his fear. Finally, in desperation, he decided to play a trick on the world. He would take a person of mortal dimensions, transpose himself into that person, and surprise the world with his magic. They would witness his power of renewal, and once again stand in awe of him."

Freddie clapped her hands softly. "That was sweet. Really sweet. But, I have to admit that I must have missed the point. What did that have to do with Chris?"

"He's in there."

"Okay, let's see if I have it? Chris had enough of real life and decided to become part of a fairy tale. Charming, quaint. It even sounds like Chris. He was very much into avoidance."

"Bear with me, Freddie. My fairy tale wasn't a cop out. Fairy tales, on the surface, may seem quaint and intended for entertainment, but below the surface are parables about bitter realities. In this fairy tale, Chris walked into a living hell. Avoidance? No. Fate grabbed him by his hand and wouldn't let go."

Freddie was fidgeting. "You've lost me. Look, I harbor no illusions about being in the same league with you. I'm supposed to be picking up on something here, but I'm not. And Chris's fate may be a lot less important to me than you think. Do you mind if I keep my own fairy tales about what happened to Chris?"

"And what are those fairy tales?"

Freddie let out a resigned sigh. "Isn't all that your and Paul's concerns? Koan, how often do I need to say it? I have no further interest in what happened, and, hand on the Bible, I'll never ask. Looking at it objectively, Chris's disappearance elevated my life many times over."

"But what if Chris were alive and as close to you as I am right now?"

Freddie frowned. "Then that's a reality I don't care to know. The only reality I'm good at is creating illusions, ones that sell. Isn't that the partnership you want from me?"

Koan shrugged his shoulders. "Okay. I guess I am beating a dead horse. But I do have one last request involving Chris."

"And that would be?"

"I was hoping that at least you and Chris would finally say goodbye to each other."

"If that's your pleasure. Okay. Goodbye, Chris. Did that sound sincere enough?"

"It'll do."

21

It could have been darker. The silver disk of the full moon cast a pale light on the countryside around Windy Hill, and shadows around Koan and Moss, who were sitting on its summit.

Moss gazed up at the star strewn heavens. "There's something 'bout bein' up here, like ya can go all the way back to the beginnings of time."

Koan sighed. "The infinity we call God. Sadly, the closer we come to understanding all truths, the more we focus on the immediate, the moment, ourselves. In my youth, I thought I saw things pretty clearly, then it seemed to get all muddled up. Now I'm old, and it's finally coming back."

"I s'pose it's that way with most everyone. When we see ole death comin' up the road, all the sudden a lotta things seem more important, and others we thought meant so much just fade away." Moss coughed, then blew into his cupped hands to warm them. "Koan, ya think much 'bout Christ?"

Koan laughed. "Your mind moves faster than a shooting star. Let's see, Christ? My first thought? Why did he have to be a human?"

"Chris and I useta think he shoulda been a ghost."

"Why not a bird, or a fish?"

Moss chuckled. "Them things had their shit together." Moss was enjoying the exchange, humming between statements. "It'd been a whole lot better, if Christ had jus' been a spirit, like God. We'd all be sharin' and knowin' the same thing, and not fightin' about seeing and interpreting it all a little differently."

"Maybe we do share the same thing?"

"I wish. Heard jus' the other day that there's a big fuss goin' on about whether Christ was white or black."

"And a spirit has no shape, size, or color? You're right, Moss."

Moss let out a blood-curdling yell, which Koan also tried, but with a lot less amplitude. A wave of wind came up and swirled the grasses around them.

"Koan, ya know, ya've got Chris's spirit in ya."

A chill jerked Koan's body, but he ignored Moss's statement. "Moss, sometimes I believe I can sense what Christ felt. He must've known that after he was gone, people would claim him to be something, each a little different than the other."

"Ya mean like the Baptists, Catholics, and Methodists, building up their churches and tackin' Christ's name on 'em, like he lived there? I bet he'd scream like Moses did, when he came down from the mount and found 'em worshippin' all them idols."

Again, Koan shook from a chill. "Why'd God even want

Christ on Earth? It only confused Man even more about who God is. Think God had a weak moment?"

"Or He underestimated the weaknesses of human bein's. There ya go. Maybe Christ was only a spirit, and people felt 'em, understood from feelin' what he was, but then they got weak and mushy-minded 'bout it, started thinkin' too much 'bout how they was gonna tell others what they felt, so they decided they'd have to make a good story outta it, creatin' an image of Christ, and then the churches."

"That's great, Moss. You hit it right on the head. And right here we've got the best church in the world. Right here on Windy Hill."

A gratifying silence fell over them, one finally broken by Koan.

"Moss, I'm ashamed of myself."

"Why?" Didja pee in yer britches?"

"No, I shit on you. Moss, my name's Koan, but I'm really someone else." Koan tensed up in anticipation of Moss's response, but he got a laugh.

"I was a waitin' for that. Ya coulda been an eagle swoopin' down here, and I'd still have recognized ya. Yer Chris."

"You've known?"

"Yeah. And what does it matter? It's like debatin' what Christ may've looked like. I didn't believe Chris would've told anyone all the things ya know. And my mind kept sayin', this man thinks like 'im too. Butcha see, all that don't matter a hoot to me."

Koan was dumbfounded. It took him awhile to accept that Moss didn't want an explanation. Tears began to well in Koan's eyes, and he leaned toward Moss, who reached out and embraced him. "Thanks, Moss. You know, right now, I wish I were an eagle and could soar up above it all. Way up high above it all."

The softest blush of bluish purple began to work its way

into the eastern horizon. The long night on Windy Hill was drawing to an end. Moss reached out and pulled a plumed piece of grass, snapping the shaft with his hands. "What we talked about before, whether you're Chris or Koan, it ain't important. You ain't Chris anymore than I'm still Moss. Not no more. A lot's changed, a lot more than the wrinkles in our faces."

Koan gazed at the pastels creeping into the morning sky. "What's bothering you, Moss?"

Moss got up, jamming his hands into his pockets, hunching his shoulders up.

"Ya know, Koan. You've been acting apologetic ever since you came back here at Christmas. Like if I knew you were Chris, I wouldn't like ya." Moss sat back down, drawing his knees up, his head sagging between them. "We used to talk real bad about the church, didn't we?"

"Yeah, we sure did."

"Well, guess who became a preacher there?"

"Not you?"

"Yes. Bonnie Sue got to insisten' that we go to church more regularly, but there in church, I didn't like what was happenin'. People didn't get all dressed up no more, they'd bring in folks to play hymns wit those electric guitars and drums. I kept thinkin' how much more I liked the way it used to be. Then one day, well, it just hit me. Ya don't sit back and jus moan about things, ya gotta get yer ass movin' and see if ya can change it. I asked to become a lay preacher. Even Bonnie Sue thought I was nuts or somethin'. But I did it. And, hell, I made a fine preacher. I wanted to shake that church back to what I remembered, somethin' like the way God use ta shake us up here, and mosta the folks just loved it. I was good. But a few years later, I just up and quit."

"Quit? Why?"

"Wadya call those things that have two meanings?"

"Paradoxes?"

"Yeah, that's it. One of them paradoxes. I wrapped my

arms around the past, like it was my true love, but it wasn't the real past. Only sorted out memories, the ones I liked the most. My mind and recollection was doin' all the seein', not my eyes, nor my soul. Well, one night, I came up here on Windy Hill, and I felt God shake me, tellin' me He isn't our memories, or our dreams, no, He is the next moment, the next breath. There I was, preachin' in a house called God's house, but I'd shut God out, made him as dead as Jesus, somethin' outta an old book, not somethin' alive in us."

"I'm truly amazed, Moss. You a preacher? I mean, if you'd preached half the things we used to talk about together, your congregation would've declared you a heretic."

"Ya don't think I told 'em all those things? I preached from my heart, not my head. And I expected one or the other to cry out and argue with me, say what I was preachin' isn't so. But that's what hurt so much. No one was listenin'. No one was a rantin' and ravin', just noddin' their heads, like I could've said most anything to 'em, jus' because I was the preacher and we were in a house of God. It finally came to me just how crazy I was thinkin'. Ya can't preach God into people. They have ta let Him into their hearts. And church ain't particularly the place where that happens."

A warm cloak of mutual agreement settled over the two men again for a while. Koan even smiled, imagining his old buddy Moss preaching in their church. Then the thought came that his father may've been sitting in the congregation.

"Moss, remember what you said about my dad, his attitude toward the community and all that? Until you and I talked about it, I never understood what set him and me apart. I had guessed a thousand things, but missed that one. He did, he lived for the community. Maybe I owe it to all those people out there, and maybe they'd see it that way, that my sacrificing for them would be my way of living for the community. The way my dad meant it."

Moss slapped Koan's shoulder. "Yer gonna beat yourself ta death with that. Wadja expect from yer father? That he punish you? When Moses came down from the mountain, he was angry, but he didn't ask God to bring down his wrath on the people, did he? He went back up on the mount, because he knew he had to accept them as human beings." Moss's hand went up and scratched on his neck. "Yeah, that's another way a' seein' it. Yer dad was just a human being, Koan. But you been treatin' him like a god, someone you gotta please somehow."

"Moss, I don't want to please him. I simply said I wanted to sacrifice, like he did."

"What is it, Koan, thatcha want to sacrifice?"

"We've set up a philanthropic trust."

"Philanthropic?"

"Yes, we're going to give money, lots of money to different places that need it, like the poor, the ghettos of the inner cities, to help those who haven't had fortune on their sides."

"I'm sure your daddy would have been proud of ya."

"You think so?"

"Sure, 'cept one thing I heard ya say. You said you want people to see what you're doin', what you're sacrificin'. Ya know yer daddy didn't like to hear such a thing, that people noticed what he was doin' for others. He'd just say, 'That's the way it is, we all do such things fer each other.'"

"Maybe in that respect he and I will always differ. In fact, I feel a need for some recognition."

"Why that?"

"Probably because I never got any from Dad. Experiencing the gratitude of the masses would be a redemption."

The eastern sky had been flowing through permutations of pastel tones, gaining ever so slowly in brightness. Peering intently, Koan and Moss thought they could see rays reaching up from over the edge of the world.

Moss yanked some dried grass and twisted it in his fingers until it was braided together, then he handed it to Koan. "Look, ole Buddy, we're as close as this. We'll always be. Ya remember how, back then, we became blood brothers?" Moss whacked Koan on the back, but his enthusiasm sounded sad.

The first hint of the rising sun burned the tops of the distant hills. Koan stood up, stretching himself to the limit. "Moss, sometimes I think I'm looking too hard for something, and I don't even know what that something is. Maybe someday, up here on Windy Hill, it will just drop down out of the heavens into my lap, like it did with you."

"I can tell yer still searchin' fer something, Koan."

"Maybe it's in a word called holda."

"Holda? What in the dickens is that?"

"You don't remember the old hermit using that word?"

"Ah guess. Was that what he was a mutterin'?"

"Yeah. Supposedly it's how all things relate to each other. The man I'm supposed to be used that word, too. Sort of like all things are one. It's funny, I can say, I've grasped the essence of that word, but inside me, I still don't feel it."

"Ah remember now. Yeah. When the old hermit said that word, I sorta took it that he meant all things have one soul. You think that's so hard to feel?"

"Maybe that's why you never left Shepherdstown, Moss, and I did."

"How d'ya mean that?"

"You didn't feel a need to go out and search for anything, the truth, yourself?"

"Ya wanna know the truth, Koan. I was tempted, when you up and left, but then I figured there wouldn't be anything out there any different than what's here, not really, so why go lookin' when ya can stay put and do the lookin' right here?"

"I felt I had to leave."

"Butcha say ya still haven't found what yer lookin' for?"

Koan let the discussion die.

Moss stood up. "Windy Hill, you're the first place that's touched by the new light of day!"

Koan grunted in agreement, but added, "But it's a more friendly place at night."

22

Koan stopped at the gatehouse of his estate. Mounted on the high stone wall was a large, shiny brass sign, "The K-Light Trust." One may have expected this sight to elicit a swell of pride within Koan. It didn't. It irritated him. The sign had been erected while he was away, and it hadn't been cleared with him. He suspected Freddie had something to do with it.

Coincidentally, soon after Koan walked through the hallway of the main house he ran into Freddie, who greeted him with a stiff-lipped peck on the cheek.

"Welcome back. We've been gearing up. You'll have to watch out for the workers. We're starting renovations on the whole western wing."

Koan wanted to mention the sign at the front gate, but Freddie was quicker, suggesting he talk to Paul about something urgent.

When Koan reached his office, he walked in, stopped, and looked around.

"Well, Paul, at least this room's still the same."

Paul tried to smile, but his jaw muscles were clenching. "She'll probably want to preserve your office as a shrine."

"You mean like a museum?"

"More like a destination for pilgrimages."

Koan laughed. "This is Freddie in her finest form. And what about you, Paul? Are you finding all this exciting? Freddie used the term 'gearing up' but failed to say for what?"

"That's not inconsistent. She leaves a lot of people guessing."

"Does that include you, Paul?"

"Yes. It's like the tail wagging the dog. Since you decided to put her in charge of promotional activities, she's acted as if that were the mission of the trust."

"Paul, you know those weren't my intentions. I thought you'd have your hands full with scoping out and organizing the projects we want to cover. In giving Freddie the other activities, I saw it as relieving you of those distractions."

"Well, in her eyes, what you so flippantly call distractions are the centerpiece. I have to confess, even I'm unsure exactly what your true intentions have been. The old man kept Angstrom Industries deliberately low profile. Now we're headed in the complete opposite direction."

"Oh, Paul, how can a little limelight hurt us?"

"It casts doubts, Koan, most importantly, on what our motivations might be. Are we out to quietly and invisibly support programs we feel are worthwhile, or are we looking to build our own image and reputation? I've already had an in-depth discussion with a project leader who warned me it would hurt their cause if they were explicitly associated with Angstrom Industries."

"Why that?"

"Because their project represent the disenfranchised in a society that favors those with wealth and power. They have very successfully inspired a large number of non-profit community self-help programs. All through private donations and voluntary initiatives. They've turned down any type of corporate donation. I was convinced it was the type of thing you're seeking to get involved with, but we can't if we're going to accompany it with such high-profile fanfare."

"Sometimes you have to accept strange bedmates to get where you want to go."

"Is that what you want me to tell that program director?"

"Why not?"

"Because he beat us to it. He flatly but politely explained that his program would continue to move forward without our financial support."

"That's his choice." Koan noticed Paul wasn't pleased. "Look, Paul, when are you ever going to lighten up? I recall way back when that you were coaxing me on by promising there would be big rewards awaiting me if I stuck it out. I feel like you're implying I shouldn't collect those IOUs. Frankly, I'm not opposed to Freddie dragging me out into the public as part of our promotional efforts. She definitely understands what sells."

Paul glared at Koan, saying cynically, "Non-profit organizations aren't supposed to be into sales."

"You know that's bullshit, Paul. My mail used to be full of letters from non-profit organizations, all putting the hard sell on. It's a big business."

Paul just shook his head. "I don't care to discuss it any further."

Koan went around his big desk and lifted his feet up onto it, crossing them. "By the way, Paul, Freddie's half-obsessed with a notion of elevating me to some kind of mystical status. You've often described the old man as a half-god. It wouldn't be inconsistent, would it? What do you think? Do I have the makings of a holy man in me?"

"Spoken with Chris's cynicism." Paul swept his slick hair back, riveting his eyes on Koan's. "Koan, I want to be perfectly frank with you. Something's bothering me."

"Fire. I'm all ears."

"First of all, I don't truly believe you trust Freddie to be running the show for you."

"There's some truth in that."

"Good. Despite that, you've given her a free reign. So which is it, are you losing it, or is there a more subtle motive in the background?"

"Such as?"

"Such as you putting me on trial."

"On trial?"

"Yes, a test of loyalties."

Koan stared sedately at the ceiling. "Paul, Paul. Are you suggesting I should never've given one big question any thought, namely, who you've been most loyal to, the old man or me? Or asked myself whether it's really me you've been looking out for, as opposed to those larger than life challenges that ignite fires in you?" Koan got up and walked over behind Paul, patting him on the shoulder. "Paul, you are without question one of the most loyal beings I've ever known. Still, you have something in common with Freddie, something I've imagined might eventually weld you two into allies. Just like her, you are a master at creating realities out of illusions. You're looking at your most successful creation, me."

Paul took a deep, protracted breath, but then chose not to respond.

Koan went back to his desk and sat down. "Paul, you must be torn apart inside. Freddie greeted me like I was a corpse. Remember all those times when I was wallowing in self-pity, insisting I'd be better off dead? Seems a terrible irony now, doesn't it? If I were to walk into Freddie's office and suggest I die, that I'm tired of all this and ready to end it, she'd probably jump for joy."

Paul had slumped over. When he lifted his head, his eyes were damp. "Beware of her, Koan. I've spent the last two days trying to get her to understand that selling you and the trust is going to take time, that people will counter with skepticism, and that we need to gradually flesh out the new image and unique personality of a relatively unknown man. You're well aware the old man recorded very little about himself. The idea came to me to collaborate with you. I understand you're a rather good writer. You can press my recall for bits and pieces of things the old man said, and together we can draw up a profile. Dare I say, there's also a more hidden motive in that."

"What might that be?"

"Such a laborious process could cause Freddie to lose interest in all of this. We've paid her a tidy sum for her work, more money than she'll ever need. I don't think she'd care to wait for us to slog through the long cerebral endeavors of putting together the uniqueness of the old man."

Koan lifted his chin, pressing his eyes tightly shut. "Paul, why are you so hellbent on getting rid of her?"

"Because she's a threat, Koan, a serious one."

"C'mon, Paul. Are you really convinced that Freddie has some sort of evil intentions? There's a difference between playful speculation and real deeds. She's talked off the top of her head about me being more worthwhile dead than alive, but it was mere nonsense."

"Koan, I am convinced she can't let go of ideas she's created in her mind. She doesn't tune in well to reality checks. Her ideas make a slick, smooth transition over to dogma, quite quickly, and the dogma translates into obsession. The other thing she seems to consider nonsense is when someone doesn't see things her way."

"Hey, Paul, maybe this will placate you." Koan smiled boyishly. "Recently I was talking with my old boyhood buddy about becoming a hermit, donning a robe, growing a long beard, you know, the whole thing. Just imagine, we could add some theatrics, like occasional sightings, blurred photographs. And, picking up on your comments, how about an old hermit writing cryptic messages, little beads of wisdom written on dried leaves?"

"High marks for imagination, Koan." Paul leaned close to Koan. "Take a deep breath, and no loud reactions."

Koan's forehead wrinkled, but then he caught the deep burning in Paul's eyes, an almost menacing look. "Okay, what is it?"

"A sense of loyalty won't allow me to act on my own, but act we must. I'll say it again. Stay cool. I know you well enough that you're not going to like what I have to say."

Koan couldn't imagine what Paul wanted to share with him. "Okay, agreed. I won't pop off."

"Good. You don't have to consent to what I'm going to relate to you, nor even acknowledge any support. I feel our situation requires a readjustment. You can't pull out square pegs that have jammed themselves into round holes. You have to destroy them in order to dislodge them. To the point, I am going to arrange for Freddie's exit."

"What? From the estate? Her contract with us?"

"No, Koan. Her obsession wouldn't allow her to accept a retreat. She must quietly pass on."

"Pass on to where, Paul?"

"Easy, Koan. We agreed, without emotions."

Koan bit down on the corner of his mouth. "Okay. I did agree. But, please, be more precise."

"Okay. I've looked at it as a hard, sober trade off, her finality versus yours."

"I'm sorry, Paul. I don't understand. You sound so grave, so somber."

"I have no doubts that that's where we're at. Freddie doesn't talk in hypotheticals just for the sake of discussion, does she?"

"Oh, I don't know, let me think…no, I guess not."

"I've come to understand her that well, too. She doesn't use hypothetical discussions to test ideas, she uses them for fine tuning. And the reason why she doesn't float ideas is her paranoia that someone might steal them. But to the point, she's spoken to me, a number of times, hypothetically about what would happen if you had an accident, more exacting, if you died."

Koan pondered a moment. "I see where you're headed, Paul. But, no, what you have in mind is unimaginable for me."

"Koan, I said at the outset, you don't have to give it your blessing. Just stand aside, close your eyes, look the other way. That will do."

"Look, Paul, I may seem to be a person with no deep values, but I have a few. I was brought up in a church, and I respect the ten commandments."

"Enough to be a target of one of them?"

"I don't believe that, Paul. That talk about a myth, that's trash. Little flights of the imagination."

"Freddie's not able to differentiate between imagination and actuality, illusion and reality. She creates her own real world as she goes along. There's nothing holy in her eyes. Answer this, Koan. Is it not within my role to protect your life?"

"Perhaps. Yes. But only if my life's really threatened."

"Fine, Koan. Your eyes don't need to be opened. But when it's passed, don't ever acknowledge this conversation to anyone, not even your special woman friend. That much I need affirmed, your agreement to silence."

Koan chewed on his lip. He was painfully aware that he trusted Paul more than Freddie. "Is there nothing I could say that could stop you, Paul?"

"No, nothing. You know I could have acted without holding this conversation, but, in the name of Jesus Christ, we are in this together, Koan. That I honor. So, back to normal. As far as I'm concerned, this conversation didn't take place."

Koan ran his hand firmly across his face. "Fine, Paul. I'm

delighted with the weather, too. Couldn't be happier."

After Paul had walked out, a chill coursed up and down Koan's spine, causing him to involuntarily shudder.

How will I be able to live with that? It was I who invited Freddie into this. Not even looking away can alleviate me of responsibility. It's not Freddie, per se. She's denied any allegiances to Chris, not carrying if he's dead or alive. I should feel no concerns about her life. It's Dad.

Dad, oh, Dad. I have to assume you believe in those commandments. You never broke one. If I now do, are we cut apart forever? Until the end of eternity?

Oh, God, it's not just Dad. I face him after I die. Now, in this life, I have but two people to save me from complete loneliness. Moss and Hope. Could I ever look either in the eye again, speak from my heart, without this bloody secret showing through? If I lost them, I'd just as well be dead. And Freddie wouldn't be around to give me the coup de grace.

Damn you, a thousand times, damn you, old man! This is another one of your goddamned inevitabilities, isn't it.

I can't stop Paul, because Paul's always on target. His assessments are never statements of probabilities. I know by now he knows when he speaks. As always, he will be right.

Okay, Paul. That conversation never took place. I will tell myself that over and over again until it becomes true. I'll start right now. Yes, our mission is more important than anything else, including Freddie. Sad, she's no longer with us, but practically irrelevant to where we want to go. My place is not here, not here listening to promotional schemes. I belong out in places like Southside. Yeah, that's the focus.

That's where I've got to go. I want to be away from here when it happens. What happens? Is something going to happen? I'm going to be surprised, and shocked.

During a brief exchange with Freddie, a few weeks earlier, Koan had reminded her that Father Nick and his group might play a useful role in helping create an image for the trust. To his surprise, Freddie was all enthusiasm, recommending that Koan take an active role in assessing what kind of alliance Father Nick might agree to, that is, using him and his programs in promotional spots for TV. She even asked to be involved in setting up the dates when Koan would meet with Father Nick.

The first such discussion had already taken place, and for the second time Koan was sitting with Father Nick at the Southside Community Center. The direction of the talks were predictable. Koan hadn't required any great intuition to anticipate Father Nick's opposition to publicity. In fact, the subjects they focused on wandered far from their agenda. Koan simply wanted to spend as much time there as possible, away from his estate, anticipating a phone call that something tragic had happened to Freddie.

"Mr. Koan, ya remember dat Thanksgivin' dinner? Ah was feelin' bad about wad happened, old Cornelius, how he ranted and raved atcha. Id's funny, but dat left a big impression on a lotta people 'round here. Day thinks a lotta you and whatcher doin' for us, but it was sumptin' fer dem to see old Cornelius stand up ta ya. Dey see old Corny as one of 'em, and he got respect. Id made a lotta people feel day were bein' recognized as human bein's. Ya know what ah'm sayin'?"

"I understand, Nick, I do. I also respect Cornelius. There's a lot of truth in what he says. There's an idea. Maybe he'd be the one to say something on TV?"

"Old Corny?! Hah! Don't see no big chance in dat. But ya can talk wid him. Dat would be sumptin', now wouldn't it, to see dat old bag a bones on the TV?"

Father Nick chuckled in a way that was familiar to Koan, a chuckle that engendered a sense of being at home.

Suddenly, a man, huffing and sweating, ran into the room. "Nick, ya gotta come! There's big trouble out dare!"

As Koan and Father Nick walked out of the Southside Community Center, they heard loud shouting coming from around a corner. It wasn't the shouting of a few people, but many. Turning onto the street from which the noise was coming, they stopped in their tracks. A few hundred people, mostly the homeless, were chanting. Further down the street were vans and police cars, a bull horn blaring. The policemen weren't in uniforms, but riot gear.

Koan stopped, his face pale. "How do these people merit this? God, Jesus, look at your imperfect world."

Father Nick stood next to Koan, twisting his meaty hands in anguish, muttering over and over, "Jesus Christ, Jesus Christ…"

Suddenly, the hollow-eyed face of Cornelius was in front of them. "They're going to kill you, Koan!"

Neither Nick nor Koan knew how to react to Cornelius's accusation.

"Corny, wad da hell is goin' on here?!"

"Supposedly a large number of people were refusing to vacate a building, and some of them were rumored to have weapons. At least that's what the police are saying got them out here. But there isn't a grain of truth in it. This was all organized. Staged."

Koan saw a cloud of tear gas explode at the front of the crowd and flinched.

"This is mad. Why, why is this happening?"

"It's you, Koan. I learned about it yesterday. A couple of the guys sent in to prepare this recognized me. They couldn't believe I was here. I guess they worshipped me back then, when I was on top. It got their egos all pumped up. They couldn't resist telling me what was going on."

For Father Nick, Cornelius was being too long-winded. "Well, tell us, come on, wad's happenin'!"

"Okay, okay. They barfed the whole thing out to me. That woman you were with, Koan, that Freddie Folkstone, she's behind this."

"Freddie?"

"Yes. She set this up like a high-priced commercial spot. Getting the police in here was to establish a cover. They needed a bit of chaos, and it looks to me like they're pulling that off very well."

Koan rubbed his temple, anguish written over his face. "But why the hell? People are going to get hurt!"

The grin that came over Cornelius's face was perverse. "Hurt? You're worried about people getting hurt?" Cornelius broke out laughing.

"Wad's so goddamned funny?!" Father Nick's face was red with anger.

"I'm sorry, but hearing Koan being concerned about someone getting hurt. You don't have a clue, do you?"

Both men looked at Cornelius in baffled silence.

"Okay. This is their plan. Sometime soon, all hell's going to break loose. They assumed people around here would know how to put together things like Molotov cocktails. Right. Street people are really a clandestine lot of sophisticated urban terrorists. Anyway, they wanted some real big explosions. More confusion and chaos. Yes, they want blood, dead people. And they want you."

Koan pointed weakly to his chest.

"Yes. You are going to be hauled out there, put right in the middle, hoisted up so the cameras can get you, full portrait and all. They're counting on your acting heroic. Then, wham! The finale. You're gone. Charred ashes. Beyond recognition. Dead among the people you've chosen to lead out of their misery. Pretty good dramatics, huh?"

Father Nick seemed to doubt Cornelius's claims, but the violence already going on in front of him had him terribly agitated as well. Koan stared into Cornelius's sunken eyes, as deeply as he could look, and suddenly, with a deep shudder, he recognized truth.

"I'm supposed to be killed. Goddamned, it's true. It's as Paul said."

Father Nick's face was tight. He studied Koan. Koan's apparent acceptance of Cornelius's explanation satisfied him. "Wadda we gonna do?"

Before Cornelius could respond, Koan broke in. "Why should I fear dying? Maybe this is the right place, the right moment, the right way to end it all. My life seems to be inevitabilities."

Cornelius looked at Koan in disbelief. "Such noble crap! You want to die as someone else's sacrificial lamb? I've come to think more of you than that. You're a fuckin' fool. I even got to believing you were making some rather grand choices, ones that might even make a difference. And now you simply want to let someone pull your strings? A two-bit promo queen with a morbid mind? Well, I'm not going to be out there doing her the honor. No, if this happens, it gives me one last mission in life, to put poison in the lady's drink. She needs to be exterminated."

A twinge of trust in Cornelius came over Koan. "Okay, tell me, then, what do you think we should do?"

"First of all, we go quietly back to the center, as inconspicuously as possible, no looks of panic or whatever. I'll make sure no one's right behind us. You go to the base of the stairwell, then we'll disappear."

Without another word, Koan and Father Nick did as Cornelius said. Waiting at the stairwell, Father Nick suddenly broke out yelling he was going to die with his people.

"They've needed a leader like you, Nick, they were waiting for you, and you want to take that away from them? You can't do that. Tomorrow they'll still be here. And you have to be too."

Koan was surprised at himself, how impassioned he spoke, how pleading, that he actually threw his arms around Father Nick hugging him. It worked, snapping Father Nick back to sobriety.

Cornelius showed up. "Let's go."

They descended the stairs to the basement of the building. Not even Father Nick knew there was a half-boarded up opening to the basement of the building next door. Once they got through this, they followed passageways, crawled under old wooden studs. It was as if Cornelius had a cockroach's knowledge of every local nook and cranny. After awhile,

Koan had no idea where they might be, perhaps blocks away from where they'd started.

They finally entered into what appeared to be an old coal cellar. The thick door had levers on it to hold it shut. Suddenly, a white light flashed through Koan's head, and he sank to the damp, concrete floor, immediately losing consciousness.

23

Paul stormed into Freddie's office, yelling, "What in the hell's happened?"

Freddie was reviewing papers spread out in front of her. She looked up at Paul with a perverse smile on her lips. "So you've heard? Sit down. Please."

Paul walked up to Freddie's desk, leaning against it, his body quaking. "Is it true?!"

Freddie leaned back, grasping papers in her hand. "Yes, it's true. Koan's dead. And here are the press releases. We have it, Paul. The future is ours."

As Paul muttered under his breath, Freddie moved her chin upward in a defiant gesture, the smug smile still pasted to her face. Paul's instinctual self-control grabbed a hold of him and pulled him back from Freddie's desk to a chair, which he sank into with great heaviness.

"So, it's over?"

"Yes, Paul. It was a masterpiece. Clockwork. Brilliant. The news coverage has been perfect. The police in their riot gear, like a Roman legion moving in. Boom. Balls of fire. Perfect execution."

"Execution. What an appropriate term. And now you have the martyr you wanted?"

"Oh, Paul, don't be so cynical. We have reason to celebrate. I admit, I owe you one. I left you out, but I had to. You were too attached to him. Still, underneath those superficial emotions, I was certain you'd approve. You wanted this outcome as much as anyone, why, because it elevates the game to a new level. And like me, you live for the challenge. You see, I know you very well."

Paul's eyes narrowed. "You're worse than he described you."

"Who?"

"Koan. Or didn't you ever suspect Koan was Chris?"

Freddie maintained her detachment, continuing to grin diabolically at Paul.

"Paul, I understand if I wounded your pride, and I offer my apologies, sincere apologies, but, please, no games. Not now. We don't have time."

Paul rose and leaned over Freddie's desk until his face was level with hers.

"You didn't even suspect, did you? Callused bitch!"

Freddie started, but recovered immediately. "I don't take well to such words."

"Or any other description of reality. Listen, Freddie, and listen good. You talked with him, tried to charm him, and I suspect wanted to be his lover, but never once did you recognize who you were with. Koan was your husband."

"Come on, Paul. This is cheap, below you. Where's the ice

cold master Koan so raved about?"

In an uncharacteristic outburst of rage, Paul swept the papers off of Freddie's desk. "Those releases should all be headlined, 'Wife Executes Ex-Husband!' You wouldn't notice you were in way over your head even if you were drowning. You don't even know who you killed."

Freddie finally accepted that Paul wasn't merely peeved. "Okay, Paul, if there are some small details I wasn't aware of, we have a few minutes to hash them out. Speak your peace."

"Freddie, the truth is very simple. Chris, your husband, wasn't dead."

"So? It would've made little difference to me whether he was dead or off on some South Seas island. Yes, there was a time when I was bent on proving he was dead, so I could finally collect his insurance, but then you offered me a lot more, and that was the end of that chapter. Basta!"

"You still aren't listening, are you, Freddie? You found Chris. You stood eye to eye with him. But you never asked, or listened. He wasn't a good actor. I'm sure he gave himself away, many times. But you didn't want to hear it. My God, I was so sure the two of you were going to approach me, hand in hand, and tell me the whole things over with, that you wanted back together. I was so sure that I had a whole set of options worked out. I was prepared to restructure everything."

"What the hell are you talking about, Paul? Where was Chris that he could have been standing there with me?"

Paul's eyes were wide open and glowed. "Goddamn you, Freddie, wake up! Koan was Chris. Chris was inside the old man's body."

"You know that's nonsense, Paul." Gradually the self-confidence in Freddie's voice was eroding.

Paul turned his head to the side, as if he couldn't face his own cynicism. "Freddie, you want so much to be a master of illusions, yet you didn't catch one right in front of you, your own husband becoming the most powerful man in the world, a man you wanted to be so close to, and now wanted to kill and make a martyr."

Pathetically, Freddie tried to test Paul, but the more questions she fired at him, the more apparent it became that he was stating the truth. Bits and pieces of things Koan had said to her drifted back, causing her body to twitch. Even though she had put calls on hold, her phone buzzed, signaling something of great urgency, but Freddie ignored it. She fidgeted, breaking off a nail and cursing. Finally, she picked up a paperweight and threw it against the wall, the crystal globe exploding into a thousand splinters.

"Goddamn him!" Freddie got up and paced around the office. "That bastard! He played games with me. Telling me Chris wanted to say goodbye. That asshole! He never was capable of speaking straight to my face. That goddamned deceitful bastard."

Freddie made her way back to her desk and sank heavily into her chair. "Well, fuck you, Paul, and fuck him as well. Do you really want to stand there in judgment of me? You? Whatever ungodly thing you did to Chris, it must have been you behind it. Does that make you any better than me?"

The only sound in the room for the next quarter-hour was the repeated buzzing of the phoneset on Freddie's desk. Paul had raised his chin, several times, as if to speak, but refrained each time. When he finally spoke, it was in a softer tone.

"Okay, Freddie, we can let the issue of guilt rest. Tell me, though, why'd you choose to go it alone? My instincts tell me I should let you fry."

"Fry? Why should that happen? And assuming something went awry, why me, and not you?"

"Because you've burned the only evidence that could tie Angstrom Industries back to Chris. Or are you suddenly going to claim Koan wasn't really Koan? Prove that."

"What about setting up my company?"

"That was a monthly event in Angstrom Industries. Capital ventures, acquisitions, divestitures, partnerships. Purely coincidental. Don't think I didn't ponder that a long time, how to package it. You're free to read the files. It was business as usual. Of course, you could plead insanity, or don't you think that's what people would conclude, if you told them your little fairy tale, your myth?"

"And you don't think I was just as meticulous as you were?"

Paul smiled diabolically. "Where did I hear about this martyrdom scheme of yours? It wasn't today. A week ago? No, it was even longer than that. It was a caller from the Southside Community Center. Someone who knew you. I heard most of the details, and if there's anything I can damn myself for it's not acting quickly enough. But you ask if you were meticulous? That call makes one wonder how many other people are speaking."

Freddie covered her face with her hands, then dropped her head to the desk, but Paul didn't relent. "I guess you didn't need me. You had the perfect execution worked out. My input may have weakened your plans."

"Shut up! Damn you! Shut up!"

An hour later, Freddie sat in Paul's unlighted office, the gathering dusk engulfing them.

"Paul, I can't go on with this." After she had repeated this a second time, Paul asked her whether there were any alternatives. "A reality has occurred, you're tied to the consequences. Something has to happen."

"Who cares? I've only had one real phobia in my life. Guilt. My mother recognized how effectively the fear of guilt motivated me, and she twisted and turned it into my soul to get me to perform."

"Guilt often transforms itself into obligation."

Freddie, her makeup gone, stared without expression at Paul. "Are you always so coldblooded? Such a wiseassed bastard?"

Paul was unruffled. "I'm trying to listen and understand."

"Well, why do you think I run instead of walk? It's the guilt of a child who could never live up. Don't belittle it, you sorry son of a bitch. "Freddie continued bemoaning her childhood, but then struck out again at Paul.

"You don't possess one ounce of empathy. I loved Chris. And you? You simply used him. That separates the two of us. I'm hurting."

"I don't buy that, Freddie. There's a kind of love that helps a troubled soul find peace. Chris was searching for peace. Love would've picked up on that. I'm not sure what kind of love Chris felt toward you, but he cared, cared enough to try to tip you off when he felt your life was in danger. But enough. We aren't addressing the clock, which is ticking toward the end of a day." Paul got up and paced around the room. "Whatever pieces are left, the world's looking, and someone's got to deliver a clear message to them."

Freddie looked up, the light from outside reflecting on a stream of tears across her cheeks. "Does that mean you're still in this, Paul?"

"I've had one allegiance in my life, to Koan, and that will always be firmly anchored. I'm not speculating on where things go from here. To start with, I'll have to know everything. Underscore that ten times. Everything. And if it's in any way tainted, you're on your own, Freddie."

"Paul, what am I supposed to do?"

Paul stood up and looked at his watch. "I doubt if you have more than twenty-four hours to present your case. I'm available between now and then. But I won't be dragged into anything. All I want to hear is where there were loose ends, and what you've done about them. That was past tense. Loose ends, after one or two days, become fixtures, and, then, I'm afraid, it's all too late. Nothing in writing. Verbal only. And in person. At my home." Paul started to leave, but turned back around. "Freddie, personal ambition kills. Living for something makes death less important. I'll be available."

• • •

"Ah'm glad ya could come, sir." Father Nick was standing on a cluttered sidewalk right up the street from the old Burning Bridges bar. Next to him was Cornelius.

"This is a strange time and place to meet anyone, but you said it was of extreme importance?"

"That depends." Cornelius had stepped toward Paul. "Are you shedding tears for Freddie Folkstone?"

"She is to me only a past tense."

"As is Koan Angstrom?"

"He isn't dead."

Paul's reply visibly startled both Father Nick and Cornelius. Cornelius gathered himself, asking Paul how he meant that.

"In some form or another, Koan Angstrom will live on. I personally have no other mission than that. But can we come to why we're here? Your community center would've been a more hospitable place to meet."

"Sir, ah knows. Cornelius and ah'd rather no one hears what we gotta say."

"But can we come to the point, the purpose?"

Cornelius moved up to Paul, their faces only inches apart. "You said Koan Angstrom, in some form, will continue to exist. We know that is so."

Paul stared into Cornelius's deep eyes. "You have his body?"

"In a sense. We know where it might be. How do you respond to that?"

"To use your phrase, that depends. That depends wholly on what your motives are for calling me here to tell me that. If we can establish that, I can be more clear about my response."

Hope wiped away the tears swelling in the corners of her eyes as she stroked the brush over the unkempt hair of Freddie, who was sitting in front of her, wearing only a light blue hospital gown.

"Would you feel better if we put a little makeup on you, prettied you up a bit?"

Hope's question was ignored. In fact, Freddie hardly made eye contact with her, Freddie's eyes peering as if there were a group of people standing behind Hope.

"I know I should have stayed with the name Fay. I lost the magic of that name. I could have become the good fairy. I would have sparkled, kept my magical wand. People have so many wishes. I could have made them all happen."

On the surface, Hope wanted to humor Freddie, lift her spirits from the deep depression the medical staff said she had lapsed into, but Hope's forte was in hooking into the bedrock of reality, not encouraging delusions. With obvious discomfort she said, "I'm sure you would've made a good fairy, Freddie."

A dim smile lit up Freddie's pale face. "Yes, I would have taken everyone to a fantasyland where they could be happy. And I would have done away with all mothers and fathers. Children don't need parents to tell them what to do. Are they going to let me be the good fairy?"

"When you get better, Freddie, maybe then."

Freddie reached out and clutched Hope's upper arm so firmly that it hurt Hope. "Is that evil old man, Koan, dead?"

"Yes, Freddie, I'm afraid so."

"He didn't like fairies. Did you know that? I shouldn't have told him my name was Fay. I think he would have tried to kill me. He didn't want to see everyone happy. Not the way I do. Do you think I'll get wings so I can fly around?"

"Like an angel?"

"Do angels have wings?"

Hope was at her wit's end. She was asking herself why she had even come to the psychiatric ward to witness Freddie in such a state, knowing at the same time that she had no on or off button for her own compassion.

"Yes, Freddie. I believe angels have wings, I guess so they can fly above all the pain and suffering of this world."

"Maybe I could be an angel too? But don't you have to be dead to be an angel?"

"Why worry about that right now, Freddie? What you need now is to rest." Hope tried to take Freddie into her arms, but Freddie fought off the embrace. Backing away, Hope tried a more familiar tone on her once friend. "Girl, you've gone through one helluva ride. I understand the pain. For now, I wouldn't be questioning things so much. Just try to come back down to earth and prepare for some kind of fresh start."

Freddie's eyes darted around reflecting her agitated emotions. "But I've got to fly. I hear everyone asking for the good fairy. I've got to get wings. They want me. Don't you hear them shouting?"

Hope's head sank, then she twisted around and got up, moving toward the door with a slow-motion gait. Her finger pressed the button to call the orderly to let her out of Freddie's locked room. It was all she could do to fight back a wave of sobs.

The door was unlocked for her. Hope half-turned to Freddie, but seeing Freddie trying to reach around to her shoulder blades murmuring why she didn't have wings was too much for Hope. Without saying goodbye, she walked out.

Outside in the hall, Hope broke down and cried. A nurse saw her and came over, circling her arm around her, asking if there was anything she could do. "If I were to have a wish granted, it would be that two so promising lives could have found some better direction. But that was too much to hope. Even I see that now."

24

Time, events, even Koan's own identity, had lost all significance. His breathing, bouts of hunger, the telltale sensation of insects creeping across his face, were the only testimony he might still be alive. Gradually it became apparent that he'd again made a detour around his own finality. He recognized the man who forced water and nourishment to his lips. It was Cornelius. The man, who had spoken so vehemently and impassioned on other occasions, remained oddly quiet, the hollow sockets around his bulging eyes making his head look like a lifeless skull.

Koan had difficulty pulling himself into a state of consciousness, and his will waned. He did, however, talk, often very coherently. Frequently the name Shepherdstown was uttered. Most of the time, though, Koan hung in a sleeplike state.

Koan was awakened by voices and tugging on his body. Cornelius was still there, but he had been joined by Father Nick and, to Koan's surprise, Moss. Koan whimsically smiled at what seemed an affirmation that it was his funeral or burial. His body felt lighter, was being lifted, and a caress of cold air brushed over his face.

To be gazing into the warm dark eyes of Moss, who was sitting across from him, gave Koan a sense of comfort, the kind that comes from recalling simpler times, a state of being that one could oversee and control. The setting was also reminiscent of childhood. The room was as basic as a shelter can be. The cabin, if it was worthy of that name, was just one room, wood slats nailed to poles, the floor dirt. Furnishings were conspicuous through their absence. Moss and Koan were sitting in cheap, folding lawn chairs on either side of a simple wood table. Otherwise, there was a lantern, a portable kerosene heater, an old army cot with a few blankets on it, and a crudely boarded together cabinet for provisions.

"The man who had ya with him, Cornelius, he was dead certain ya were a goner." Moss shook his head slowly. "At first I thought so too. Ya know, Bonnie Sue and me, we saw in the news where you'd been killed. We were mighty surprised ya were such a big shot. We were feelin' real broken up when this fella called Nick showed up at our place. I can't relate to ya how spooky I felt. I'd seen you'd been killed, and a man comes askin' for me, takes me outside and tells me I have ta to come and getcha. I still thoughtcha were dead, when I saw ya in that old building there in Pontifica. Mumblin' around the way ya were, ya seemed like a ghost."

Moss ladled soup into a bowl for Koan, then chuckled, as Koan carefully guided a spoonful to his mouth.

"Not often ya get to speak to a dead man. Ole Chris

woulda been proud. He used to believe people never really died. Sorry. Ah shouldn't be makin' fun. Yer in a sorry state. They told me, 'Don't bring 'em back, or tell a soul who he is.' Least ah got this old cabin up here, where no one'd ever come. By the way, we ain't far from where we built that ole tree house. That's why I put this old shack up here. Couldn't get up in the tree, like we did back then, but I wanted to be able to come up this way sometimes and think. There's a little pond not far with good fishin'. Had a rock slide, years ago, that blocked up the creek."

Koan looked up, his bloodshot eyes fixing on Moss's. "Guess things've turned around full circle. I was gonna help the world, and here's the world helping me."

"Don't go talkin' 'bout who's helpin' who. Just concentrate on mendin' yerself."

Weeks passed. Koan's whitish hair had grown down to his shoulders, merging at his jaw with a beard that framed his mouth. Moss had brought him razors and a mirror so he could shave, but he'd chosen not to. Looking at himself in the mirror, Koan concluded, if it weren't for the sweatshirt and khaki pants he wore, he could have passed for the old hermit of the woods, the one he and Moss had befriended in their youth.

Koan's physical condition had turned out to be a lot less serious than initially suspected. The explosions that were intended to kill him had caused the building he, Father Nick, and Cornelius had been hiding in to collapse. Koan had been struck on the head by a falling block of concrete, suffering at least a severe concussion that had kept him in a state of unconsciousness for days. Also, Koan hadn't taken in much nourishment and had suffered from exposure. To everyone's relief, he hadn't required a doctor, something no one wanted to risk. When Moss remarked he was looking as fit as ever, Koan joked it had to be Bonnie Sue's excellent home cooking. A part of him was celebrating his return to the simple roots of his life.

Reality caught up with him one day. Moss had brought Cornelius and Father Nick to the cabin, quite an ordeal for Cornelius, whose health seemed to be rapidly deteriorating. From them, he learned they had contacted Paul and met with him.

"Why?! Why does he have to know I'm still alive?"

Cornelius struggled to lift his head. "He doesn't know. He doesn't know you're alive. We didn't say so, directly."

"Id's true, Mr. Koan. Ah think he believes we got your body stashed away somewheres."

"Paul's clever. He picks up on the tiniest hint. I'm sure he's asked himself why you got in contact with him. You didn't ask for money, did you?"

"No, sir."

"It would've been better. He probably would have paid you something, figuring you were just trying to milk a fantastic thread of hope. That you didn't want anything, that's going to bother the life out of him. Goddamned it. You may not understand me, but it's been good to be dead."

There was silence, except for the sounds of the woods outside, until Cornelius went into a dreadful fit of coughing. Koan was overcome by a feeling of compassion, an emotion he wasn't used to.

"Can't you get to a doctor, Corny, or a hospital?"

"What good would that do?" Cornelius had to cough some more. "I'm dying."

Koan helped Moss and Father Nick get Cornelius to his makeshift bed.

"Corny, tell me, why did you feel it was important to contact Paul?"

"I can't offer you logic, Koan. I've learned something, living on the streets, in abandoned buildings, putting up with the likes of old fatso here, Father Nick. As long as there's still a few breaths left, there's meaning. I've helped others, kicked a few butts, right Nick?"

"Ya sure has. Ah gotta give you credit fer dat."

Koan laid his hand on Cornelius's skeletal hand. "I see. You feel I should be going back to help, however I can. I haven't ruled that out, or anything else. I would like it to be on my terms, though."

Cornelius looked up at Koan, his head swaying slightly to the side. "I understand what it means to be preempted. That wasn't…" Cornelius had to blow phlegm from his throat, "…that wasn't my intention. It's your choice."

Cornelius and Father Nick had to stay overnight, as Cornelius wasn't strong enough to make the trek back. The next day, with Moss's assistance, they left, leaving Koan pondering his next move.

"Moss, I've decided. I'm going to be alive."

Moss raised his eyebrows, then laughed. "Seems a pretty basic decision."

Koan laughed with him. "What I mean is I'm going to let them notify Paul, what we talked about the other night. He can tell me what the situation is, what choices I may have. I can't do a thing without knowing more."

"What's going to stop him from telling others?"

"Moss, Paul is a lot like we were. He wouldn't share a secret with anyone. Except for maybe you, I've never met anyone I could trust more."

"He sounds like quite a man. It'd be nicer if we could go on down to the house, but who knows who might come by?"

"Paul will be willing to come up here. He's a city person, but he's got a will that's tough as nails. He'll come."

Cornelius had made a slight comeback and was strong enough to meet Paul again, along with Father Nick.

"I trust you're still not willing to tell me what I'm supposed to find. I'm willing to trust you, though. I've sensed we share an attachment to Koan, though we may be coming from different places."

Cornelius peered intently at Paul. "You love him, don't

you."

The statement agitated Paul. "Love? No, I prefer attachment. Respectful attachment. But the semantics aren't important. Are they?"

"I guess not."

Paul was told he should call Father Nick and tell him when he had a full day available, as it would require as much as twenty-four hours. He called the next day, saying he was holding the whole weekend free. Father Nick told Paul to wear outdoors clothes and shoes for hiking. Just before daybreak, Saturday morning, Paul drove up at the Southside Community Center. Father Nick was standing there, but he said little, directing Paul to another car. A blindfold was put around Paul's head, and the car sped off with Moss at the wheel.

Koan couldn't remain still. He walked around outside the hut, checking regularly whether anyone was coming around the hill off to the north. Finally he heard voices, but it was another five minutes before he saw Moss and Paul coming into the clearing.

Koan had never shown any real affection toward Paul, other than an occasional pat on the shoulder, or a hearty handshake. Koan gambled purposefully toward Paul, then threw his arms open, the two men embracing and smacking each other on the back many times.

"Koan, I had hoped…who says there aren't miracles? God, it's good to see you."

After some more hugs, Koan said to Paul, "I would've thought you'd be rejoicing to finally be rid of me."

Paul hesitated in responding. "It's true. There were positives in your death. But as you're witnessing, I've felt a loss. A paradox, if you like."

The weather had cooperated wonderfully, providing a late spring day with a deep blue sky, brilliant sunshine, but without oppressive heat. Instead of sitting inside the hut, they brought the chairs and table outside. Paul showed great discomfort at being so immersed in nature, swatting bugs away with an occasional look of panic. Soon, however, his mind took over and blocked these things out.

It took awhile for Koan to explain everything that had transpired, but Paul listened attentively, talking very little.

"Some people seem to care very much about you. Your experience must have been enough to cure any old vestiges of cynicism."

"Not completely. I've been deathly curious about how you would take my being alive. My departure, and Freddie's arrest, I can imagine that's close to a perfect set-up for you? By the way, how's Freddie doing?"

"You still care?"

"I guess I do."

"Then you haven't heard. The news was to be released this morning. She committed suicide. I say it with no malice, but it's just as well. She'd gone off the deep end. You knew they'd put her in an institution?"

Koan confirmed that Moss had given him that information from the news.

Paul swatted at a pesky fly, then cleared his throat. "There's great irony in all that's transpired. I'm not sure the old man could've wished a starker contrast between the forces of good and evil. The press has had a field day with it. Freddie's been personified as obsessively greedy, power hungry, self-promoting, devoid of an moral restraints. It's as if they were waiting for someone to come along so they could pile all the woes of our society on them. In their little tragedy, Koan is being depicted as the bigger-than-life hero, dedicating his life and resources to the betterment of mankind. One prominent conservative columnist is drawing an analogy to the crucifixion of Christ, calling Freddie the inherent sin in mankind, and the profound message in Koan's death is a reiteration of the message that our sins through Christ will be forgiven. It's a real carnival atmosphere, and I wouldn't feel sorry about missing it. One more thing, the ultimate irony. If she were still alive, Freddie would probably be claiming this to be the perfect outcome she envisioned, the birth of a great myth."

Neither Paul nor Koan showed a trace of amusement. Koan sighed deeply, his hands folded in his lap. "Paul, I've never felt so at peace. The turmoil you describe seems light years away. And it comforts me that I instigated none of it, that I don't have the slightest smudge on me. My ego feels both inflated and humble. So much ado about me."

Moss, who had left after bringing Paul, returned with a large cooler, which contained food prepared by Bonnie Sue and refreshments. Bonnie Sue had even insisted Moss take a checkered table cloth. The simple, picniclike atmosphere was relaxing. Even Paul got into joking around about earlier times. After they had eaten pieces of blueberry pie, Paul's face got tight, signaling Koan something important was about to be discussed.

Finally Paul asked, "Koan, I don't know if it's a subject you care to discuss, but have you considered the possibility of coming back?"

Koan frowned. "Returning to Pontifica?"

"Yes. As Koan Angstrom."

Koan's laugh was one of disbelief. "I don't understand, Paul. Aren't you perfectly satisfied with the way things are right now?"

"My question wasn't in jest, Koan. I would welcome you back. I'm sure plausible explanations could be given. I haven't given it sufficient thought, but there's even a possibility of leveraging it to good advantage. Surely, you don't wish to stay here?"

"For now, yes, I'm quite satisfied to remain here."

"But you're not closing the door, that is, to considering the other?"

"No, I won't close the door, Paul. For now, though, I'd rather not discuss it."

Koan did feel a slight sadness when Paul departed. The emotion annoyed him, because it implied a chunk of his self-identity was somehow tied to Paul. Also, in the following days, Moss pushed Koan to consider Paul's offer, creating a sense of resentment in Koan. It was as if the complete freedom of choice his situation offered him was being challenged. The emergence of small pangs of guilt finally broke Koan.

"Moss, can you do me another favor. I hate making you my messenger, but there's one other person I'd very much like to see."

Two days later, Moss came into the clearing with a woman, Hope. Her eyes were puffy and red. Moss had had to tell her why she should go with him, and hearing Koan was still alive unleashed her emotions.

Just as with Paul, there was a long series of hugs. Hope kept pulling back and looking at Koan as if he were a ghost, then hugging him again to her with all her strength. Once again, Moss went to get fresh provisions. Koan discovered he was in great need of comforting, which Hope most generously provided. Most of the rest of day was consumed by small talk and soft words.

Moss looked at his watch. "It's gettin' time to move on out."

Hope gazed at Koan with a look of tender affection. "Any reason why I can't stay here tonight?"

"We won't fit on that cot."

"There's the ground. I've never slept on the earth, but I've also never felt such a strong desire to do so."

Neither Koan nor Moss argued strongly against Hope staying. Later, the lantern the only light, the nocturnal sounds of the woods all around them, two bodies pressed close together, as if wanting to merge into one. Sleep didn't adequately describe the night. Koan and Hope wrapped themselves in bliss.

When the sunlight finally awakened them, Koan felt rejuvenated. He teased Hope into joining him on a sprint to the pond, where they both ran into the water stark naked. Koan couldn't remember when he felt so playful. Hope also acted more youthful and unencumbered. Finally, they threw themselves on the grassy bank, letting the warm sun dry their bodies.

Hope reached over and took Koan's hand. "You've never seeded life?"

Koan looked over at Hope with a frown. "You mean, gotten a woman pregnant?"

"Yes, that's exactly what I mean."

"You're not suggesting you'd…"

"I'm not suggesting anything. Motherhood's never entered my mind. There was just this feeling, like I was being inseminated. A glow."

"A glow? Hmmm."

An hour later, Moss arrived, and Bonnie Sue had outdone herself. There were fresh-baked biscuits and air-dried ham. Moss quickly fried eggs on the small stove. Several times Moss and Hope murmured their satisfaction. Awhile later, Moss excused himself, saying he had chores to do but would be back mid-afternoon.

Although Hope didn't bring up the subject of Koan returning, Koan wanted to discuss it. He felt a need to find a balance for the arguments Paul was sure to have when he next came to visit.

To Koan's surprise, Hope immediately took Paul's side. "Even if it has to be packaged as a miracle, hey, you're looking at someone who already believes it's one. You've died twice on me, you know." Hope lowered her eyes. "There's also a selfish motive for my wanting you back. I'm one of those common people you've set out to help, so you can now associate with me, publicly, or?"

That brought a pleasant laugh and hug from Koan. "Sounds good to me. But you do understand, don't you, why I'd love to just disappear?"

"I understand the emotions. You've got simplicity. Not an obligation in the world. Yes, I understand that."

"I hear a 'but' wanting to come out?"

"Okay, yes. I've always felt there was an unselfish you wanting to come out. I think that's what the decision boils down to."

"But why is it selfish to desire peace? Real peace?"

"My dear friend, desiring peace is not making peace. I mean, it sounds like you're trying to tell me that somewhere like this is peace, birds singing, no sirens or cars honking outside. Personally I'd find it kind of spooky after awhile. How can one be alive without interacting with other human beings? Koan, if I've read all that pain in you, even back as the dashing Chris, the pain wasn't in your ears, or eyes, it was in your soul. Isn't that where you desire to find peace, in your soul, not merely peacefulness around you?"

"Do you understand me that well, Hope?"

"I pray that I do."

25

After the two days with Hope, Koan felt pumped up and ready to face Paul again. The night before Paul was to meet him again, Koan dreamed profusely.

One set of dreams focused on Hope. The key event was establishing a bond between them. The accompanying emotions were scattered across a full spectrum. Dominating was a sense of wellness, fulfillment, security.

Koan rarely dwelled on his mother, primarily because there were no outstanding issues to resolve out of the past relationship. His mother had been simply that, a mother, the womb from which he'd emerged, the nurturer, his comforter during infancy, teething, the emergence of crawling and walking, mobility, and the freedom to discover the world around him. His mother had remained completely detached from conflicts Chris had with his father. How she managed such detachment was still a wonder to Koan, but she had executed it so successfully that right up to her death, Chris addressed his parents as two wholly separate entities.

In his dreams, Hope offered the same nurturing his mother had provided him. Hope was warmth, soothing, an offerer of peace, deep inner peace, a buffer against the agitation and conflict of the world around Koan.

These dreams, coming repeatedly during the night, ended, though, with a cutting stab into the engulfing state of serenity. Unlike his mother, who had more often than not remained silent or spoken in the softest of tones, Hope would suddenly blurt out statements, challenging Koan's wish to ball himself like a fetus in her arms.

Hope couldn't accept that as an end in itself. In one such dream sequence Hope suddenly shouted, "There's nothing I desire more than to comfort you when you're in pain, but, goddamn, you can't be in pain all the time!"

The other most frequent kind of dreams involved Koan going back to lead the new movement. In these, his being inflated, his image grew light and soared up above the heights of the tallest buildings in Pontifica. In one dream, he was illuminated by spotlights, bright white against the dark heavens above him. There was also chanting, simply his name over and over again, from thousands of voices. The sense of elation was overwhelming and awoke him, so strong was his desire to yell with joy.

These dreams too ended abruptly. In one, Koan, hovering weightlessly above the towers of the city and, waving to the masses below, turned to see a point of light in the blackened sky, the light becoming ever more intense. It appeared to be something like a fighter aircraft, on it a needle-shaped nose. Koan became frightened when he realized this aircraft was headed right at him. At it closed in, he made out the face of the person piloting the aircraft. It was his father. The expression on his face was intense, however, with no other discernible emotion. Seconds later, just as the needle nose of the plane was about to hit him and explode his inflated being, Koan awoke with a loud wail.

Only one of these dreams ended differently. His father had again appeared to prick the bubble of his celebrating, but this time Paul appeared, grabbed his father in a headlock and squeezed with all his might. His father's tongue hung out, he gasped and choked, then withered up and disappeared. Koan's emotions were a blend of terror, relief, profound sadness. Paul, having rid him of his father's image, walked over to Koan, embraced him, saying, "It was time for me to take his place. We will understand each other, Koan. You will have your peace."

The new day broke, and Paul returned, this time more relaxed. He'd also gone to an outfitter and wore attire better designed for a trek in the woods. Koan couldn't suppress a laugh, and Paul joined in, the two demonstratively happy to be together again.

"So, Paul, what remains of the new beginning, the great myth?"

Paul's smile was wry. "More volunteers than we could ever use. Freddie was right about one thing. I still find it a bit incredible, but your death has made Koan Angstrom even more mystical. Overnight, something like a cult following has arisen. We're struggling with that. It may be but a brief reaction, but if it isn't, we need to find ways to harness all the sudden energy. I have to admit, it borders on the overwhelming."

With his usual hesitancy and choice of words, Paul asked Koan whether he had come closer to a decision on coming back. "I've had a special someone ask me the same thing. I admit her reasons had more appeal. Do you know, Paul, I've never done that thing people call settling down? Maybe no life's complete without it."

"I wouldn't know, Koan. I've thought about it, and there's every reason in the world for you to come back. And the biggest of all has to do with you. Your causes. In the time I've known you, nothing has lit you up more, Koan. The attempt on your life has totally distracted from any suspicions as to why you suddenly want to be so generous. The old man would be proud. As fate would have it, Freddie's scheme and its failure have validated your causes. Groups who were wary about coming near us, for fear of the associations that might create, are now ready to fly. I can't imagine anything that could fulfill you more."

Koan peered at Paul as if trying to extract his bottom line motives. "Paul, what I don't understand is why my reappearance would make any difference. From what you've told me, Koan Angstrom's alive and well. At least his myth. Frankly, I fail to see why I'd be needed."

"I disagree with that, Koan. A myth can be interpreted and embellished in many different ways. It's like an uncut diamond. The world's more receptive than ever to hearing exactly what kind of person Koan Angstrom was, what his motivations and values were. Sure, even if we do nothing, he'll become, at the very least, a colorful folk hero. But I know you recognize there's a lot more potential in it than that. Koan, you can influence the outcome."

Koan's head sank as if a weight had been placed on it. "Paul, I feel incapable of living up to the picture you're painting. You know damned well how often I've screwed up in the past. You put me out in the public and people are going to start wondering just how wonderful Koan Angstrom is. I mean, have you really thought about that? What do you expect, to have a tape recorder implanted in me so that I say exactly the right things? And what in the hell would the right things be? Has that all been worked out?"

Paul recognized that his appeal wasn't fleshed out enough. "Koan, I'm sure this won't be our last discussion. I want you to know, I haven't made any assumptions, nor attached any timing to this. It's a process." Koan nodded. "Tell me, if you don't come back, what would you do? I can't imagine you staying here. Not after summer has passed."

"Why not? I'm sure this place could be rigged up sufficiently to make it through a winter. No, the truth is, the more I've thought about it, the more I feel I'd be perfectly happy to go up to a place called Windy Hill and just meditate. Like a Buddhist monk. Focus on paradoxes. The world's full of them. And, yes, if I'm lucky, I might gain enlightenment, before I die."

Paul sensed that Koan was only half-jesting. "Koan, you may see me as someone who's driven only by challenges, but there's more than that singular dimension deep inside of me. I question too. I've asked if the will of the old man hasn't been fulfilled? He's become immortalized. I've asked if that wasn't the goal, a goal now accomplished? What if that was the finale? What is there left for me? Dwelling within myself, I've found old, unfinished bits and pieces of a life. There was a love, one not consummated. There were glances at fathers with children. Or a fleeting but gripping ambition to write. We all reflect on those roads not taken."

"With regrets, Paul?"

Paul smiled. "No, if I did have regrets, it would be the right time to act on them. No one's standing next to me to hold me to the mark."

"Are you trying to put a guilt trip on me, Paul?"

"The old man never put one on me. I did what I did because I had faith in something greater than I could ever be. I had faith that we can become greater by becoming one with that which is greater than us. I'm certain the old man would've let me walk away, if I so chose. Faith held me."

"Which I lack?"

"Why are you trying to place judgments into my mouth, Koan?"

"Sorry. I am."

Sensing the conversation was in a rut, they walked to the

nearby pond. Paul proved he hadn't spent much time out in the natural world. When they tried skipping rocks across the surface of the water, Paul managed no more than three skips. But he was lighthearted about it.

"It's a little like your life, Koan, the rock barely escaping from sinking, like your brushes with death."

Koan's next stone skipped all the way over to the other bank. "I'd like to think that's symbolic, that this time I'm in safety."

"I can only wish you that, Koan."

They wandered back to the hut.

"You know, Paul, this is familiar territory for me. Make that territory I trust. The innocent kid comes out in me again here."

"Was that such a time of innocence?"

Koan shut his eyes. "No, actually it wasn't. I did a lot of questioning, so much that I wore out my welcome in Shepherdstown."

"I hope I was clear, Koan. There's nothing inherently bad in questioning, only if it gets in the way of acting."

"Meaning you're still wanting to hear my decision?"

"That wasn't implied, but if you wish."

"Good, Paul. Tell me how you envision it. We label it a resurrection. A true miracle. Don't sell me short, Paul. In some ways Freddie and I weren't that far apart. I understood where her obsessions were headed. I listened to her. It was an exciting idea. Too bad I don't have a messianic complex. Imagine the possibilities that would've offered. Kidding aside, there is something that attracts me to that. It's a vision of the old man smiling at me and patting me on the shoulder, telling me, 'Well done, Chris. You did it well.'"

Koan expected Paul to respond, but he simply asked Koan to continue.

"Okay, why isn't that enough? To be honest, I'm scared shitless. Of what? There was talk that he was somehow immortal, something I didn't buy into, not at first. The more

I tried to understand him, though, the more I saw him in such an aura. My problem. I'm humble enough to consider myself damned mortal. And that's remained the chasm between him and me, or me ever being him."

"Koan Angstrom was a mortal."

"Paul, even if you were to explain to me how you come to such a logical conclusion, things have gotten way beyond that. You even say his death has elevated him to a myth. That, in my book, is immortality."

"Koan, I don't think that changes much. You're Koan Angstrom, mortal or immortal. You put energy into the vehicle. In that respect, things haven't changed."

"Maybe they changed a long time ago. Do you know what one of the biggest moments of truth in my life was? It was the first time I considered lying to my parents. I remember how I felt, like my life would change forever if I went through with it. My life would become a deception. I lied to them anyway, and what I feared happened. Being Koan Angstrom has only taken it to a higher level of deception."

"I'm sorry, Koan, but I feel your comparison is invalid. A lie is a lie. To emulate and carry the standard for something you have faith in, that's no deception, if faith is the driving force."

"My God!" Koan got up and stomped hard, taking a swat at a low-hanging branch. "Are you ever at a loss for consummate wisdom? Maybe I'm relieved to be away from you."

Almost immediately Koan regretted his outburst. Paul, however, wouldn't allow his ego to be bruised and changed the subject.

"It may surprise you that I have my hands full with a serious threat."

"I thought Freddie was dead?"

"In all seriousness, not everyone's overjoyed with your, sorry, Koan's popularity. Some of the first people on the doorstep were religious interests, all wanting pretty much the same thing: endorsements."

"Endorsements? That sounds like I became a sports star or something."

"At first it had the character of endorsement requests, but that quickly changed when it became apparent just how big your appeal had become. Rather than wanting statements of association with their organizations, the stakes escalated. As one evangelist put it, they wanted Koan to embody their ministry. You might imagine, we distanced ourselves from such things, and that's when the threats arose. First came attempts at defaming Koan Angstrom. When the first such attempt backfired and seemingly destroyed the organization behind it, the threats were taken to a higher level. This past week, just as an example, charges were made that Koan Angstrom was in fact antichrist. Accompanying this have been 'or else' suggestions, the demand being that we publicly distance Koan Angstrom from anything religious and label him instead as nothing more than a shrewd businessman who decided to give his fortune away."

"I'd say you do have your hands full, Paul. And to be quite honest, that sounds like a wasp's nest I don't care to get close to."

For the first time, Paul acted impatient. "You're just not getting the point, are you?"

"What point?"

"The ballfield's yours, the blank canvas. You were the one who set out to do something for the people in Southside. Nothing's cast in concrete. It's yours to define, Koan, the whole damned movement. If you need reminding, I'm the facilitator, not the creator. I'm telling you, you can come back and take it in any direction you wish. I'm offering unconditional support."

"This is it, isn't it?"

"Yes, Koan, I feel you need to focus yourself on a decision."

"Good. For one, I don't know how to act like an immortal. Two. I've spent a lifetime trying to figure out who I am. I've been given a rare opportunity, one I'm not sure I deserve, an opportunity to dig into who I am and with a little luck come to peace with that. Your offer is little more than an invitation to sink deeper into a mire, playing out an identity rather than finding my own. My response to that should be obvious to you."

After Paul's visit, two days passed without Koan getting any sleep. It made him anxious that Paul might never return. He even went through several bouts of paranoia, imagining Paul engaging someone to eliminate him.

Koan went to the path the led into the clearing where his hut stood. Digging back deep into his childhood, he devised some ways of warning himself of anyone approaching. He dug a hole and laid branches and leaves over it. He also devised a "whip branch," a branch bound back by a piece of vine spanned across the path, when broken by a the leg of an approaching person the branch whipping painfully across their upper body.

Koan wanted to see Hope again. He was mulling around asking Moss to summon her, when he came up with new provisions the next day. Suddenly, there was a sharp cry.

"Oh, my God! Ohhhh."

The sounds came from the path, the voice female. Koan hurried over to find Hope had been slashed across the face by the whip branch, a cut bleeding on her cheek, as was her nose.

"Oh, Koan. Shit. Guess this is foreign territory to me."

Koan was relieved that Hope's injury was superficial. He took her to the hut and cleaned up her wound.

"How the hell did you find your way up here?"

"I guess I've always had a good sense of direction"

"Or you felt my soul calling out to you and you followed it. I'm sorry…Oh, I'm glad to see you, Hope."

Hope, her accident forgotten, couldn't wait long to ask Koan when he was returning to Pontifica. Instead of telling her he wasn't, he tried to reconstruct the discussion he'd had with Paul. Hope listened patiently, but finally couldn't hold back any longer.

"What's really holding you back, Koan?"

"I'm not really sure what it is."

"Am I detecting an old, familiar feeling-sorry-for-myself tone? Grab the opportunity, Koan. Take that self-pity out in the woods and bury it." Hope wrapped her arms around Koan from behind, kissing his ear. "Isn't it enough that I'm standing here with open arms, ready to massage your soul whenever it gets bruised."

"I couldn't ask that of you, Hope."

"Who said you had to ask? I've been there, from that first time I found you crying at your father's side in the hospital. You didn't ask then, that I hold you and let you purge your grief."

"How can any soul be so unselfish? I wish I could believe, that, that such a thing exists. It might give me the peace I seek?"

Hope released Koan, walking away, her back turned to him. "Peace? It's funny, isn't it. When I hear you say that word, no meaning comes to me. It's like you're talking about inscriptions on tombstones, rest in peace. You toss that word around as if it's something that comes over you, warm and fuzzy, when the whole world stops turning. Maybe it does, after our deaths."

Hope drew herself up tightly, then let out a soulful sigh. "No, I'm not going to cry, mourn. You aren't dead. Your faith is." Hope turned toward Koan. "What's wrong? Is it all too intangible for you, believing, having faith? You can't count it, accumulate points, come up with a winning total, declare yourself on top of others? You know, you had me convinced, convinced as an old man you no longer needed all that. Was I so wrong?"

"No, I had changed, Hope. Come on, I'm just struggling with something I don't understand."

"Is it because you'd have to accept a compromise, something short of perfection, something as imperfect as mankind is? Is it not the ultimate giving of ourselves to declare ourselves one with all else, regardless in each case to which level that takes us, no matter how unclear or uncertain the outcomes? I thought you were doing that, with those people in Southside? Wasn't that your motivation, to find a common ground with them?"

"It's deeper than that, Hope. Sometimes I have this irresistible urge to emulate my father, who was altruism personified, and other times I simply hate him for what he expected of me."

"Koan, everything has a side that stands in the light, and a side that's in shadow. Having had a childhood that was hell taught me that life's about sorting out the positive bits and pieces and discarding the rest. If that's what you're doing, go for it. I'm with you. I'll give you endless choruses of the old Hope cheerleading routine. But, please, please, don't come at me with that old urge to deny and flee. That's the ultimate no-win option. You know me. I know no other way than to take the cards I'm dealt and play them the best I can."

"Hope, I've wished so often I had your wisdom."

"You do. You only have to live it."

Hope visited Koan again, but after an exchange of tenderness, cracks in the harmony broke open. When Koan announced that he had pretty much decided to grasp his solitude and live out his life that way, Hope tried to whisk it away with levity.

"Koan, is there room for another person up on that place you call Windy Hill?"

"As far as I know, it's public land. You know, that might not be that bad. I could die up there, make a last appearance, and when I'm gone, the whole world could make pilgrimages there."

"The whole world, including me?" Hope paused to swallow her cynicism. "Koan, say it to me, say, 'I don't wish to be alone.'"

"Hope, I have to remind you of something you beat into me long ago, that one has to stand alone in their choices."

"Yes, one makes their choices alone, but choices beg for support, comforting, nurturing, sharing. Choices aren't a victory, or an end, rather a beginning, a difficult and challenging beginning." Hope tried to look impish, but her face betrayed grave thoughts. "I speak from my heart, Koan. You've always known you get the truth from this gal. It's part of the package."

Koan fell into Hope's arms, pressed his head into her chest. "Oh, Hope, yes, you can come with me. But can't it be without any further discussions about all that back in Pontifica? Can't we just take in the simplicity of all this out here until we one day die peacefully? Don't I have the right to that?"

"I wish I could say yes." Hope let her head sag, but then jerked it up high.

"Koan, my profession speaks for who I am. I can't stay here. I can't view life, as you seem to do, as a cruel hoax perpetrated by an angry God. You once muttered that to me with bitterness, that you thought God was so angry that he created mankind, and he vented that anger through constant torment. If we need personify God, it is a being who inspires us to celebrate life. I can't see death as the culmination of a God's punishing anger. No, I see it as the close of something wonderful, the final ribbon tied onto the gift of life, an active and giving life."

Koan waved his hand downward. "Nice words, Hope, but as strong as you are, you have one glaring weakness: your unquestioning compassion. People manipulate that." A rare show of disdain burned in Hope's eyes. "I'm sorry, Hope. That was too harsh. I shouldn't speak for you, just for myself. If I go back to Pontifica, I'd be used for a thousand different ends. I've had enough of manipulation, no matter from whom or from where it comes."

"Koan, Koan, my dear Koan. That's what separates us.

Your world of could be's and what if's. I don't question all that. I go with it believing where it takes me is right. Not a right I have, but the right place to be headed. Things just become apparent along the way. I have no complex explanations. Just faith. And a little hope."

"Here we go again. I know, I lack faith."

"I hear Chris, except that he used to say he lacked the balls. At least I now know that's not true." Hope smiled, hoping it would be catchy. "Come on, Koan, it's no big thing, open your heart up for a little hope."

Hope reached out to embrace Koan, but he pushed her back. She tried again, but with the same response.

"Damn it, Hope, leave me in peace!"

Hope's eyes were ice cold. "I can weather your bouts of frustration and anger, but not that. Not telling me to leave you in peace when I'm reaching out to offer you just that. I can't reach a blind soul."

"Then fuck off, Hope."

Hope did just that, and after she had departed, Koan walked out into the forest and yelled at the top of his lungs, over and over again until the jugular veins on his neck were bulging.

"Fuck all you who find me a selfish little imbecile! You haven't looked deep inside of me, at my torment! You've only guessed at what might be there! It hasn't been your cross to bear! Fuck you and all your self-righteousness! Fuck you for finding me selfish…"

Koan refused to see Paul again, though Paul tried with great persistence. Hope came once more, but Koan asked her to leave. While Koan felt he'd made his choices, Moss rudely confronted him with his disagreement.

"Old friend, you can't stay up here forever. Someday someone's gonna come up here a-snoopin'. It's high time yer decidin' where yer gonna go."

Numerous times Koan had tried to get into a conversation

about his dilemma, the arguments being thrown at him about going back to Pontifica, but Moss simply didn't understand enough of the background to pursue it.

It was clear to Koan that he'd worn out his welcome. One day, eating in the cabin with Moss, Koan declared he was going to clear out, go back deep into the forest and fend for himself. Moss expressed doubts about the wisdom of that, making it clear, however, that he wasn't going to stand in the way.

"Koan, I still think goin' back would be a lot better for ya. But no one's goin' to stop a man who's made up his mind. Even if it's not for his well bein'."

Just before Moss was going to leave, Koan let his head sink and couldn't hold back a bout of soft sobbing.

"You know, Moss, at the bottom of it, I guess there's one thing I can't escape. I'll never quite measure up."

Moss sighed deeply. "You know, Koan, that sounded exactly like Chris talkin' about his father. I may not know much, but ya gotta let a dead man rest."

That was the last time Koan saw Moss.

26

Koan crawled over wet leaves, between stalks of plants. All sense of time and direction had left him. His only goal was to make it to the top of Windy Hill. He shook a slivering millipede off his hand, gasping at the sight of a grimy foot, the joints of the toes arthritically swollen and gnarled. Koan drew back, losing his balance, and fell onto his back. Looking up, he saw a leathery, weathered face framed by a wild mane of white hair that flowed uninterrupted into a great, white beard.

Earlier, while drinking from a pool of water, he had seen a reflection of himself that almost mirrored the person he was seeing. Focusing, he realized it was the forest hermit, the same one he and Moss had so often encountered in their childhood.

"I came because I heard you saying the world had died. I wanted to see what your eyes were seeing. I couldn't imagine such a thing, the end of all things."

During his childhood the people of Shepherdstown warned of a crazy hermit in the forest. It now seemed terribly ironic to Koan that he might be the crazier of the two of them. As he crawled along on the forest floor like a blinded serpent, he had been mumbling, at times incoherently.

"You heard me?"

"Yes, my ears hear most everything. You said the world was dying."

"The world? Oh. No, not the world. My world. I said my world is dying."

"Your world? What world do you possess?"

"A figure of speech. I once was someone else. And that person died. Well, not really died. An old man died, and I became him. Why am I trying to explain this to you? He died, the old man, and now I'm dying. It's like the whole world is dying."

The old hermit looked upward. "We are not the whole world, and neither we nor it die."

Back in his childhood, the riddles the old hermit presented were a fascinating challenge, but now the play on words was irritating Koan. "Good. I know only that I am going to die." Koan pawed his soil-smudged hand over his eyes, as if he were hoping to chase an unwanted hallucination away, but when his eyes opened again the old hermit was still there. "You must be terribly old. I would've thought you'd long since died."

The old hermit smiled whimsically. "Old? Do you mean like the trees? Some weren't here when I last saw you, others were smaller, but I can also recall when the moon shone on this place before there was even one tree. Do you mean the moon? Or the stars? Some have gone, others are already past, and new ones are being born. Perhaps they measure old for you? But all this comes and goes, and comes back again. How do you measure that?"

Koan questioned his naive childhood acceptance that the old hermit existed in the same worldly context he knew. The hermit had looked old then, but now no older than Koan recalled him. The conversation exasperated him, yet not having dialogued with a living soul in days, speaking made him feel alive again. "Do you know why I came back here to the forest?" The hermit shook his head. "I couldn't go back. They want me to reappear, like some god resurrected out of the ashes."

The hermit interrupted him. "A god? What is a god?"

Koan stared in confusion at the hermit, then let out a perverse cackle of laughter. "What a relief! Somehow I expected this unbearable revelation that you'd turn out to be God. Thank God. Yes, thank you, God."

"I see no one named God, nor have I ever known anyone by that name."

Koan looked up, his head shaking. "You are a strange animal. It's just as well. God's someone who puts big guilt trips on people."

"Guilt? I'm sorry for you that you know such a person. But why did you thank him, if he makes you feel so bad?"

"Because feeling guilty makes us get our asses in gear so we can get out and bust our humps." Koan laughed again, waving his hand toward the hermit. "But don't ask me now why that's good. It already killed my wife."

"I'm sorry for you."

"Don't be." Koan was bothered by the hermit's innocent sympathy. "I can't imagine you killing anyone, or anything, but somehow you instill fear in me, a fear I never felt with you when I was young."

The old hermit's smile was childlike. "You're a grown man. You may think my eyes are very weak, but I recognize that. Yes, it's true, children don't fear who I am. But their parents say they should."

Koan just nodded. The old hermit mimicked his nodding, and the two sat there, for a long time, just smiling and nodding at each other. Finally, Koan felt moved to make a confession.

"I said before that I thought you were dead and gone. Well, I actually played with the idea of taking your place, being you. I wanted to roam around out here and do nothing but commune with nature. Great idea, but I guess there's no opening."

The hermit seemed only mildly amused. "Why not look outward away from yourself? I cannot become you, or you me, but we can embrace all of this around us, and each other, and we can then disappear, no longer be important. We become no one, and have nothing to look back at. So is it with me. I have become nothing, nothing you could become."

Koan pondered what the old hermit said, then he climbed to his feet. "Thanks for the riddle, the paradox." Koan reached out and grasped the hermit's upper arm, squeezing it as if to assure himself his being was real. "I've been in desperate need of something to occupy me, to meditate on, something that may finally bring me enlightenment, up on Windy Hill, before I die."

The old hermit shook his head, apparently discouraged from saying anything further. With a slow nod and wave of the hand, he turned and walked away, disappearing out of Koan's sight.

Koan continued on his way to the top of Windy Hill. By evening he had made it, sitting with his legs folded in front of him, watching the great red sun slowly dip below the horizon.

It's an ending. A tidy ending. Koan Angstrom alive and well in Pontifica. Yes, finally alive because he's dead. More powerful as myth than mortal. No more loose ends to deal with. Loose ends, that's good. No more shit. No more shit from me.

I didn't see it coming. Maybe I didn't want to see it. Clues were there, plenty of them. Did I want the heroics so badly that I was blinded to Freddie's intentions? I don't know, and who cares? This I wanted too. This is the ultimate freedom, here alone on Windy Hill. Solitude. No one showering expectations over me. I can be master of my fate, what little of it's still left.

Chris, get away from me! You're still yearning for your wake and the ears to hear it. You want to hear them mourning, the way you couldn't when your father passed away. But why? Why do you need one last great celebration? Why won't a small dot to punctuate your end do? As Hope so often said to you, Find peace, Chris.

Who would've been at your wake? Freddie? Her ghost? Posthumously applauding what she so wanted? You'd finally give her the hook line of her advertising jingle. "Death could not consume his spirit."

No, I wish to die as I lived, alone. Koan got the super celebration, tens of thousands who didn't know him coming to memorialize him. Those masses have no idea it was I who pumped life back into the old man. I stepped in for him, and now he's the greatest there is. Nice move, Hickory Harry. Yeah, that I'll miss. That little celebration. My old boss standing there, with the whole firm around us, saying, "Man, Chris, it's a miracle you pulled that off." Hot stuff. I'd really be hot stuff.

As the sky darkened, a wind with a chilling edge arose. Koan hunched himself together in a fetal position.

Putting things right with Dad? I'm still no wiser how that could've happened. What kind of relationship did Jesus have with Joseph? Funny that Moss and I never tossed that one around. Moss would've liked that question. Wasn't Jesus supposed to honor Joseph as his father? Jesus took off and never looked back. He completely ignored the father who held him as a child and taught him to work with wood. The irony. The carpenter's son dying on a cross fashioned from wood. But did he and Joseph ever make peace? Where was Joseph at the end? An absentee father? Or was it like me? Was it Christ's will to take off, make it on his own, and leave his father in the past?

I know what Dad would say to that. "Why are you thinking about such things, Chris? Why ain't you spendin' your time with others?" Yeah, he'd also be saying, "Why ain't you goin' back to Pontifica?" To emulate your selflessness, Dad? No, we walked in two different pairs of shoes, Dad. Jesus didn't emulate Joseph.

The wind became very still, then from far down the flank of Windy Hill, Koan heard a roar that steadily increased in volume. Tree limbs cracked, and debris began to fill the air. Koan balled himself tight together.

"So, is that you, God, coming up to get me? Is this the finality I've continually evaded? Well, come on. I've been ready before, and I'm ready now."

The torrent of wind finally arrived, buffeting Koan as he clenched at the roots of the grasses around him. The swirling dust blew into his eyes and blinded him.

"Go ahead, God, take me!"

Koan twisted around and pressed his body flat against the earth, his arms stretched straight out from his torso.

"God, whatever your purpose was, I never found my script, no destiny, no outcome or purpose. Even when I thought I had that sweet fruit in my grasp, it soured and turned rotten. You win. You've made a tired, beaten old man of me."

The wind whipped harder, tearing out vegetation by its roots, and fear crept into Koan's heart.

"Even if I've failed, you must give me credit. I searched for a set of rules. There's got to be credit for good intentions."

Koan listened for an ebbing in the wind, a speck of hope in him desiring a short reprieve, one last dialogue, with anyone.

"God, listen, please. You must have known the old man Koan. Maybe you two were into something together? I found that scribbled note from him, the one that he wrote inside the cover of the Bible. 'Who we are is letting go of the need to know.' That's what the old hermit was saying, wasn't it? Is it enough for you that I'm also willing to give up my life? To die without needing to know who I was supposed to be?"

Suddenly, like a miracle, the wind ceased completely, and the air was still chokingly thick, as if the heavens were only tentative in their silence. The brownish-black clouds continued to churn and roll above and around Koan, threatening to descend and engulf him once again. Koan wondered whether it was nothing more than a freak of nature, rather than a response to his pleadful praying.

Then, from out of the murkiness, Koan discerned what seemed to be two silhouettes approaching him. As they drew closer, but before he could clearly identify features, he sensed who they were, his father and the old man Koan.

Koan scrambled up from the ground, raising his arms. "Dad, oh God, thank you! I never thought I'd see you again!" Koan began to stumble toward his father, who raised the palm of his hand toward him to stop.

"No, don't come any farther. I'm not sure you are my son."

"Of course I am, Dad. Oh God, don't worry about how I look. I can explain all that."

"No, stay. It's not your appearance."

"Then what? I am Chris, your son."

"Then tell me, are you the wolf or the fox?"

"Come on, Dad. What kind of question is that?"

"You say you're my son, but I want to know, are you of the pack, or the lonely predator?"

To Koan, who desperately wanted to embrace his father, the questioning seemed bitterly inappropriate. "Okay. You always wanted to hear it. Yes, I believe I was of the pack. Things were just different with me. A different world. I had peers. I belonged. You see, I was a wolf."

Koan looked to Mr. Folkstone for an expression of approval, but he didn't respond, nor the icy look on his face change. Instead, the old Koan broke in.

"What have you learned about paradoxes?"

"Paradoxes?" Koan found the questions he was having to field incredulous, but at least it was the dialogue he had prayed for. "You mean the name we share, Koan, and its Buddhist meaning? A paradox to ponder upon to gain enlightenment. Is this why we meet, for one last paradox, the ultimate paradox?"

"You've just stated a paradox."

"I did?"

"Yes. You spoke of your pack being your peers. A pack implies bonds. Your peers, I must say, were a group of empty souls, marching perhaps arm in arm, but how can those without a soul have bonds? An interesting paradox, don't you think?"

"But, but..." Koan felt unjustly attacked, "but it was more. I don't think you knew the real me. I really was, I was trying to find some sort of permanence."

"Permanence? How easily you use that word." The contents of what the old Koan was saying came across as hostile, even though his countenance and tone of voice was absolutely serene. "Tell me, where was this permanence you sought? In mortal existence, nature, the universe?"

"Perhaps."

"There, you've created another paradox."

"I did?"

"Yes, you mention mortal existence, nature, the universe in one breath with the word perhaps. Very good. They are all part of a great, constant transformation, indefinite at all times. They are, if you like, perhaps."

"Well, uh, I guess that's true, but, see, that supports my point. In fact, that's it. Dad, you wanted me to join the Scouts, be involved in the church. Maybe those things began with good intentions, but I felt they were transformed into...let's say I didn't trust them."

Mr. Folkstone replied, "I never asked you to worship the outward images of such things. It was their uniting forces, that essence, their holda, I wished you to experience. But no, you flinched as if such things might dilute that almighty individuality of yours."

Again, the old Koan broke in. "I would hope it's been evident to you that a peer isn't someone who wears the same clothing, uses the same words. There is only one place all things are alike. It's in our holda."

Koan wanted to soft-pedal the sharpness of the conversation, hoping to appeal to the old Koan's sentimentalities. "That is an elucidation. I say that with gratitude."

"Gratitude? There are many levels of gratitude, but there is one that stands above all others."

Koan wished he knew the punch line, so that it would elevate him to the level of equal partner in the discussion and dissolve the feeling that he was on trial. "I take it you mean the gratitude we feel when another has given themselves unselfishly to us?"

"I speak of an action, not a feeling."

"We return what they have given us by giving the same to them?"

"You would not be guessing if you knew."

Koan couldn't bridle his irritation. "Then what the hell is it?"

The old Koan wasn't the least ruffled by this outburst and continued to speak with absolute calmness. "The ultimate gratitude is when we give ourselves to a sense of eternal time, become one with all, past, future, and present. Holda. Have you experienced that kind of gratitude?"

Koan felt disemboweled by the question, which he perceived as a set-up. As tears overflowed from his eyes and rolled down his cheeks, he looked toward his father pleadingly. "So, you aren't going to embrace me, Dad, even if this is our last chance?"

"Son, what would it mean that our flesh touch again? My soul has sought to embrace you, innumerable times, but your soul did not respond. Still, at this very instant my soul is reaching out to you, beckoning to you to merge with that of which I am also a part. Holda."

Koan couldn't suppress a feeling of anger at what seemed to be a toying with his emotions. "Okay, okay. Maybe I'm too testy. I did come here to meditate and find peace. So, if you're in no hurry, it's only fair, isn't it, that I be given a chance to see if I understand you?"

Koan got no response, which he took as agreement.

"Let's start with you, the man who took my life, the man I had to become. I was told you were trying to infuse your soul into me, but that part of me refused to die with my body. That's why the operation failed, because my soul wouldn't budge. In other words, I screwed up your plan. I can understand if that would've pissed you off. The question is, is this now your way of telling me you've paid me back with a shitload of misery?"

Koan only got blank, dispassionate looks, which irritated him once again.

"There's more, isn't there? I crossed you again. With your first plan ruined, you set up a new one. You intended to die there in Southside, there in that sea of anonymous human beings, symbolically, there in that hopeless hell were nothing could survive but a soul. You even used Freddie. But, voila, the old fly in the ointment, me, I didn't die. And now? Yeah, now I'm bothersome. I messed up that neat, tidy ending. And I still don't have your soul in me. Bad, bad boy. And you're here because you fear I could fuck it all up even more, by going back and letting the whole world know exactly what kind of jerk Koan Angstrom was? I could make you look very human, very humble. Right?"

That Koan wasn't getting any counter-arguments encouraged him.

"Good. I still have some of the old Hickory Harry in me. Let's strike a deal. Paul's ideas are sound. When weren't they? I could go back. Yeah, some sort of miraculous resurrection. That would elevate you to the god status Paul often mentioned. I mean, if your plans are that big, so be it. We could give it a try. I'm game. We can get the masses chanting, 'holda.' Why not? I'm sure that would satisfy both of you. I can be a very cooperative person, given the proper respect and acknowledgment."

Not only was the image of the old Koan smiling, but also Mr. Folkstone. Koan lost it. "What's there to smile about?!" the old Koan replied.

"Your offer is fascinating, if not fanciful. I'm certain what Paul has in his hands will stimulate mankind to thought and contemplation. As you yourself say, it's a search. Holda is that, something mortals search for within their souls. To your accusations that you were somehow used, one could be very philosophic. For instance, is there any other justification for being, other than in that form, to be of utility? But what you speak of is not philosophy. What you speak of in terms of being used was opportunity. Great ones were put into your hands. I think you will agree with that?"

"At times I thought so, but I never escaped the suspicion I was being manipulated." Again, Koan saw what seemed to be amusement written on the faces of the old Koan and his father. "Are you going to tell me with a straight face I wasn't manipulated?"

"How can there be manipulation if all are one? Holda. Yes, you did indeed attempt to commune with me, your father, the old hermit. In such moments of oneness, no one could have an advantage over the other. Advantage only has a context where things are separable."

Koan's teeth were clenching. "No, no, no. Those are just words. It's like I said. You set it all up. Like I was going to be your marionette."

"When did you ever relinquish your own choices, your own volition? You seem obsessed with a notion of higher powers who are angry, conniving, and vengeful, obsessed with an image of yourself as one who must ultimately be punished. It must disappoint you to find there is graciousness, generosity, yes, compassion, and joy. You see, in holda, we are all part of each other, and it follows our regard for ourselves is by definition also our regard for each other. No, if it were a choice I could have executed, I can hardly say this is an outcome I would have desired."

"Nor that you're dead," snapped Koan. "You sacrificed that, your life, didn't you, for a failed experiment. There. That's another offer I can make you. How convenient that I'm not dead. It must be worth a lot to you to get back into the world. Maybe that's the deal we can strike? Put me back into my old self. Let me be Chris again, and I'll gladly give you back your mortal form."

"There's nothing I seek to get back to. We're always there, always will be, together with all that wills to be one with us. Holda."

Koan's face went ashen white. "You don't care one bit about all this, more importantly, about me, do you? I mean, for you it's little more than an amusing game."

Mr. Folkstone leaned slightly toward Koan. "Games like the ones you and Moss played in your endless discussions?"

Furrows appeared in Koan's forehead. "Oh, I see, now you're going to come down on me and Moss for blaspheming the church. Yes, we talked about a lot of things, especially all the hypocrisy we saw."

"Son, did you believe my eyes were blind? I could have carried on the same discussions with you that you had with Moss. But that would have been like arguing over the shell of the egg, its color or texture, rather than the bird evolving inside that would some day fly. It was not the shell that would have wings."

"So, that was all wasted time, the time Moss and I spent together?"

"No, Son. It had the chance to bring you closer."

"Hooray. I wasn't that bad after all. There's a good note to end it all on. Maybe it's best if we quit now, and I get back to dying?"

The wind began to rise again, and Koan anticipated the

disappearance of the two, along with the renewal of the storm, but suddenly the old hermit was there.

"There you are again! You seem to keep getting lost out here. I remember once telling you and your friend about wandering off, minds wandering off. Do you remember asking me what crazy people were?" Koan didn't reply. "Well, it looks like there's been one big misunderstanding here. Something in passing told me. I know the old man over there too. Knew him a long time before I met you and your friend. What was your friend's name, Moses? Whatever, I figured something wasn't right the last time I saw you. You looked like the old man, but I sensed you weren't. I knew it was you from back then, that Christ boy."

"The name is Chris!"

"Doesn't matter. You and your friend, ya listened good with your ears, but not your hearts. You wanted so badly to know who you were, but not what was. Not all this. Do you remember? You wanted the tree to be a tree, when I said it wasn't. You didn't want to hear that everything is nothing except for what it serves in the world around it. Tell me, why did you never ask me my name?"

Koan began trembling. He couldn't explain why, perhaps only that the old hermit was the only adult he knew in his youth where he didn't feel he was to some degree full of shit. He had completely revered the old shaggy man. That the old hermit now joined the tribunal seemed like the last sense of innocent security had been withdrawn from Koan. "I don't know your name. But I guess I'm curious now to know. What is it?"

"I have no name. That allows me to be one with everything. But that's not important now. You have something that has to go back."

"Go back? What?"

"Your soul. You didn't listen well, did you? I told you that what you called crazy people were just minds that had wandered away for a time. Guess that's what happened with you, a soul wandered into you from somewhere else. But as the lamb finds its way back to the warmth of its mother, that time has come."

Koan's eyes reflected an inner surge of panic. "You want my soul? No! You can't do that to me! What's mine is mine! I am who I am, and if I have to die, I'll die for that."

The old man Koan glared with eyes that were both extremely intense yet also permeated with compassion. "It's been amazing to witness such a compulsion for recognition, yet if you die here, who's going to even notice? There's no recognition in alienation. We've all wanted to recognize your soul, embrace it, let it be one with us, and vice versa, holda. You've always had it in you to belong, but you've willed in the end to push your soul aside. You have, it seems, willed to not exist. I recognize now that you truly desire that, to die in the truest sense."

Koan's eyes were blurred by tears, his body quivering uncontrollably, and he again balled himself together in a fetal position. "If none of you have not one ounce of understanding for me, then go. I don't need you to be here when I die, and you certainly won't be mourning over me."

Mr. Folkstone responded. "I saw it as a good sign when you didn't mourn my death, a hope that we could commune thereafter. We cannot mourn the passing of mortality, as our holda remains together."

"Well, good. If you have no capacity to mourn, then there's no further reason to hang around here."

There was a "So be it," but Koan couldn't tell from which of them it came, or from all of them in unison. As if they hadn't even been there, the silhouettes were gone, merging into the turbulent clouds. Koan gazed upward, his eyes closing. He felt as alone as any mortal could be. "Paul, it's in your hands. I know now I won't be back. I no longer know if I exist. Or have existed. No, it's true, I never have."

From the heavens above, a furious bolt of lightning joined itself with the peak of Windy Hill. The deafening clap of thunder that followed marked Koan's last conscious thought. A small fire burned atop Windy Hill, so small that it was hardly discernible from a distance where any soul might see it. And by daybreak, it was gone.

Epilogue

Paul Wahrmacher, at first nearly overwhelmed by the response to Koan Angstrom's apparent assassination, rose to the occasion and provided the masses a focus for their hunger to learn more about the man who died on a humble mission to help the disenfranchised. A concise work was published, mostly from Paul's recollections, called "Elucidations, observations and wisdoms from Koan Angstrom." This book went into a second printing less than a month after its release, and the longer-term demand seemed insatiable.

A rumor emerged that Koan Angstrom had been sighted near a small town named Shepherdstown. No confirmation of this materialized until one day a journalist spotted a woman sitting upon a hill rising above Shepherdstown. Later, the woman was identified simply as Hope. She conceded she had known Koan Angstrom, that her reason for visiting Windy Hill was because he had spent nights there. She also admitted to having met with him after the date of his assassination. As to why Koan Angstrom chose to spend time on Windy Hill, Hope offered little more than to say, "To search for eternal peace."

Within a year, resorts sprouted up around Shepherdstown. The thousands who came there to make the trek up Windy Hill had just as many explanations as to why they were doing so. On top of Windy Hill they found little, only sparse vegetation and one gnarled tree, which was twisted around in what resembled the letter omega, its base charred deeply on one side. Miraculously, one branch of this tree sprouted leaves each spring and it lived on past most people's lifetimes.

Although she disappeared into obscurity, the woman Hope developed into a cult figure, often more powerful in attraction than Koan Angstrom himself. It was said she was Koan Angstrom's mate with whom he shared his most intimate thoughts, even the life force that provided him with inspiration and vitality. With time, the two persons, Koan Angstrom and Hope, became inseparable, the one representing striving for spiritual truths, the other for the embedidness of these truths in earthly existence.

In one final, ironic twist, Hope became a fertility symbol, revered for her powers to help bring strong, healthy lives into the world. The old, gnarled, omega-shaped tree atop Windy Hill was worshipped by many as a sign of the womb, the womb of Hope which had only been inseminated spiritually by Koan Angstrom.